DESTINY ON ICE

DESTINY ON ICE

BOYS OF WINTER #1

S.R. GREY

Destiny on Ice (Boys of Winter #1)
Copyright © 2016 by S.R. Grey

ISBN-10: 0-9979749-1-5
ISBN-13: 978-0-9979749-1-1

Editing: Hot Tree Editing
Cover Photographer: CJC Photography
Model: Assad Shalhoub
Cover Design: Najla Qamber Designs
Interior Design and Formatting: by:
www.emtippettsbookdesigns.com

GOLDEN BOY GETS A LITTLE TARNISHED

BRENT

My father was a great hockey player. Back in the day, in the era of eighties' big hair and synthesized music, Billy Oliver won not just one, but two Stanley Cups. He was awarded the Conn Smythe trophy both times and has received an assortment of other hardware throughout the years.

He's retired now, but my dad was once a star.

To me, though, he's always just been Dad.

But as his only child, I have a legacy to live up to. I pray I don't disappoint him. I pray someday I'll be as good as he once was. And damn it, I better win a freaking Stanley Cup like he did.

I have no choice, not really. Since the moment my father first laced up hockey skates on my three-year-old little feet, the look of pride on his face told me even then all I needed to know—anything short of being the best will never do.

And guess what?

In many ways, I've become the best at what I do, which is, like my dad, play professional hockey.

I've been good since the start, a natural some say. I don't know about that, but I do know that even before I was drafted—in the first round by the Las Vegas Wolves, an expansion team at the time—I was being called "The Golden Boy" and "The Next One."

These days, three years later, I'm pretty much the poster boy for the NHL. And I have a slew of endorsement deals to prove it.

Lately, though, I've been falling short.

And I really don't know why.

Something is missing for me in the game. Or is it something that's missing in *me*?

I blow out a breath and shake my head.

Things started out so great. Where'd it all go wrong?

I made a name for myself early on. Expansion teams usually struggle for years before posting a winning record. Not so for the Wolves. With me centering what was then a subpar line, I was still able to make us shine. We came out swinging that first season in the league.

BRENT OLIVER SCORES THE GAME-WINNING GOAL IN HIS AND THE WOLVES' FIRST NHL GAME, SETS UP TEAMMATES FOR TWO MORE

One month later, there was this:

THE WOLVES OFF TO A COMPLETELY UNEXPECTED STELLAR START

Then things started to slide.

Those subpar players on my line weren't enough to keep afloat a pretty much overall crappy team, even with me centering. The Wolves' owners and management made the necessary moves—they don't mess around when shit needs to get done.

We picked up a phenomenal winger, Nolan Solvenson. He started to play and things turned around.

ADDING SKILLED RIGHT-WINGER NOLAN SOLVENSON TO ROOKIE BRENT OLIVER'S FIRST LINE PROVING TO BE A MASTERFUL MOVE

ON A MID-SEASON WINNING STREAK, THAT SOLVENSON TRADE IS PAYING OFF FOR THE WOLVES!

Another trade made at the deadline gave us Benjamin Perry. A big, strong left-handed winger, he was the final piece to the puzzle. Even with far-from-elite second, third, and fourth lines, it didn't matter. Not with me, Benjamin, and Nolan on the first line. We could *not* be stopped.

Benjamin—or Benny, as he's known to the team—is adept at using his size and muscle to check the hell out of any sorry soul who happens to be matched up against him. He simply wears other players down... and then it's a fucking scorefest. Thanks, in part, to his killer slapshot.

Together with Nolan, a sniper in his own right, we were—and in many ways still are—quite a force to be reckoned with. We destroy teams, though not as much lately. But back then, man, we were racking up so many points that the press branded us the OPS line, as in Special Forces.

THE OPS LINE'S SNIPERS OF OLIVER, PERRY, AND SOLVENSON ELIMINATE THE COMPETITION WITH EASE

THERE'S NOTHING COVERT ABOUT THIS LINE'S SCORING PROWESS

We worked our reputation to our advantage. Trash-talking on the ice and taunting players became our pastimes. We also happened to get a lot of pucks in the net.

Ah, the good old days.

We still trash-talk and taunt, but we aren't as lethal as we once were.

"We just need to get back on track," I murmur to myself. "The season doesn't start for a few more weeks. I'll have my shit together by then."

I better, since I'm the captain of the team. If I go down, we all sink. And that's not fair to anyone, especially not to my linemates, Nolan and Benny. Over the past couple of years they've become my best friends, which is a blessing and a curse. It's a blessing that we play so well together, but it's a curse that we also have a tendency to fuel each other's vices.

God knows this off-season we've become far too focused on partying and women. Like me, my linemates are extremely popular. Hell, let's not mince words—we're gods. In the hockey world, it's good to be a god. Guys want to *be* you and girls want to *do* you. Multiply that all by a hundred if you're not an ogre in the looks department.

And none of us are.

Not to brag—though, I guess I kind of am—but I have the most women falling at my feet. Hell, I've had women who've wanted to *lick* my feet.

Like, literally.

There was this crazy bitch this one time…

Wait, I digress. Back to where our team is today—floundering in a sea of mediocrity.

After that first good regular season, we fell apart during the playoffs. A dirty hit that sent me flying into the boards also sidelined me with a concussion. It didn't end there. More bad luck plagued our team. Nolan went into a scoring slump, and Benny took a punishing check against the boards that broke his foot. We were knocked out of the playoffs in the first round.

I went to Minneapolis, my hometown, to sulk.

"Next year will be different," my always-positive father tried to reassure me.

He was wrong.

We missed the playoffs entirely the following year, for reasons still unknown.

Then there was the season that just ended this past spring—another disappointment.

LAS VEGAS WOLVES FOLD, KNOCKED OUT ONCE AGAIN IN THE FIRST ROUND

Needing a break from all things desert-life, I said to Nolan and Benny, "Fuck this shit."

That was over three months ago. We were in the middle of cleaning out our lockers for the summer. My linemates looked at me, confused.

And then Nolan finally asked, "Fuck what shit, Oliver? What are you going on about over there?"

"Everything," I replied, gesturing around the empty locker room. "We're done, finished. Let's get the hell out of this place for a while."

I meant Las Vegas the city—and I think Nolan was catching my drift—but Benny misunderstood.

"Dude," Benny began, "we *better* get outta here soon." He checked his watch. "We have a tee time at two."

He meant the golf game we had planned, but I was having none of that.

"Fuck golfing," I snapped. "I'm talking about *really* getting out of here. I think we deserve a much-needed break from this whole damn town."

Nolan looked intrigued. "What'd you have in mind?"

I happily shared with him and Benny what I'd been thinking about for days. "Let's head up to my house in Minnesota. We can spend the summer on the lake." I grinned, bad intentions in mind. "You know I'm a fucking rock star up there. We can party every night. Hell, we can fuck and get fucked up till training camp starts up in September."

Benny was in immediately, but Nolan had to think it over in his thoughtful kind of way.

At last, he said, "Okay, let's do it."

Since that day we've been partying like rock stars. Or, more accurately, like out-of-control hockey players.

We're still on a roll, even though it's August and we have to fly back to Vegas real soon. Until then, however, I've vowed my cool contemporary house by the lake will remain *the* place to party. It's our OPS base for debauchery, after all.

In reality, though, this craziness can't go on. We all know that.

Even wild and crazy Benny had the sense to ask me just last week, "Dude, what should we do?"

"About what?"

I was in the midst of texting a local puck bunny to see if she wanted to meet me for a quickie, so I was a bit distracted.

Benny sighed. "We gotta report to camp in a less than a month. Guess it's time to start thinking about slowing down with the girls, the booze, the—"

I put down my phone and cut him off with a raucous, "Hell no, my friend. We just need to scale it back a little."

"Scale it back in what way?" Nolan, who walked in the room just at that moment, wanted to know.

I shrugged. "Maybe have smaller parties? Maybe drink a little less?"

We all agreed to those things, but we haven't followed through. In the past seven days we've abstained from partying for all of two.

This is so not going to play well with the team. My diet is crap, and I'm nowhere near peak playing shape. Sure, my body looks all lean and cut, meaning you'd never know I wasn't ready to hit the ice rearing to go, but looks can be deceiving. I went out for a run just the other day and came back fucking winded as hell.

That was a first.

Still, I'm confident I can get back into playing shape in no time. It's the inside of my head that's kind of a mess. I just don't fucking care about winning, not anymore. I mean, I do, but I don't. Does that make sense?

Nah, it doesn't to me, either. But I better figure it out, and fast.

Where's my drive to get my shit together? Where's my commitment to winning, my obligation to my players?

I ask myself these things every day now, but I guess the answers are clouded by my drinking copious amounts of alcohol and fucking way too many puck bunnies.

Dad would be so proud—not.

Well, he would be glad I diligently use protection. I haven't gone *that* far off the rails. Still, wrapping my dick up isn't enough to keep management off my ass. My agent already informed me—this morning, in fact—that the Wolves' ownership group has a pretty good idea of what I've been up to, along with my teammates, here in Minneapolis.

I listened half-heartedly when my agent woke me up to say, "Don't blow this off, Brent. Management is *not* happy with you. There's a certain image they expect you to uphold, and you're not doing that."

God forbid I'm not the team's "Golden Boy." I'm "The Next One," remember?

Bullshit, it's all crap.

Coach Townsend called me shortly after I got off the phone with my agent. He had the same warning.

"You don't want the team to take action. You're not going to like what they have in store for you, Brent, if you keep up with this bad behavior."

"Oh, come on," I replied, laughing. "The Wolves can't fire me. And what could be worse than that?"

Coach T chuckled like he knew something.

Hmm...

"I can't worry about that shit today," I said to him. "I'll start cleaning up my act tomorrow."

"Brent..." Coach T sounded doubtful.

"Really, I will," I insisted.

That was a few hours ago. And I plan to make some changes. But maybe not quite yet.

"Before tomorrow gets here," I justify to myself, "we still have the rest of today. And that means there's time for one more party."

I stride into the second-floor living room of my house, a spacious and angled space overlooking the huge lake on my property. Peering out at the crystal blue water, I announce to Benny and Nolan, "Listen up, boys. We're having one final blowout tonight, a party to end all parties."

There's a murmur from Nolan, but nothing from Benny.

"We're going to do this one right," I go on. "We party tonight. But then, when tomorrow arrives, we're done with messing around. We start training full-on."

Yeah, right, a little voice in my head coughs out.

I look around since no one besides my guilty conscience seems to be chiming in.

It's early afternoon and the sun is bathing the room—my favorite, by the way, with the way it juts out over the lake showcasing the floor-to-ceiling windows on two sides and a massive deck with a mile-long view on the other—in a warm summer glow.

Nolan, who is lounging on an easy chair with a beer in his hand, raises his bottle. "I'm in," he says.

His words aren't the least bit slurred, even though he's been drinking straight through since last night's bash.

"And then, yeah," he continues, agreeing with me, "we'll start getting ready for camp."

Despite his ability to suck down alcohol like a fish, Nolan hasn't veered too far off course. Getting back on track won't be hard for him. He's like Mr. Discipline. And he's not fooling anyone, anyway. I caught him working out in my basement gym a few days ago. With the way he was pumping iron I suspect he's been training consistently for a few weeks now.

There's still not been a response from Benny, which is unusual. Dude's always up for a party. He's probably the worst of us when it comes to out-of-control antics.

And that's saying a lot.

"Hey, where's Benny?" I ask Nolan as I scan the shadows of the room.

He nods to a sofa that's been pushed way-ass off to a far corner.

"Oh, I should've known." I chuckle as I take in an eyeful.

Benny is sprawled out on a sofa in the shadows, sleeping like a baby. His massive chest is rising and falling in perfect rhythm with the ticking clock on the stone mantel above his head. Some puck bunny he was fucking around with last night is with him, passed out on top of him.

The sheet covering their naked bodies is hiked up just enough to afford a view of the girl's creamy thigh, which is casually slung over my linemate's muscular, hairy-as-hell leg, and positioned under his semi-exposed junk.

Chuckling at Benny's total lack of modesty, I pick up a throw pillow and lob it at his head—the one that clearly controls all his thinking.

And he scores!

As the pillow makes contact—and how could it not with a pole like that marking my target?—the sheet falls off completely. I get a quick flash of perky tits and tiny ass. And then, shit—a big honking piece of man-meat assaults my eyes.

"Dude," I snort, mock-offended. "You need to cover that shit before you blind us all."

Benny stirs to life. Sitting up, he barks, "What the fuck, Oliver? I was having the best dream ever. That is till you started tossing shit at my balls. "

Nolan lets out a low chuckle. "Only you, Benny, could find a way of using 'tossing' and 'balls' in the same sentence. But really"—he tilts his bottle to Benny's dick—"you need to do what Brent said and cover that shit up."

Throughout this entire brain-draining exchange, the girl wakes up. And damn, she looks young. Letting out a little squeak, not unlike a hamster, she gathers the sheet around her naked self and scurries off to where she seems to think the bathroom is.

I only know this 'cause she's muttering something about having to pee. But the poor girl has no idea where to go. Hamster-girl flies past me, heading down the wrong hallway, the one that leads to my bedroom.

As I rush to retrieve her, I can't help but grumble, "Why in the hell do they always think the damn bathroom's down *my* hall?"

I catch up to and redirect the girl, pointing her in the correct direction. "It's that way, sweetheart," I say in my kindest tone.

No need to be an asshole; the poor thing already looks shell-shocked. Though whether that's due to waking up in a strange house or waking up next to that monstrous thing Benny calls a cock, I have no clue.

"Thanks, Mr. Oliver," she replies.

And then she runs off.

"*Mr.* Oliver?" I shake my head. "What the fuck is up with that? If she thinks I'm old and I'm only twenty-two, then…"

Whoa, wait.

Hurrying back out to the living room and pointing an accusatory finger at Benny, I say, "That chick better be over eighteen, dude. We're in enough trouble already with the team."

Benjamin Perry is twenty-eight, but he likes younger girls. Nothing illegal, so don't get your panties in a bunch. He just happens to favor babes who either look young, or are *just* old enough.

"She's twenty-three," he replies, sounding hurt by my accusation.

"What? Five years past eighteen?" Nolan peers over at me and smirks. "Hey, Oliver, you think Benny is working up to go cougar on us?"

Laughing, I reply, "Seeing as he's on his way to fucking the full spectrum of girls in their twenties, I do indeed think he's secretly working his way up to thirty."

"Small steps," Nolan says.

"Fuck you," Benny interjects. "You're both dickheads."

I put up my hands. "Hey, don't be pissed at me. Take it up with Nolan. He started with the jokes. I only brought up the chick's age for your own protection. I'm always looking out for you, buddy."

"Yeah, you usually are," he concedes. "And thanks for that." He shoots me an apologetic grin. "You really are a good kid at heart."

I shrug, feeling a little self-conscious at being called a kid. But then I see what Benny is up to, preparing to bust my balls.

Sure enough, the next words out of his mouth are "You do know I mean *kid* in a good kind of way. Like maybe"—he smirks—"a *golden boy* sort of style."

"Ha. Ha," I retort. And since he's enjoying yanking my chain far too much, I shoot him the bird. "Shut the fuck up, man."

Benny may give me a hard time, but his underlying sentiment is genuine. What he said about me being a good guy, like a decent person, is true. Despite all the craziness of late, I want nothing but the best for my friends. And just because I've been fucking up my own life lately doesn't mean Benny's and Nolan's lives have to go down the shitter too.

Really, I probably should've never invited them to Minnesota. I should have come up to the lake house by myself. That would've been the smart thing to do, especially if my intention all along has been to piss away my career.

I don't really want that, though, do I?

No.

I just need some help in getting back on track.

But where would I find something like that?

Ah, fuck it.

"So what do you say, Benny?" I ask, back to focusing on the party. "You in?"

He stretches, covering his dick with the pillow I threw at him. I make a mental note to have all my furniture *and* their decorative accents, especially the pillows, steam cleaned.

Running his hand through his shaggy, dark blond hair, he says, "Am I in for what?"

"Party tonight," Nolan interjects in his usual no-nonsense tone. "One last blowout, and then Brent here says we're stopping with the bad behavior."

I have to laugh. Nolan is only three years older than me, but it's like he's twenty-five going on forty. He's the voice of reason in our crew.

Well, most of the time.

Not today, though. No, today he agrees to go all-out.

With the party plans full steam ahead, we get on our phones, texting and calling everyone we know.

"Tonight we party hard," I declare when we reconvene in the living room.

"Yeah," Nolan says, holding up a freshly opened bottle of beer.

"You mean hell, yeah," Benny corrects, raising the full shot glass in his hand.

"Hell, yeah," I echo, a beer *and* a shot on the table in front of me. "And just so we're clear," I add. "Tomorrow we give up the booze and the women. Tomorrow we start training for real."

The boys agree, and we drink to our plan.

Yeah, tomorrow we'll do all those things...

2

YOLO, BITCHES

AUBREY

"**N**o way, Aubrey," my bubbly little sister squeals in my ear.

Even with all the noise at O'Hare at eight thirty in the morning on a bustling Tuesday, I hear only her. Really quite a feat when you think about it.

"You're leaving Chicago in what? Like an hour?"

"Yep," I confirm. "I'm scheduled on the nine-thirty flight to Minneapolis. And then I'll be on my way up to see you, little sis."

I decided late last night that detouring up to Minnesota before I head out to Nevada for an upcoming work assignment—a job which I know very little about, except that it'll likely consume the next two to four months of my life—would be a nice surprise for both me and my only sibling.

Lainey recently returned to Minneapolis after spending the .

summer at our parents' house in Butler, Pennsylvania. I didn't have a chance to visit her, or my folks, even after I promised I would.

This is me correcting at least one of those wrongs.

Lainey is about to start her senior year at the University of Minnesota. She's majoring in marketing, and soon she'll be busy with her business classes. Same as I'll be busy readying for my new work assignment by this time tomorrow.

My little sister starts gushing, going on and on about all the fun things we can do in Minneapolis, most of which involve bars and parties.

I gently remind her, "I'm only staying for one night, Lain. Plus, I have an early morning flight to catch tomorrow."

It's not that early—the plane I'm booked on to Vegas doesn't leave till eleven—but it's safer to let on like the flight is at the ass crack of dawn. I'm hoping to deter party girl from keeping me out half the night.

"Okay, okay," she concedes. "It doesn't matter when you leave. We're still finding ourselves some kind of trouble to get into tonight. And I mean trouble with a capital T, chica."

She's referring to drinking, which I don't do much of these days.

But tonight I'll make an exception.

"All right," I say, a smile playing at my lips. "Maybe it's time I show you I really can party with the best of them."

"You're on," Lainey replies.

Gulp. I hope I can hang. The last time I had anything more than a glass of wine with dinner was on a date I went on last year. Yes, you read that right. A whole twelve months have passed since my most recent even remotely romantic encounter with a man. But even that was a bust. My date and I had absolutely nothing in common. He spent dinner texting on his cell phone, probably with another girl, and I drowned my sorrows with copious amounts of margaritas. It was all I could do to soothe my bruised ego.

While I lament the sad state of my dating life, Lainey continues to jabber on excitedly about this evening and what we can do while I'm there. Between my "yeah" and "uh-huh" responses, I have to chuckle. My sister turned twenty-one last month and everything to her is still so über-exciting.

I'm the calm one in comparison. I guess that's because I'm three years older. But it's not only that. We're just different. Really, the only thing we have in common is the way we look. Both of us have raven-black hair that we wear long, and we share the same turquoise-blue eye color.

Apart from that, we're like night and day.

Lainey is the party girl.

I'm the serious, career-oriented one.

She's the boy-crazy chick with guys lining up to ask her out.

I, as established, rarely date.

Hmm, I really need to change that, though. I've been feeling extra-lonely lately.

"Wow," Lainey says, sounding suddenly shocked, and thus distracting me from my reverie.

"What's wow?" I ask.

"I still can't believe you worked things out so you can come up and visit me. *And* all while getting ready to go on a business trip. I have to say, Aubs, this is very unlike you."

"Maybe I'm turning over a new leaf," I reply with a firm nod she unfortunately can't see.

You need to mix it up if you ever expect this boring life of yours to change, a little voice inside my head has been reminding me, thus prompting this decision.

"I hope so." Lainey sounds cautiously optimistic. "You need more fun in your life. I love seeing you take a chance here and there. It's like I always say—you never know what might happen if you throw caution to the wind once in a while."

I've shared with Lainey lately how I'm tiring of the dull and routine-driven life I lead, this existence filled with work, work, and more work. I'm married to my job, but damn it, I need a mistress. Or would that be a master?

Oh my! My long-neglected lady bits like that idea.

"Aubrey, did you hear me?"

"Yes, yes." I clear my throat. "You're absolutely right. I've been thinking about what we talked about a while ago and I'm trying to go with the flow a little more. That's why I booked the flight, totally impulsively, to come see you. Who knows, Lainey? Maybe tonight I'll *really* cut loose. We all know I'm due."

That's right. I may as well jump aboard the YOLO train and ride it to the land of wild abandon. Maybe if I do, I'll even meet someone tonight. Someone I'll never see again, of course, but that's good. I need a practice-man I can sharpen my flirt moves on. They're rusty as hell and could use some fine-tuning, especially if I ever plan to use them to land a guy some day. Hopefully that "landing" will occur within the next decade, seeing as the last real boyfriend I had was way back in college.

Damn, that puts things in perspective. And it reminds me of my sex life.

Pfft, what sex life?

"Right," I whisper. "More like lack thereof."

Beneath my jeans, I imagine my lady bits making a little sign of the cross, praying to reverse the curse of the dreaded dick-drought. Realistically though, despite all my bluster, I don't see that happening anytime soon. Not with another work assignment starting up in Las Vegas.

"So, Aubrey, this more impulsive you," my sister begins. "Does this mean we'll be seeing more of her? Like, on a consistent basis?"

"Don't expect me to be wild *all* the time," I hedge. When I hear her groan, I hasten to add, "Don't worry, though. Compared to how I've been lately, there's a lot more crazy-Aubrey days brewing up ahead."

She laughs, but then warns, "Be careful. You've gone so long without taking chances that you're at risk of getting hooked on the adrenaline rush you're bound to feel when you finally let go."

Jeez, am I really that bad? Probably, seeing as I don't do anything impulsive, like ever. My job pretty much precludes me from that kind of recklessness.

"I hope you're right," I murmur. "I need a jolt of…something."

"Hey, I'm just happy I get to spend some time with you, even if it is just for one night." Softly, she adds, "I really missed not seeing you at Mom and Dad's this summer."

"Oh, Lainey, I know."

Regret gnaws at my gut. See, this is why I need a change. My lonely existence not only lacks a man, but my relationship with my family has been suffering, as well.

"I wanted to visit," I continue. "Really, I did. But I got so damn tied up with my last client that the next thing I knew summer was over. And then there you were, back at school."

"Yeah, here I am," she murmurs. "And you're about to start a new assignment."

"Yep," I reply.

"The busy and exciting life of a life coach continues," she says with a smile in her tone.

"Hardly," I scoff. "It's busy, yes. But I don't know about the exciting part."

"Hey, I know you claim it can be grueling sometimes—and you miss out on things, true—but really, Aubrey, what a gig."

"It's not all sunshine and roses," I assure her.

Undeterred, she goes on. "So this latest client, the one you just finished with, was he another rich dude who turned out to be a handful?"

"Aren't they all?" I say on a sigh.

I like my job, but truthfully it wears on me. Being a "life coach" to troubled celebrities requires a ton of commitment. Not to mention you have to jump at a moment's notice. And that's exactly what I've been doing for the past twelve hours, scrambling like a chicken with its head cut off.

After I received a call from my boss, Mr. Delahunty, late last night, the scrambling began. I have a new client. A client I have no real info on that I need to meet with tomorrow afternoon. It's usually like this with my kind of work. I go in blind to assure the client's anonymity until all the contracts are signed.

Lainey sighs longingly into the phone. Even after assuring her that it's not all fun and games, she insists on clinging to the false illusion that my job is great.

Dreamily, she murmurs, "Difficult clients or not, you still have the coolest job on the planet."

"I guess," I grudgingly reply.

My job is pretty cool, when viewed as an outsider. I mean, come on, working with celebrities, most of who end up being hot male clients. That can't be all that bad, right?

Wrong.

It's a huge time and energy commitment. And though it pays well, I sacrifice a lot. I guess I should throw in here that I'm employed by a very discreet firm, one that specializes in helping not only troubled celebrities, but also messed-up musicians and professional athletes with issues. My job is to help the client get their life straightened out, so they can shine like the star they are.

Sometimes booze is the problem, and other times it's drugs. One time we had a client who was addicted to hookers. I got that one, lucky me. But no matter what the issue is, I'm there, playing counselor, psychologist, and friend.

Our firm is based in Chicago, so that's where I live at the moment. I could live anywhere really, seeing as I'm always traveling and spending months at a time in various locations around the country. I go where I'm needed…and stay as long as required.

"Where are you crashing tonight?" Lainey asks out of the blue. Before I can answer, she adds, "You can stay with me if you want. I'm sure my roomies wouldn't mind."

What? No.

Lainey lives in a house with three other girls, all of whom are in school. Their place is located only two blocks from campus, making it party central most nights. I might never make it to Vegas if I crash there.

"No, that's okay," I reply. "I already have a room booked at a hotel out by the airport."

"Oh, okay."

I remind my disappointed-sounding sister, "This is still part of a business trip, Lainey."

"Okay, okay, I get it." I imagine her rolling her eyes at her *not-quite-wild-yet* big sister. "But we're still having fun tonight, no matter what. I'm making sure of it."

The sensible side of me takes over for a minute and I remind her, "A good time is fine, but I need to be back at the hotel at a sensible hour. I can't miss my flight. I need to be sharp and clear-headed when I get to Vegas tomorrow. The client will be at the meeting, and I'd like to make a good impression."

"The new client is out west, that's cool." Lainey says.

"Yeah, I suppose so."

"So who is it this time around?"

"I don't know," I honestly reply, not that I could tell her even if I did. Confidentiality is paramount in my line of work. Still, it's safe to say, "My boss didn't inform me of much. Only thing I know for certain is I'm attending a meeting with the client and their management team in the afternoon. Everything about the client—what he does for a living, what his name is—will remain a secret till then."

"Sounds intriguing," Lainey muses. "It must be someone good."

"Hmm, maybe," I reply, wondering myself who I'll be matched up with.

"It's a guy, for sure, that you're helping?"

"Yeah. From what my boss indicated it's definitely a male client."

"Ooh, maybe this one will be über hot and you'll fall for him."

Hot or not, that would be a big NO! Fraternizing with the client is strictly forbidden, which is fine with me. Lainey has no idea how messed up these guys actually are. And yes, I use the term "guys" because our firm works with far more male clients than female ones.

"It doesn't matter if he's hot," I say to Lainey. "We're not permitted to date our clients."

"That's a shame."

"No, not really," I reply. "These guys are usually complete nightmares."

It's true. I've worked with two male clients so far this year alone, and both were so screwed up that each required a multi-month commitment. Dating either of them would never have crossed my mind.

"But you help them become all sweet and kind," Lainey says.

Oh, the delusions of youth.

Chuckling, I reply, "I wish I had that kind of influence, Lain. But the truth is I only help my clients straighten out enough so they become successful again. They tend to remain epic jerks."

Case in point, my most recent client, an aging quarterback, turned out to be more than a handful. He was a fallen hero with a massive pill-popping problem, and my job was to fix him before the fans figured out what was really going on. His team was close to canning him, but I finally talked him into giving rehab one final try. It worked too. But I had to hang around to counsel him and make sure it stuck. The quarterback—and I wish like hell I could share his name with you—is right now in training camp. I'm proud to report he's clean and sober, and throwing bombs like he did ten years ago.

But that doesn't mean he wasn't a terror to work with. He was. He blatantly hit on me every freaking day, begging me to go out with him, forbidden or not. The grossest part was he was freaking married!

Ugh, I need hazard pay.

And I totally do.

Before the philandering footballer, I was assigned to work with an alcoholic actor. Back in the day, this guy was every teen's dream. But now thirty, he was struggling to land roles. Even though he was half in the bag and ready to give up, I took him on. I got him sober and back to feeling good about himself. I heard just the other day that he landed a role on a hot new TV show.

Good for him, even though he was an ass. Too bad my non-disclosure agreement precludes me from sharing with Lainey how he used to find it infinitely amusing to flash his dick, like every single day I worked with him. She'd freak if she knew that. But she'd *really* freak if she knew just how tiny his lusted-after prick is.

I chuckle, thinking of how that itty-bitty thing was so not worth showing off. Even my hungry-for-dick lady bits were bored.

"What's so funny?" Lainey wants to know when I start giggling.

"Oh, nothing," I reply, pulling myself together.

"Is it something about a client?"

"Lainey," I warn.

"Damn it, Aubrey," she huffs. "You never tell me anything good."

"I can't," I remind her. "Believe me, I wish I could. But you know how it is. I sign strict confidentiality agreements with each and every client. If I told you anything specific I'd get fired from the firm."

"Someday, I swear," Lainey says, sounding mischievous, "I'm going to get a name out of you. And I bet when it happens it'll be because you fall for one of these guys."

"Never going to happen," I maintain. "You may as well give up on that crazy fantasy."

My sister groans. "Boo, you're no fun. But you bet your ass I'm holding you to the having fun-rule tonight. I know just where we're going too."

"Oh no, what am I about to get myself into here?"

"A text popped up while you were talking. Apparently there's a party tonight at some sweet lake house just outside the city. I've heard of the place. I think it belongs to some rich baseball player."

"Sports, huh?" I start chewing on my nails. "I don't know about this, Lainey."

"Oh, come on," she pleads. "This isn't one of your clients. You told me yourself you've never worked with any fucked-up baseball players."

"That's true," I murmur, considering.

The only problem is that Lainey doesn't know a baseball from a football. I guess I'll have to trust her on this one. I can't back out now, not after all my "new me" talk. Nonetheless, I picture all the files I've recently seen at the office, ones for everyone in our firm. When I'm satisfied there's never been any baseball clients in Minneapolis, I say, "Okay. I'll go."

"Cool. Promise me you won't change your mind at the last minute and back out."

"No, I'm all in," I assure her.

"Thank God."

"After all," I continue, trying to convince myself more than her. "What possible harm can come from attending one little party?"

"That's the spirit," Lainey says.

Yep, this is the new me, throwing caution to the wind.

"You're about to see a whole new side of me tonight," I tell my sister. "Someone wild and fun and free."

Crap, I hope I don't end up regretting this tomorrow.

I DON'T HAVE A F*CKING PROBLEM

BRENT

"**D**ude, you have got to see this bullshit."

Benny has just come out of his bedroom, and he's mad as hell.

I look behind him, expecting to see a girl all upset and shit. But no, he's alone. At least, I think he is.

"What's the problem?" I inquire, wavering on my feet. I'm a bit unsteady, but happily buzzed. The party is in full swing, and I've done my fair share of imbibing already. "You got a girl hidden in there that you're trying to ditch?" I crane my neck to see past big Benny.

He shakes his head. "No, no girl. Not yet, that is." He winks and smiles, but then his smile fades. "Check this shit out, though."

He shoves his cell under my nose, and I try to read what has him so irate. But in my current state the words are too fucking blurry to make out.

"Fuck, man," I grumble. "You're holding it way too close for me to read anything." I take the phone from him and hold it at a bunch of different angles. At last, I find one where I can see the words.

Well, sort of.

As I sort-of read the fuzzy message, I mutter, "Dude, this is nuts."

"Yeah, see. I told you it was bad."

I blink and the e-mail comes into better view, so I read it once again.

Handing the phone back to Benny, I shake my head. "Wow. I can't believe the team's threatening to trade you. That's harsh."

Benny brushes back his mop of blond hair and rolls his unfocused green eyes. He's almost as fucked up as me.

"Yeah, well, a trade is imminent only if I refuse to admit myself to some fucking treatment center out in goddamn Arizona. One the team has handpicked for me." He pockets his phone and sighs. "I have to be there, checked in, by tomorrow night."

When Benny grabs for the bottle of Grey Goose I've been nursing, I let him have it. With this news, he needs it more than me.

After he downs what's left, he says, "Goddamn management. I don't have a fucking problem."

Some random girl walks by us just then, a full bottle of vodka in hand. In my best take-care-of-me-babe voice, I ask her if I can *please, please have it*. She gives it to me, of course, and then tries to stick around. Benny and I shoo her away. We don't have time for bitches tonight.

Unscrewing the cap, I raise the bottle and declare to my friend, "I don't have a fucking problem, either."

As I'm taking a long pull, I spy Nolan coming around the corner.

"What are you two little bitches whining about back here in the dark?" he asks when he reaches us.

"Fuck off," I say, lowering the bottle.

Nolan laughs.

Benny then fills him in on what's going on, and when he's done, I ask him, "Have *you* heard anything from team management?"

He shakes his head. "No, not a word."

I'm not surprised. Even though Nolan has spent the summer with us, and he's done his fair share of partying, he's not the hot mess Benny is. Along with those workouts in my basement gym, Nolan's been diligently stocking the fridge with loads of healthy shit.

Twenty-five going on forty, remember?

"What about you?" Nolan asks me. "Any e-mail ultimatums for the captain of the team?"

"Not a one," I reply, feeling rather smug.

I'm pretty confident I'll *never* receive an e-mail like that. I mean, come on. The team would never trade *me*. Or force me to do anything I didn't want to do.

Benny, taking note of the cocky expression on my face, says, "You're forgetting something, Nolan."

"What's that?"

"Our 'golden boy' is untouchable, remember?"

"Good point." Nolan laughs in his low, even timbre. "I almost forgot that Brent Oliver can do no wrong."

I call them out for what they are. "You're both pricks."

Benny gestures to the living room, where it's noisy as hell. And getting noisier by the minute.

"Come on, Golden Boy," he says good-naturedly. "We better get our drink on, party our asses off, and make this night count for something.

Looks like this party has just become what you said it would be—the last blowout of the summer."

"Speak for yourself, Perry." I laugh. "I'm not the one receiving e-mails shutting down any of *my* extracurricular activities." I raise the vodka to my lips. "I don't, nor will I ever have a fucking problem. I handle my shit just fine, thank you very much."

I take another long pull from the bottle, all while Benny laughs at my over-confident ass.

He pushes past me to head back to the party, patting my shoulder as he goes. "Keep lying to yourself, dude," he says.

Benny is joking—I think—but the look Nolan gives me tells me everything I need to know—I *am* lying to myself. Because, let's admit it, I clearly have a problem. And it's a rather big fucking one. In fact, it just keeps getting bigger, this problem of mine, when not five minutes later I receive a text from my agent.

It's a warning that my ass better be on a private jet tomorrow.

Huh?

Apparently, there's a mandatory meeting with management in Vegas. And if I miss it, I'm toast.

What in the hell could this possibly be about?

PARTY LIKE A ROCK STAR

AUBREY

"This party is the best, Lainey," I scream over the noise. "Have I told you lately how much I love you? I do, little sis, and I'm so happy you brought me here."

Lainey smiles over at me. "I'm glad you're having a good time, sweetie," she says. "Like I said this morning, when we were on the phone, you deserve a night like this, just some good, old-fashioned reckless fun."

She hugs me and when she pulls away, everything goes blurry. "Whoa, don't move so fast," I say.

Worry creases Lainey's brow, and she peers down at the red plastic cup in my hand. "I think it's time to start pacing yourself, Aubrey. You don't drink much these days, so maybe slow it down a notch. At the rate you've been going, you're either going to get sick or pass out."

I'm definitely drunk, but to Lainey I maintain, "Nah, not me. I'm a trooper."

Belying that point, I shift my weight from one foot to the other and almost topple over. Lucky for me Lainey has fast reflexes and grabs my elbow.

"I'm good, I'm good," I insist as I right myself with her assistance.

"Pacing, Aubrey," Lainey repeats. "Learn it, live it, make it a way of life."

"My stumbling wasn't on account of me being drunk," I huff.

She laughs, and I point down to the four-inch shiny black heels I borrowed from her to complement my shimmery red party dress. "It's these damn shoes you gave me to wear. They're deadly."

"Yeah, sure they are," Lainey replies, shaking her head. "Good thing *I'm* the designated driver this evening."

On that, I can't disagree. "Yeah, good thing," I concede.

And then, for no reason other than the fact I'm buzzed to the gills, I yell to the crowd, "Party like rock stars, dudes!"

That earns me some interesting looks. Okay, clearly I am beyond buzzed. Lainey is right; these vodka tonics I've been slinging back are catching up to me.

"I'm going to be so hungover tomorrow," I groan as I finally admit I'm inebriated.

"You can sleep it off on your flight to Vegas," my sister says reassuringly. Much more of a partier than I, she's well-versed in next-day hangover remedies, which she proves when she adds, "Drink lots of water when you get back to the hotel. And eat a couple bananas. That'll replenish your potassium."

"Thank you, Dr. Lainey."

She shakes her head at me, but in a good way. I can tell she's glad

I'm cutting loose and goofing around, just like I promised.

"I'm proud of you," she yells over the ever-growing crowd noise. "You're really sticking to this 'new you' philosophy of having fun."

"I sure am," I agree, raising my cup. "But this reckless me is making an appearance tonight only. It's fine to get a little crazy in a place where no one knows me. Speaking of which, thank God I'll never have to see any of these people ever again."

"Here, here." Lainey taps her water bottle to my cup. "Get wild, crazy girl."

"To one night of absolute abandon," I declare.

As I polish off what's left in my cup, Lainey says, "Hey, on a serious note, I'm glad you came out with me tonight." She makes a little hand flourish in front of me, like I'm a prize on a game show. "You look stunning, Aubs. That dress is amazing. You should consider wearing it to your meeting tomorrow. You know"—she puts her fists up in a mock-fighting stance—"knock 'em dead and all that."

More like get fired and all that.

I peer down at the cute and clingy red number I stuffed in my suitcase before I left this morning. I packed it on the off chance I'd actually venture out at some point on this trip. And wow, here I am, already wearing the dress and partying like a rock star. But a dress like this, all sexy and low-cut, is best reserved for nightlife only.

"I think this might be a bit much for business," I state.

"Still, it's a good thing you brought it. Otherwise you wouldn't look so fabulous tonight."

"Thanks, Lain." I smile over at her. "I'm glad I threw it in my bag at the last minute. I almost didn't."

"Why? What do you usually pack for these work trips?"

"Business suits for meetings and lots of leggings and comfy shirts for the downtime."

Lainey lets out a little laugh. "Talbots and LuLaRoe, right?"

"You know it."

I sway a little from side to side, moving to the music someone just turned up.

Lainey smiles and says, "You're kind of funny when you're tipsy."

Still swaying, I remark, "I may be a little more than tipsy, Lainey, m'dear."

She laughs, and I decide it's probably best to stop moving so much since it's making me kind of dizzy.

Lainey is peering into the crowd, so I do the same. There are lots of guys, and she's eyeing them up and down, checking each one out. I don't usually assess men, but then again, maybe that's my problem.

What the hell; let the assessing commence...

Guy with a mullet, that's a no-go.

Oh, hey, there's one who's kind of cute.

Oh wait, crap. He's with a girl already. I sigh. *The good ones are always taken.*

Whoa, wait, who the heck is that?

A stunning specimen of hot maleness comes into view, and blinking to be sure I'm seeing correctly, I muse, "Wow, is he real?"

I fear he may be a mirage. You know how thirsty people imagine seeing water out in the desert? Maybe that's what's happening now. This man—if he's even real—could actually be hideous. Maybe the dick-drought has finally affected my brain. Can that even happen?

"Is who for real?" Lainey asks, interrupting my drunken panic that I'm losing my mind.

Before I can point out the model-caliber dude who's captured my attention and confirm he's not a mirage, Lainey sees him for herself.

"*Who* is that?" she exclaims.

Thank God, he's real. "That's what I'd like to know," I murmur.

"Shit, Aubrey, that guy is hot enough to qualify as bona fide book boyfriend material."

Whoa, this is serious.

I shoot my sister a look. She has an insatiable romance novel obsession, along with a slew of what she terms "book boyfriends." I hear about them all the time. There's a Christian, some dude named Barrons, and a Gideon in there somewhere. That's just three I can name off the top of my head, thanks to my current drunken state.

But back to this guy, this real-life, incredibly delectable man… Wow! I don't know if he's a book boyfriend come to life, but he definitely personifies masculine perfection. He's tall, has olive-toned skin, thick dark brown hair, a strong jaw, high cheekbones… Oh, hell, you get the picture.

Gah!

Oh, and let's not forget about his oh-so-sculpted bod. Or, at least what I can discern of it under his dark jeans and tight black tee.

Dreamily, I lean against Lainey and say, "Look at him, Lain. I bet your romance authors would have a blast writing about a guy like him."

"They would, and they do write about guys like him," she assures me. "All the time, in fact. Why do you think I read so much?"

"It all makes perfect sense now. I clearly need to load up my Kindle."

"You do," she agrees. "I'll send you some recs. You've totally been missing out."

Lainey, though she's talking with me, sounds somewhat distracted. So I follow her gaze…

Hmm, she's staring beyond my dream guy to some other hot male that my guy just stopped to talk to. This new hot guy is a huge mass of muscle, with longish blond hair that's wild and unruly. My sister is riveted, and I think I know why. "Hey, that blond guy looks a little like Thor. Didn't you go see that movie, like, ten times?"

"Shut up, Aubrey." She nudges my shoulder playfully. "I only went to see it twice."

"And the DVD?"

"Okay, yes. *That*, I may have worn out. Along with a couple of battery-operated devices."

I roll my eyes. "I don't even want to know what that means."

"Oh"—she winks at me—"but I think you do."

"You and your sex toys," I say, laughing. "You're shameless."

"You will be too," she says, "once you finally break down and buy one."

Pointing back into the crowd, I say, "Just get back to staring at Thor. You can use him for fantasy material later."

"You bet your ass I will."

We share a smile that it's cool we can be so open with each other. But when we look back into the crowd, Thor is gone, lost in the growing sea of people. My guy is still there, though. My real-life book boyfriend. And he seems to be getting closer, seeing as he's walking toward us.

Wait, what?

"Shit," I murmur.

Lady bits go on high alert, and I can almost hear the whistles sounding, "Incoming, incoming projectile."

I'm safe—and they're safe—as I soon realize he's not even looking at us. Me. *Whatever!* Book Boyfriend is too busy pushing through the mass of people while staring intently at a smartphone in his hand.

At one point, he stops and lifts the device to scowl at whatever's on the screen. When he lowers it, he bites out what appears to be a curse.

He then lifts the device again and shakes his head, like he can't believe what he's reading.

Well, I can't believe how hot you are. So color us both surprised, buddy.

As he nears me, I start to feel like I'm in the best dream ever. You know the kind, where you never want to wake up because everything in dreamland is going the way you wish things would go in real life. You know—perfectly.

Our eyes meet, but only for a second. I don't think he even registers my existence, but it's enough for me.

I lift my hand to wave him over, but Lainey stops me. "What the hell are you doing?"

I shrug, hand poised in the air. "I'm making a move, taking a chance." I start waving my hand like a nut, all while yelling, "Yolo, yolo, yolo!"

"Stop that," Lainey hisses. "Oh my God, you've completely lost it."

She grabs my hand and lowers it to my side. "No yolo crap in this sea of people. If you're attracted to the guy, fine. But there are better ways to get his attention. Why don't you get him alone for a minute? Talk to him. Find out if he has a girlfriend. If he does, she could be here. You don't want to embarrass yourself, do you?"

Lainey is clearly not onboard the YOLO train. I need to get her a ticket. But for now, I refocus on the crowd.

"Okay," I say, "I'll be good." And then, "Aw, shit, Lainey. My guy disappeared, just like Thor. Damn it."

Lainey places her hand on my shoulder reassuringly. "Hey, if it's meant to be you'll find him again."

"I don't know about that." I shake my head. Finding him seems like a daunting task when I can barely walk a straight line.

"Come on." She takes my hand. "I need more water."

"Ooh!" I lift my cup. "And another drink for me?"

Lainey narrows her eyes as she gives me an assessing once-over. "I don't know about that. I think you need a break from the booze. Pacing, remember? Let's grab you a bottle of water for now."

She's no fun. "Okay," I say, complete with a pout.

As we head downstairs to where there's a big tub of ice filled with bottled water, I think about Book Boyfriend.

"I can't quit thinking about him, Lainey," I admit as I carefully navigate one stair at a time. "Did you see his eyes? They had to have been the prettiest shade of brown I've ever seen."

"You could make out the color from that far away?" Lainey sounds doubtful as she helps me down the last step. "And while intoxicated?"

I smack her arm, and then end up holding onto it for support. "Shut up. Seriously, did you not notice the rich deep color?"

"Um, no, can't say that I did."

"Well, I did."

I'm insistent, though truly I'm not sure now if I'm imagining things.

Still, horny and sexually-deprived girl that I am, I go on. "God, that body. And that *face.* Those eyes too. I bet I could out-romance your romance writers with a spot-on description."

"Oh, this should be good," Lainey snorts. "And just how would you describe his eyes?"

I scramble to come up with a fitting literary description. Only problem is I'm not a writer. The best I can do is this...

"His eyes are like the color at the center of a sunflower. The fuzzy part, you know? Where it's all dark brown and inviting—"

"Fuzzy? Inviting?"

"Shut up, I'm not done. And, yes, fuzzy and inviting. Like you could cozy up in—"

My sister stops me. "Jesus, Aubrey, please no more. Whatever you do, do *not* take up writing. That may be the weirdest comparison I've ever heard of to describe a hot guy's eyes." She shakes her head. "Really, Aubrey, *sunflowers*?"

Nudging her, and suddenly in touch with my inner comedian, I say, "You have to admit it was a flowery description. Get it, Lainey? Flowers, sun*flowers*."

Lainey rolls her eyes. "You're killing me, Aubrey."

Just then her phone buzzes, thus putting an end to any more talk of Flowery Eyes. Or was that Sunflower Eyes?

She grabs my arm. "Hey, hold up. Margeaux is texting me something about another party."

Margeaux is one of Lainey's roommates and also her best friend, so I throw out, "You should invite her to the party."

Lainey, still reading the text, murmurs, "Hmm, I don't think so. There's another party that's closer to campus. That's what the text is about. Aubrey, it sounds really fun." She looks up from the phone, eyes pleading. "What do you think? Tell me you'd be okay with us taking off and heading over to that one?"

The only thing missing is a "please, please, please," like Lainey used to do when we were kids. The writing's on the wall, like in neon graffiti. A party close to where Lainey lives means she can park her car at her house and walk over. And then she can drink, like I've been doing. I don't begrudge her wanting to have fun too. I'm sure it's boring for her to watch everyone get drunk while she's stone-cold sober.

There's just one little fly in the ointment.

I'd prefer to stay at *this* party, seeing as there's a guy here, one who looks like a book boyfriend, and one I may actually have a chance of meeting and talking to before the night is over.

"Go ahead and go," I say to Lainey, with all this in mind. "I need to head back to my hotel soon, anyway."

Lainey frowns. "Wait, how do you plan to get back if I leave you here? I'm your ride, silly girl."

More like drunken girl. But hey, I'm a drunken girl with a plan.

"I'll just call for an Uber," I state, like this is such a given it shouldn't even need to be articulated. I can't let her in on my real motive, or she may try to talk me out of it.

"I don't know." My sister scans the crowd. "I don't think I should leave you here by yourself. You could get into some real trouble, seeing how drunk you are."

My baby sister, the voice of reason. And me, living on the edge. The world has truly gone crazy.

"Alone?" I gesture to all the partygoers. "I'll hardly be alone. And hell, Lainey, almost everyone here is drunk."

I'm not exaggerating; there are lots of people stumbling about. Lainey crosses her arms as she takes them all in.

"That's the problem," she says, at last. "Plus, there are more guys here than girls. And since they're all drinking, who knows what they'll be getting up to later."

The wheels in my head are turning as I try to come up with a plan to convince Lainey to leave without me. "Okay, tell you what..." I begin.

"Yes?" she replies, arms still determinedly crossed.

I whip out my phone and open the Uber app in front of her. "I'll order my ride right now in front of you. This way you can go ahead and leave, all with the assurance that your big sister is in good hands."

"It's not Uber's hands I'm worried about," she mumbles under her breath.

I let out a groan. "Oh, come on, Lainey. Go have fun at this other party. Think about it. My hotel's out of your way, anyway. You shouldn't have to drive me all the way across town. If I went with you to this other party I'd probably end up calling for a ride, anyway." I look down at the phone and start tapping at the screen. "You'd like to at least have a couple of drinks before the night is over, right?"

"Yeah," she says. "I guess."

"So, go. You deserve a good time too. Your boring old sister has had the whole evening to cut loose. And trust me, I've had a blast. But it's time for me to get back to being responsible. And that means returning to the hotel and getting my ass to bed."

"You did say you have an early morning tomorrow," Lainey mutters, more to herself than to me.

I can tell she's almost where I want her to be—comfortable with leaving without me.

I hurry her along to that end. "Yes, yes, I have a really early morning," I fib.

Lainey appears torn, chewing at her bottom lip. She always does that when she's unsure of something.

I hold up my phone to show her there's a ride on the way. Hopefully, that'll assuage her concern.

"Look," I say, nodding to the screen. "My ride will be here in eighteen minutes."

Crap, she needs to leave, like now so I can cancel the Uber and start searching for Sunflower Eyes. Hmm, maybe I should think of a more manly-sounding name for him? But until then, back to the point— who knows when I'll have another chance to be so reckless?

Lainey takes a deep breath, and then releases it on a loud sigh. "You sure you'll be all right?" she asks.

I peer down at the phone. "For seventeen… No, wait, sixteen more minutes, yes, I think I will survive. "

"Okay, then. Since you have a ride on the way I'll go."

Yes!

Her phone buzzes again, and I place my hand on her back to give her an encouraging little shove. "Go, go. That's probably Margeaux, wondering where you are."

Lainey turns around and hugs me. I hug her back, holding onto her tightly. "Bye, Aubs," she says in my ear. "I love you. I'm glad we had this chance to hang out tonight."

"Me too, sweetie. And I love you too. Bunches and bunches."

"Call me once you're settled in. You can tell me all about your new client." She leans in close and whispers, "I know you can't give me any specifics, but you can at least let me know if he's a sex god."

"You're so weird." I playfully push her away. "No names, though, remember?"

"You're no fun."

"Go, go," I say again. "Get out of here."

Lainey turns to leave, but before she walks away, she says, "Text when you arrive in Vegas so I know you got in safely."

"I will, I will."

I watch as Lainey finally departs. Once I've lost her in the crowd, I immediately cancel my Uber ride and toss my cell back in my purse.

Then, I begin my search.

But distractions keep me from my goal.

I stop several times when I'm corralled to down shots with various groups of friendly partiers. So much for pacing myself, I get drunker than ever. And—who knew?—drunken me likes to talk to random strangers. Soon, I forget all about the hot guy I was hoping to corner.

"I'm having too much fun," I mutter to myself as I stumble around. "Everyone is so nice."

I accidentally wreck into a group of girls at one point. They help me find a downstairs bathroom when I share that my bladder is about to burst. In the bathroom, two of the girls listen to me lament about the state of my current—read: nonexistent—love life.

"I haven't had what could qualify as a real boyfriend in so long," I share as I fluff out my shiny dark hair in front of a mirror. "And my last date was a complete bust. I swear I'm cursed. I only meet losers or players. That's why I've pretty much given up on the dating game."

"Don't lose heart," one girl tells me as I gloss my lips. "You'll find someone."

Ha. She's as drunk as I am so I don't put much stock in her trying-to-be-encouraging words.

As time passes, and back in the party fray, I lose track of my new friends and wander back upstairs. Strolling around the big living room where most of the guests are hanging, I sip at a beer.

Maybe beer isn't such a good idea, though. It makes me have to pee. Again, like now.

With no one around to help me find my way this time, I'm left to wander on my own. I go down what feels like many halls in my quest to scope out a bathroom.

But I have no luck.

Until, finally, I venture down a hallway I pick at random.

"I don't know, though," I say to myself. "This one seems pretty empty."

As I continue down what feels like an endless corridor, I find myself squeaking out, "Yikes, it sure is dark back here."

I should probably turn around; this is clearly an off-limits area. But then I come upon a huge room where the hallway ends. I step inside since the door is open.

Holding onto the wall for support, I feel around for a switch. When I find what feels like one, I flip it up.

A lamp flickers to life, illuminating what appears to be a spacious bedroom. There's a huge bed in the center, some funky black furniture with chrome accents, and lots of windows. There's also a very masculine-y feel to the room, leading me to conclude it must be the party-thrower's room. You know, the baseball player.

There are some photos on the walls, and they appear to be sports-oriented, but my feet are killing me far too much to go check them out. I don't care for baseball, anyway.

I toe off the offending pumps by the door, and then make my way over to the massive bed. Taking a seat on the edge, I rub my poor soles. Seems even large amounts of alcohol can't silence screaming arches.

Lucky for me, when I look up I spot an ensuite bathroom. "Finally!"

My bladder urges me to go take care of business, even though I'm so sleepy I could pass out right here.

And I might.

But nature calls.

Forcing myself to stand, I stumble to the bathroom. When I'm finished, I'm so out of it that I push my lacy red panties all the way *down* my legs instead of pulling them up.

"Oops. They go *up* your legs, goofball. Not down." Giggling, I add, "Unless you were planning on having some fun."

Yeah, right, if only.

Sadly, I never found the stunning specimen of man I was eyeing up earlier. My real-life book boyfriend, my Sunflower Eyes, he may as well have been a figment of my imagination.

When I start to tug my panties back up my legs, I lean way too far forward and almost face-plant off the throne. I decide to just leave the damn things on the floor. "Really, why must we wear underwear all the time, anyway?"

Okay, so all the alcohol I've consumed has clearly left me befuddled. "Too much to drink," I mutter as I return to the room and fall back on the big bed.

I'm ready for sleep, but my eyes feel drier than the Sahara desert. My extended-wear contacts need a break. Good thing I brought a case and my glasses. Rolling to my stomach, I feel around in my purse for a contact case and my eyewear. Once I find what I need, I pop out my lenses and put on my glasses.

Scooting up to the top of the bed, I wiggle under what has to be the biggest, softest, puffiest comforter ever.

"Mm, this is nice. I'm jus' gonna lie here for minute."

Three seconds later, I'm tossing my glasses onto the stand by the bed. "Maybe make that fifteen minutes."

I close my eyes and I am out, dead to the world.

5

WHY DO THEY ALWAYS END UP IN MY BED?

BRENT

Around ten o'clock on the night of our awesome party, and after receiving an annoying e-mail that requires me to fly out to Las Vegas tomorrow—for who-the-hell-knows-what reason—I run out of vodka and switch to single-malt scotch. By two in the morning, I am obliterated, stumbling around and searching for my bedroom.

"I think it's down this way," I say to myself. And then chuckling at the confusing array of hallways in my place, I add, "No wonder girls get lost in here all the time."

But since it is *my* house, I find my bedroom just fine. At least I assume that I do, seeing as when I wake up the next morning it feels like I'm in my bed, all warm and snug under a thick white comforter.

But something's not right.

I open my eyes and am promptly blinded.

Fuck, why does the morning light streaming in through the window have to be so goddamn bright? Come to think of it, why do I have a big window like that in my bedroom to begin with?

I roll to my back, my head pounding like a woodpecker on crack as I forget all about windows and morning light. I know what the real problem is, anyway. Draping an arm over my achy eyes, I mutter, "Mixing hard liquor, never a good idea."

"Ugh, I am right there with you, pal," a feminine voice groans out from next to me.

Wait, what? I don't recall bringing anyone back to my bed. And what's with this chick calling me "pal?" Not the term of endearment I'm used to hearing once I get through with 'em.

I sit up abruptly. "What the fuck? Who the hell are you?"

I receive no answer, as Mystery Woman drifts back to sleep.

Huh, this is a first. Not that there's a girl in my bed; that's happened before. What's weird is that I have absolutely no recollection of nailing this particular one. It's a real shame too, since she's hot as hell.

Did I hit that, though, and just can't remember?

Nah, I don't think so, seeing as I'm sporting some impressive morning wood.

My cock strains against the comforter, pointing over at Mystery Woman like he's a divining rod. Yeah, that wouldn't be happening if I'd been laid properly.

Shit. Maybe we did do it and she sucked, and not in the good kind of way.

Mystery Woman, who may or may not be a good lay, finally comes to. She sits up next to me, stretching her lithe form. Yawning, she rubs her eyes, not bothering to look over at me. She must be half asleep and unaware I'm here. She probably thinks the guy she replied to a minute ago was part of a dream.

I check her out more thoroughly before she notices she's not alone.

Hmm, I don't think she's a puck bunny. Although if she is a PB she must be a wildly popular one, based on how sexy her body looks in that tight-as-sin red dress. The confident air surrounding her, though, screams to me that she's no dingy pushover. Nope, not with the kind of fire I see in those pretty turquoise eyes.

Oh, shit.

She just discovered she's not alone. And those stunning eyes are trained on me, narrowed in what appears to be anger.

Yeah, I definitely didn't fuck this one. She wouldn't be so mad if she'd gotten some Brent Oliver cock.

"Who the hell are you?" she asks as she pulls the comforter all the way up to her chin.

Maybe her eyes aren't narrowed, after all. I think she's just squinting. Can she not see me all that well?

"Hey." I wave a hand in front of her beautiful face, which she quickly smacks away.

Okay, not blind. Maybe near-sighted, though.

"Ugh. Boundaries, please," she snaps.

I suppress a laugh. This chick is cute, all worked up like this.

I try again to make nice by holding out my hand. "Hey. I know this is awkward and weird as hell, but I guess we should introduce ourselves. I'm Br—"

She winces and holds her head. "Can you just shut up for a minute? My head is killing me."

Wow. No one ever talks to me like that. "Talk about rude," I snap.

She squints over at me, still like she can barely see me. But see me, or not, she has no qualms about reading me the riot act.

"Whoever you are, mister, next time you fall into a bed you should check and make sure it's not already occupied."

Is she for real?

"Wait a goddamn second," I volley back as she's busy reaching for something over on the nightstand. Glasses, it looks like. "For the record, lady, this is *my* bed. Maybe you're the one who needs to check before invading someone's personal space."

"Invading *your* personal space?" She fumbles with the glasses, drops them once on the bed, and then picks them up. "That's rich coming from you, especially when it was your big, warm body, among *other* things, pressed up against my ass—"

She's gotten her glasses on now, which incidentally make her look even sexier, in a hot librarian sort of way.

"Why'd you stop?" I ask.

Behind the lenses, her pretty eyes are widened in shock. "Oh shit," she utters as she stares at me intently. "This can't be happening."

"What can't be happening?" I query, at a loss.

"It's—it's...*you!*"

Her appalled tone catches me off guard, prompting me to say, "What the hell is that supposed to mean?"

Glancing away, she says softly, "Uh, it doesn't mean anything."

Okay, if she's going to play games, then so am I. And do I ever have one for her. It's called: If I Can't Fuck You, Then Let Me Fuck *with* You.

"Hey," I begin, smirking, "I have a question for you."

"Okay?" She eyes me warily.

I lean in close and lower my voice to my sexiest rasp. "Did we"—I gesture between our bodies—"you know."

She jumps away from me, seemingly horrified I'd suggest such a thing. "Absolutely not," she states.

Good God, I don't want to give her a coronary.

Toning it down a notch, I say, "Relax, sweetheart. I know nothing happened. I'm just giving you a hard time."

"Why would you do that?" She's cute when she's perplexed.

I make an "isn't it obvious" face, nodding down to how our bodies are positioned, almost intertwined, in the bed. When she still doesn't get it, I lay it on the line for her.

"You're in my bed, honey. And, well, you know what *usually* happens when a man and a woman end up in bed together."

"True." She blows out a breath. "But though I ended up in your bed, I can assure you *that* didn't occur."

"Yes, yes"—I roll my eyes—"we've established that. But if I didn't bring you back, which I know I didn't, then how'd you end up in here?"

"It's not important," she murmurs.

Really, I don't think she knows. "Okay," I say.

Mystery Woman starts looking really uptight. Well, she's been looking that way since she put on her sexy librarian glasses, but this is more. Truth is, she probably could use a good roll in the hay to loosen her up a little.

Hey, I'm up for it—in more ways than one—if I can get her to agree. And I hope I can. Not only am I horny as hell, but look at her. She's gorgeous, even if she is a little weird. But, damn, weird or not, those turquoise eyes are mesmerizing. And all that shiny black hair would look good splayed out against my pillows. Don't even get me started on that sexy dress. The curves and ample cleavage it's showing off make me want to tear that red fabric away so I can see more.

We should definitely nail her, my dick urges. *Make a move, stupid.*

Leaning back against the pillows and lacing my fingers behind my head, I let my cock "dick-tate" my next words.

"So, we clearly missed our chance to hook up last night, seeing as we were both crushed." I flex my chest and arms, a move I *know* makes girls wet. "But you know what they say, right?"

Wary, she asks, "No. What do they say?"

"There's no time like the present."

She gawks at me like I've grown an extra head, and not the one I'm hoping to show her. Oh well, it was worth a shot. It's always a risk, letting the unreasonable head speak for the reasonable one. The guy below the belt is so impulsive, and, really, only ever has one thing in mind.

Gathering the comforter around her curvy little body, and providing her with more than enough coverage considering she also has on the dress, Mystery Woman scoots away from me, like I'm some kind of a pervert.

Really?

"If you didn't bring me here, then how do you think I got in your bedroom?" she asks, still clearly suspicious.

This again, please.

I lean forward and fold my arms across my chest. "Good question. Why don't you think about it a little harder so *you* can tell *me*?"

I really don't need an answer, though. I think I know exactly how she ended up in my room. This woman, like so many others, wandered down the wrong hallway while searching for a goddamn bathroom. It's happened too many times to count. And I must admit that sometimes one of the lost and weary—or should I say hot and horny—finds her way to my bed. If they're really sexy, like this one, I let them stay. And then I give them what they want—superstar cock.

This one, however, appears to be truly stumped as to how she ended up in here. Biting her full bottom lip, which makes my dick twitch, she glances around.

Finally, her tone turning apologetic, she says, "I don't really know how I ended up in your bed. I don't remember much of anything from last night, just bits and pieces."

"What do you remember?" I softly inquire.

I'm easing up since she is kind of adorable, all confused like this. What I'd really like is for her to stick around a while longer. Not so I can seduce her—though I won't rule that out—but so I can look at her some more.

Shit, I'm turning into a creeper.

"Well," she goes on, while I evaluate my motives. "I remember my sister bringing me to a party. And then I drank, like, a lot. I really don't drink all that often, so it hit me kind of hard."

She raises a hand to her head, like it's still hurting, so I say, "Hey, I have some aspirin in my medicine chest." I jerk my chin to indicate it's in the attached bathroom. "You can go grab some if you want. Or I can get it for you."

"Thanks, but that's okay. I think only time can heal this hangover."

She smiles, and I hope it means she's feeling more comfortable around me. Why that matters, I don't know. But since she's right about the hangover healing in time, I say, "I hear ya."

We share an understanding nod and a commiserating smile. *Ah, we're finally getting along, this is good.*

I then ask, "Can you tell me what else you do remember?"

"Sure." She smiles again, and shit, she's so fucking pretty, smeary dark eye makeup and all. "I remember wandering around by myself by the end of the night. I remember having told my sister to go ahead and leave a while earlier. I think I called for an Uber to take me back to my hotel."

Hotel, eh? So, she doesn't live around here. Wonder where's she's from?

I plan to ask, but before I get to that I need to know, "Did you call for that ride? Did they cancel on you or something?"

"No. I canceled it."

She's full-on chewing on her bottom lip now, like digging through these glimpses into last night is taking all she's got in the memory department.

"Why'd you cancel your ride?"

I'm curious as to why a woman would want to remain alone at a party where she obviously didn't know anyone.

"Good question," she says.

I figure we're at an impasse. We'll never know how, or why, she ended up in my bed. But then, all of a sudden, she starts blushing like crazy, like she may have just remembered the reason why she canceled her ride.

So, of course, I again ask, "Why'd you cancel your Uber?"

"Uh, no real reason."

"Oh, come on now."

In the faintest of whispers, I hear her say, "I was kind of hoping to meet a certain someone."

Good thing I have good hearing.

She makes a move like she's going to get out of the bed, and all I can think is: *No, not yet.*

"Wait." I grab her arm—lightly, mind you—but when she gives me a *what-the-hell-are-you-doing* look, I release her immediately and apologize. "Sorry."

She doesn't bolt, thank God.

Pulling her knees up to her chin, she buries her head in the comforter wedged between them. "This is so embarrassing," she mutters into the fluffy down.

"Who were you hoping to meet?" I press.

I'm insanely curious as to who it could have been. Maybe Nolan? Or perhaps it was Benny she'd set her sights on? Both are good-looking men. But then again, maybe, just maybe, she was hoping to meet me.

And assuming that was the case…

When she lifts her head and looks over at me, I take a chance and smile. I make sure it's a sweet smile, not a leering grin, lest it land me back in pervert territory.

She smiles back, and her eyes tell me all I need to know—it *was* me she was hoping to meet. And here we are, like it's goddamned fate or something.

Just like that, I am intrigued.

Something about this girl hits me in the right way. I sense she may not be in my bed because of my fame. Maybe she simply likes the way I look, nothing more than that. It'd be refreshing if she has no agenda, no long game of landing a hockey player for a boyfriend or a husband.

Over the course of the next few minutes, we don't utter a single word. And it's not even weird. Even when we let our eyes do all the talking.

I kind of like you, Mystery Woman.

I sort of like you too.

You look really good in my bed, kind of like you belong here.

I could stay a little longer, if you want?

Okay, that last one is a reach, but it's what I'm hoping she's communicating.

Is there a connection developing between us?

Yeah, I think so.

Until, suddenly…

A look of horror dawns on her face. Everything in her expression suddenly screams *you are not the guy I thought you were!*

No more eye-talk. I flat-out ask, "What's wrong? What just happened here?"

She backpedals away from me to more than halfway across my king-size bed.

What the hell?

Feeling under the comforter, and then what looks to be up under her dress, she gasps, "Where are my panties? You didn't take them off me last night, did you?"

"What?" I'm aghast. "Fuck, no."

Still, she persists, "If you did, that's really creepy. And I totally want them back."

Okay, now *I'm* aggravated. We just went from something nice to something shitty. I shouldn't be surprised. If it's not a girl with an agenda, it's a fucking psycho. I have the worst fucking luck when it comes to women. That's why I simply love 'em and leave 'em. It's just easier that way.

"I swear I didn't take your stupid panties off you," I snap. "I get enough pussy on my own, thank you very much. And to clarify, that would be conscious pussy. I certainly would never stoop so low as to undress a passed-out girl for a free peek."

Eyeing me like I've just been placed on a sex offenders list—hers— she asks in a snarky tone, "Well, what happened to them, then?"

"Shit, I don't know."

Okay, enough. Pretty or not, connection or not, I've had enough. I obviously misjudged her. She's one of the crazy ones, like foot-licker. Why do so many of the hot ones turn out to be psychos?

Who cares? my dick interjects. *Let's fuck her, anyway.*

"Shut up," I mutter.

"Did you just tell me to shut up?"

"What? No."

Psycho Girl—who's gone from Mystery Woman to Crazy Town territory—scrambles from my bed. She just about falls off the edge in doing so, but once she's standing she spins back to face me, hands on her hips.

Glaring at me like I'm the devil, she snaps, "You had to have taken my panties off me. I have no memory of taking them off on my own."

Fuck, she won't leave this alone.

"I told you I don't have your goddamn underwear." I let out a sigh. "But you know what?"

She cocks her head. "What?"

"I think it's time for you to go."

"Oh, that's just great," she fumes, flashing eye-daggers my way. "You not only steal my panties but now you're kicking me out of your house. To go forth in the world underwear-less! You're a real prick, you know that?"

I hold my tongue. I've learned it's best not to rile the psychos. And this one is clearly bat-shit nuts.

Still, I can't resist a little fun, seeing as she's hating on me big-time now anyway.

Grasping my morning wood under the covers, the clear outline giving her an idea of just how big I am, even semi-hard.

—Semi-hard, you ask? How can that be?

What can I say? My dick likes conflict.—

I raise a brow and smirk at her. "Hey, I bet I know what happened to your stupid panties." She gawks at me—and also at my dick—as I clamor on. "I think *you* took your own panties off last night, hoping to get some of this." I wiggle my junk for effect. "And let me tell you, honey. You wouldn't be the first to do something like that."

Scrunching up her face, but not before adjusting her glasses and surveying my cock once more, she hisses, "You are such a pig."

"Oink," I reply.

She throws up her hands. "God, get me out of here."

"Gladly." I let go of my dick and reach over to the nightstand for my cell. "Let me call you a car."

"Don't bother." Psycho Girl grabs her purse from the floor and, whipping out her own phone, politely informs me, "I'm perfectly capable of calling for my own ride."

"I was trying to be nice," I grind out between clenched teeth.

This chick is making me nuts. Her strain of crazy must be contagious.

"I don't need your twisted version of nice, Panty Stealer."

"Whatever," I mutter. "If you want to call for your own car, knock yourself out, honey."

Walking backward toward the door, she points at me and warns, "Quit calling me *honey*."

As she turns, hand in the air, ready to dismiss me all haughty-like, she clumsily trips over what appears to be her discarded pumps.

Chuckling, I can't stop myself from blurting out, "Watch your step, *honey*."

"Go fuck yourself, whatever-your-name-is."

Oh my God, she really doesn't know who I am. This is classic.

"Whatever you say, tough girl," I reply.

"Ugh!" She's spitting mad now, and spouting off the weirdest things, like, "I hope you get hit in the head with a fly ball. I hope a wild pitch takes out your junk."

"Huh?"

Does she think I play professional baseball? Wherever would she get an idea like that?

Suddenly, I start laughing at the utter absurdity of this entire morning. Of course, she thinks my amusement is directed at her.

"Stop laughing at me," she snaps.

That just makes me laugh harder. I'm not laughing at her, though. I swear I'm not. I just find this whole ridiculous encounter wildly entertaining. How often does a bona fide psycho, one who thinks you play baseball, end up in your bed?

"Wow," I mutter, "what a whacko."

Psycho Girl reaches the door and spins around. Stabbing a finger my way, she says, "You're an asshole and a prick. God, I am so stupid. To think last night I thought you were ho... Uh, never mind."

"Whoa, wait, you thought I was what? Hot?"

"Shut up!" she shrieks. And then, in a softer tone, she says, "Just please stop talking now."

Shit, she looks like she's about to cry. But that doesn't mean she's done cussing me out. "I hope I never again lay eyes on you. And I mean never, ever, ever... Like for the rest of my life. Even that might be too soon."

Good God.

"Fine," I say, defeated. I'm too tired and hungover for this shit. My amusement is waning, along with the semi I was sporting.

I close my eyes and listen as the door slams.

Thank Christ, she's gone.

Still, despite her obvious need for a mental health assessment, I can't erase her from my mind. There's something about her. Crazy or not, her calling me out—even if she was wrong about the panties, and *way* off on the weird baseball thing—felt sort of refreshing.

It certainly made me feel more alive than I have in a long time.

Women never challenge me the way Psycho Girl did. They're usually too busy trying to get to my cock…or to my wallet. Not Psycho, though. Of course, it helped that she didn't know who I am.

Still, the girl was real with me.

And I need more real.

Maybe if I had more real in my life I wouldn't be so damn determined to fuck things up like I've been doing lately. I test the fucking boundaries simply because I can.

Too bad a girl like her can't be around every day—to challenge me, to keep me on my toes. I could use someone like her in my life.

But alas, she's gone, forever out of my life.

6

LOOKS LIKE I'M GONNA NEED THAT UBER, AFTER ALL

AUBREY

Who cares if he's scorching hot? He's an epic jerk...and a panty-stealer.

"Yeah, what a freak," I mutter as I scamper from the jerky baseball player's room, the pumps that nearly tripped me dangling from my hand.

Forget about his washboard abs. He probably paints them on.

I bend in the hallway to slip on the heels. "For sure, that's what that callous, arrogant ass does."

Forget about his chiseled good looks. They'll fade with age.

Faltering, I murmur, "Yeah, but aging for him is a long way off."

Hey, pay attention here. You're wavering.

"Good point. You're right."

Let's not forget he messed up your awesome descriptive simile from last night. His eyes aren't even sunflower-brown. They're more of a whiskey shade.

"Another good point!"

Wait a minute. Enough is enough. I'm supposed to erase him from my mind. Plus, I need to pee. My bladder's screaming that we better find a bathroom or the floodgates will burst.

Stumbling down the stairs, I luckily come upon a powder room. I do what I need to do, and then I'm on my way, out of this stupid lakeside house for good.

Digging my phone from my purse, I sigh. "God, I pray I never step foot anywhere near this place again."

My head is pounding, and I'm furious with the arrogant ballplayer. I'm never watching baseball again. Not that I ever do. But this assures I'll never start.

I glance around. I'm out in the middle of bumfuck-nowhere.

Tapping at my phone, and praying for reception, I muse, "Looks like I'm gonna need that Uber, after all."

A ride can't get here soon enough.

I shake my head, boggled by my own stupidity as I order the Uber. I can't believe I thought that pompous ass was one of the most gorgeous guys I'd ever laid eyes on.

You were drunk last night, remember?

Yeah, nice try, but that doesn't work. Jerk-o still looked damn good this morning. I may hate him, but I can't deny he has an epic level of hotness going for him.

That's all he has, though.

"Except for maybe that big dick," I murmur.

No maybes about that one, chica!

Yeah, that was no magic trick under the covers. No rabbit in a hat illusion. Maybe it was a carrot. A really long, thick—

That wasn't a vegetable under there, sweetie. That was some pure man meat.

"Mmm…" Happy that I'm not a vegetarian, I think about how I'd like to take a big bite, and maybe a lick or two for good measure, of his pure man m—

"Wait a minute." I stop myself. "You're supposed to be hating on that dick, not lusting after it."

The dick can't help who it's attached to. Maybe a little lusting is okay?

"No!"

Seems even my voice of reason is a traitor when it comes to cock.

I hit the phone against my head to punish myself, but that just hurts like hell. "Ow." I rub my temple and check my phone.

Seven minutes till my escape from this latest embarrassment.

"See, this is why you're better off staying focused on work."

Yeah, work. Speaking of which, I have obligations today. Luckily, it appears I'm still on schedule for my flight. I just need to stop at the hotel so I can take a shower, put my contacts back in, and grab my stuff.

Oh, and I certainly plan to put on some damn underwear. Everything under my dress feels so exposed, all thanks to that pervert absconding with my panties.

Just then, as if to emphasize that point, a gust of wind blows up my dress. I smooth the material down in the nick of time, seconds before the Uber driver pulls up.

Someone almost got a peep show.

God, now I'm even thinking like the pervy baseball dude. I swear I can't get on that plane to Las Vegas fast enough. I'm ready to put this whole crazy morning behind me.

And Mr. Panty-Stealer?

Well, he's being erased from my mind, never to be thought of, or spoken of, ever again.

When I arrive in Vegas there's a limo driver waiting for me. He's in the baggage claim area, holding up a large placard with my name spelled out in letters so big even my tired and hungover self can't miss it.

It's stuffy and warm inside the terminal, making me more than ready to turn my bags over to the driver. He takes them off my hands, and I proceed to follow him out to a far worse inferno.

As he begins to load my luggage into the trunk of the waiting limo, I remark, "Wow, it must be like a hundred and ten degrees out here."

I fan myself with my hand, a sorry attempt to cool down. The black business suit I put on at the hotel seemed comfy and fine back in Minneapolis, but here in hell I feel like I'm about to die from heatstroke.

"It's not that bad today," the driver replies as he busies himself with shifting my many bags here and there, making sure they all fit. "Though it's been pretty rough lately. You're lucky. We're on a cooldown now. Last I checked it was only ninety-seven."

"*Only* ninety-seven," I mutter. "That's some cooldown."

Smiling kindly, he assures me, "I'll put the AC on high in the car. You'll be comfortable in no time, Miss Shelburne."

Once we're in the limo, and the AC is indeed pumping full blast, I remove my makeup bag from my purse so I can at least attempt to freshen up after the long flight, a flight where I, thankfully, had a chance to take a much-needed nap.

All in all, I'm not in too bad of shape. Especially considering I had such a rough night…and a fucked-up morning from hell with the baseball player jerk.

Nevertheless, I'm looking forward to a stop at whichever extended-stay hotel my firm has me in for the duration of this assignment.

That reminds me to ask the driver, "Where exactly are we going?"

Peering back at me in the rearview mirror, he says, "I've been instructed to drive you straight to the meeting with management and the new client."

"Wait, what? We're not stopping at a hotel first? I was hoping to drop off my things and freshen up."

"I'm afraid that's not possible," the driver informs me. "And I wouldn't count on a hotel stay, ma'am. Based on where I'm supposed to take you following the meeting, it would seem your firm and client management have decided you're staying somewhere other than a hotel."

"Oh, great," I mutter, irritated at the ridiculous amount of secrecy for this assignment. "So where will you be taking me after the meeting? I'd like to know where I'll be living for the next couple of months."

"I'm sorry, but I'm not at liberty to divulge that information just yet, Miss Shelburne. I've been instructed to inform you that everything you need to know will be covered at the meeting."

I don't press. Orders are orders.

But I am curious.

If I'm not staying in a long-term residence place, I guess I'll be put up in an apartment. A place of my own would be nice, but it also tells me I'll be residing in this lovely sauna known as Nevada for quite some time.

Wow, this client must really be a handful. Better prepare for the worst now.

But I can't, seeing as I still have no idea who the new client is.

And though the driver wouldn't have that info, he can definitely let me know where exactly we're going. If I have that info, then maybe I can guess what *type* of celebrity I'll be working with—actor, musician, or professional athlete.

Reaching for a bottle of water from a cooler in the back, I casually ask, "So where is this meeting taking place?"

"At Desert Sports Complex," the driver replies.

Hmm, sports. An athlete, it would appear. Oh joy, like I haven't had enough of them after this morning.

"There's no baseball team out here, is there?" I cautiously inquire, holding my breath.

Not that the jackass from this morning would play for a team in Vegas. He's clearly a Minneapolis player since he lives there. Still, I'd hate to run into him at a game or at a professional baseball function.

I breathe a sigh of relief when the driver replies, "No, there's no professional baseball team in Las Vegas."

"Thank God," I murmur. And then I ask, "What professional teams *do* play at the sports complex?"

"Why, the Las Vegas Wolves play there." The driver beams like a proud fan.

Wait, I've think I've heard of that team.

"Ah," I murmur as it dawns on me. "They're a hockey team, right?"

"Yes, ma'am."

Sooo, I must be assigned to a player. Too bad I don't follow the sport more closely. If I did I might have a clue as to who their troubled players are.

The driver continues to make small talk as we drive to our destination. I don't catch everything he says, but I do perk up when he excitedly announces, "The Wolves' new season is starting up real soon.

Every September I try to take my son to at least one of their preseason scrimmages."

I don't have children of my own, not yet, but I hope to some day. Still, I'm always awed by the love that's so clear when parents speak of their kids. My driver seems to be no exception.

I pick up on the longing in his voice when he sighs and adds, "I'm hoping someday I can take my boy to a regular season game. For now, though, those tickets are way out of my price range."

"How old is your son?" I ask softly as I make a note to give him a really great tip.

"Twelve," he replies.

"That's a pretty fun age."

He nods and agrees. "Yeah, it is. He's old enough to understand the game and how it's played."

I laugh and tell the driver, "I could probably use a few lessons from your son."

"Not much of a hockey fan, huh?"

"Not really," I admit. "I know team names and stuff, but not much beyond that."

We fall into a comfortable silence, but then I realize this man, a fan, might have some valuable insight into who I'll be working with.

"So," I begin, "living out in the east, I don't hear much about the Wolves. Are they any good?"

He shrugs. "They're okay. Been to the playoffs a couple times, but they never seem to do much once they get there. It's crazy too. As a fan, you expect more. With that OPS line of theirs, you'd think they'd go deep in the playoffs every year." He sighs. "Oh well, what can you do? Just hope they turn it around this season, I guess."

OPS line, what the hell is that? I have no clue. And I don't care to ask. But I would like to know, "Have you ever heard any rumors of troubled players on their team?"

The driver throws a disapproving glance back at me, probably wondering why I'd ask such a thing. "No, ma'am," he finally replies.

"Oh, okay."

After a minute, he clears his throat and asks, "Where you from back east?"

"Oh. I'm from a small town named Butler. It's a little north of Pittsburgh. But I live in Chicago currently."

"Ah, so does that make you a Hawks fan? Or do you still root for the Penguins?"

"Well, like I said, I'm not a huge hockey fan. But I'll always be a hometown girl at heart. If I were to root for a team, it'd definitely be the Pens."

We reach our destination and our hockey talk comes to an end. But my brush with hockey is about to go much further.

7

SHIT, NOT YOU AGAIN

BRENT

After the crazy—though very much intriguing—girl leaves, I head to the bathroom for that aspirin.

When I stop to take a piss, aspirin dissolving on my tongue, I discover a pair of lacy red panties on the floor in front of the toilet.

"What the…?"

These must be the panties Psycho Girl was going on and on about. Figures she left them on the bathroom floor all on her own.

"What a crazy girl," I say, chuckling as I drain the monster.

Later, after a refreshing shower and a few more aspirin, I pack for my impending trip to Vegas. When I remember that I need to throw a toothbrush in my bag, I head back to the bathroom. The panties are still balled up on the floor. That red scrap of silk and lace is the only reminder I have that this morning really happened. It's already starting to feel like a faraway dream.

I don't know why I do what I do next, except maybe just to hang onto something tangible so I don't forget Psycho Girl. In any case, I grab the undies and throw them in my bag.

And then it's time to go.

Nolan drives me out to the regional airport, where the team's private jet is waiting for me to board. The whole way there I bitch about being kept in the dark as to why I'm required to fly to Las Vegas today.

"Why would the Wolves want an in-person meeting with me?" I ask Nolan since he's like Yoda—all-knowing, all-seeing. "Haven't they ever heard of Skype?"

"Probably not," he replies. "If you recall, management only recently discovered text messaging."

"Unfortunately for me," I murmur. "If they'd stayed in the dark ages, I'd probably be off the hook."

"I doubt that," Nolan says, chuckling. "It was your agent who sent the text."

"Good point. He is a savvy bastard."

Once we reach the tarmac where my plane awaits, I reach around to the cabin in the back of the truck to retrieve my bag. "Thanks for the ride," I say to Nolan.

He knows I'm starting to stress about this meeting, and why shouldn't I? I've been a bad boy in the eyes of the team. Hell, I've been a bad boy in the eyes of just about everyone.

"Hey," he says, "whatever is going on, just keep in mind that it can't be as bad as what's happening to Benny right now."

"Yeah, that's for sure." I lean my head back against the headrest and think about how poor Benny is on his way to an airport as well, but not this one. "Not only does the sad bastard have to enter that rehab facility out in Arizona by tonight, but he has to fly to Phoenix commercial."

It's a message from the team, a smack in the face to wake the hell up. The good life could end at any time—for me, for Benny, for anyone. We're all fair game. Maybe not Nolan, though, since he's basically kept his shit together.

Sighing, I say, "I should've followed your example, man. You've been working out, eating good stuff, doing all the right things."

He pats me on the shoulder. "You're going to be fine, kid."

Let's hope Yoda is right on this one.

In Las Vegas, my agent—a middle-aged man, trim and fit and with silver-streaked hair—is on the tarmac, waiting to pick me up.

His name is Jock Sosarelli. With a name like Jock, how could you not be involved with sports? Before he became an agent, Jock played professional baseball. When a career-ending injury took him out of the game for good, he went into sports management.

Jock's a great agent—one of the best, with a killer rep. He's slick, polished, and professional. He expects the same from his clients. That's why I'm not the least bit offended when he lowers his four-hundred dollar sunglasses and eyes me up and down with a shake of his head.

I have to chuckle. Already evaluating and assessing, and I've only been off the plane for three minutes.

"Glad to see you arrived cleaned up," he says. "You look more or less ready for a meeting of importance."

"Hello to you too, fucker," I retort.

Laughing, Jock holds out his hand.

We shake, and he tells me, "You don't pay me the big bucks to kiss your ass, Oliver. You pay me to land you seven- and eight-figure deals. *And* to make sure you retain them."

He has a point.

Glancing down at the navy blue suit I threw on at the last minute, I remark, "Dressing like this seemed the wise thing to do." With a quick glance up to the blazing sun—and I mean quick, so as not to scorch my corneas out of my head—I add, "Even if it is like hell on earth out here, and I feel like I'm melting."

Jock chuckles as he indicates we should get into a waiting limo.

Once we're settled in the comfortable, air-conditioned car, he says, all cryptic-like, "You think this is hell? Just wait till we meet with the team."

"Jesus, Jock, what could this possibly be about?" I scrub my hand down my face. "So I partied a little extra hard this off-season. I fucked a few more women than usual. I didn't do anything any other hockey player out there isn't doing."

"You're not just any other hockey player, Brent. You're the team's biggest asset and their chief investment. You're their golden boy—"

I hold up my hand. "I hate that fucking moniker, man."

"I know," he tells me. "But it's true. And the team pays you a shit ton of money for the privilege of calling you whatever the hell they want. I'd suggest you learn to like all the names they come up with." He catches my eye. "Or at least pretend like you do."

"Duly noted," I reply dryly.

I want to ask Jock more about the content of this meeting, but the drive to Desert Sports Complex is a quick one, meaning we arrive in what feels like no time at all.

I'm surprisingly calm on the way into the building, but that's only due to familiarity. Knowing that the ice I practice and play on is so close kind of soothes me. It's all very Zen, or whatever. I just love hockey, okay?

Despite all the business bullshit I deal with, like this upcoming mystery meeting, the game is what I live for. Skating, the smell of the ice, it's all a salve to my soul.

As we walk to a bay of elevators, I say, "I think everything is going to be okay, Jock. Really, this is all just a big misunderstanding. Once I talk with management and assure them my head's in the right place, we should be good."

"Maybe," Jock murmurs, doubt coloring his tone.

I blow out a breath. "Who should I expect to see at this meeting?"

I'm curious as to how many asses I'm going to have to kiss.

"Just Dolby," he says.

Mr. Dolby, who we call Dolby, is Director of Player Operations. His lone presence at the meeting begs the question, "Why isn't ownership attending? If this meeting is so important they should be here, right?"

"Not necessarily." We step into the elevator, and I ready myself to be whisked up to my possible doom. "Don't be fooled by the lack of attendees, Brent. This meeting is vital for your career."

"Sure it is." I make a face as Jock hits the button for the top level.

My agent isn't one to hem and haw—he tells me shit straight up—so it's only mildly surprising when he informs me, "Now that you're in town, ownership wants you to stay put. That means there'll be plenty of opportunities for them to talk with you in person."

Okay, this is unacceptable.

"No, no way." I shake my head. "I'm going back to Minneapolis the minute this thing is done. I'll come back to Vegas when preseason training officially starts."

"Consider it starting for you, as of today."

"Fuck!"

"About this meeting, Brent, there's more." Jock looks uneasy, and that's a rare occurrence. There has to be something coming up that I absolutely will not like.

"More?" I ask, wary. "What's that mean?"

He crosses his arms. "There's someone management wants you to talk with. Maybe even spend some time with her. Well, actually, there's no maybe about it. You'll be meeting with a woman today, one who's here to help you. She flew in from back east, like you, just a little earlier."

Now I'm worried and confused.

"What are you talking about, Jock? Help me with what? And what's with the 'she' and 'her' crap? I thought the team wanted me to stay away from women? Now you're telling me they want me to hang out with one?"

Jock looks guilty, and that's never a good sign. "This isn't some random woman, Brent. You're meeting with Aubrey Shelburne. She's worked with a lot of high-profile figures, and she's very good at what she does."

"What exactly does she do?" I ask through clenched teeth.

"She's what's called a 'life coach.'"

"A *life* coach?" I hit the Stop button, and the elevator shimmies to a halt. "My life is just fine, thank you very much. What exactly is going on? Talk to me, Sosarelli."

"Just meet with Ms. Shelburne, Brent." Jock hits the button and the elevator resumes its ascent. "This is going to happen whether you like it or not."

I'm tired of fighting. It's always a lost cause when you're nothing more than a commodity. And that's what I am to the team.

"Fine," I concede.

I guess I'll have to meet with this life coach, whatever the hell that means. We'll just see about spending time with her, though. Maybe if she's hot I'll give her a day or two, let her "coach" me, preferably in bed.

Outside the conference room where the meeting is about to take place, I stop so I can say to Jock, "Okay, let's do this. But for the record, I still think this is total bullshit."

"Duly noted," he says, throwing my words from earlier back at me. *Smartass bastard.*

All things considered, I'm actually in a pretty good frame of mind when he pushes open the door.

I'm good that is, till I walk in the room and see *her.*

What... the... ever-loving... fuck?

In a tone betraying my utter shock and horror, I say, "Shit, not you again."

THIS IS BRENT OLIVER?

AUBREY

"This is Brent Oliver? That can't be right. This guy plays baseball, not hockey."

That remark earns me many confused stares.

"Uh, never mind." I wave my hand.

I'd like to leave, but I know that's not an option. This is my job. Though one thing is clear. The guy who threw the party—you know, the one I woke up to this morning, *kill me now*—does not play baseball.

Damn Lainey. I knew she had it wrong.

What are the odds of this happening? Pretty slim, I'd say. But not for me. Oh no, I have the worst luck.

This is what happens when you're left in the dark. No one told me anything about this guy before I flew in. If the team had e-mailed me, say, a few photos of the new client I would've known last night to avoid him like the plague. I would have seen him at the party and, cute or not, run the other way.

But noooo.

This team is so secretive that even the file I was given when I first came into the conference room contained no photos of the client. Not a single one anywhere in the contents.

There are team logos all over the thing—a profile of a red wolf's head on a black background—but nothing else in terms of images.

Now that I know what I know, I have to ask myself why *would* there be a picture of Brent Oliver. The guy is a superstar—a fact stressed over and over again in the file. The implication being that everyone must know his face.

Everyone that is, except for me.

Oh, but I do know that face. It belongs to a panty-stealing pervert, one whose damn bed I was in this morning.

Please, let me disappear now.

The new client also happens to have the distinction of being the jerk who kicked me out of his house, sans the underwear he stole.

"I am *not* working with this woman," I hear Panty-Stealer murmuring to the man next to him, like he's the wounded one in this scenario. "I absolutely cannot be around her, Jock."

I glare over at him. Brent Oliver has some nerve.

He can't work with *me*?

He probably has my panties in his possession right now. I wouldn't be surprised if they were tucked away in the pocket of that on-fleek suit he's wearing, the one that looks freakishly good on him.

Yet here he is, acting like I'm the problem.

While I can't believe this is actually happening, the agent guy is telling Brent to simmer down.

"This subject is not up for debate," he snaps. "We discussed this in the elevator. You *have* to work with her."

"But she's fucking crazy," Brent states, loud enough for everyone to hear.

"How do you know that?" the agent asks.

"I just know."

"That's enough!" I jump up from where I'm seated at a long conference table and point my finger over at him. It's not the one I'd like to raise high in the air and shove in his face, but rather the more innocuous one to the left. "I am *not* crazy," I go on, defending myself. "If there's any weirdo in this room, it's *you*."

Oh my God, did I really just say all that out loud?

This man makes me lose control of everything—my body, my mouth, just about every damn part of me. All heads pivot from me to Brent then back to me. They gawk at us like we've both lost our minds. Well, everyone does except for Brent's agent. That guy is chuckling. I even catch him muttering under his breath, "This is going to be more fun than I expected."

"Whatever," I grumble.

The man who introduced himself earlier as Mr. Dolby, Director of Player Operations, is seated directly next to me. He hammers his fist on the table and calls for order in the room. There are two interns who were passing out files earlier, and who are currently filling our glasses with water. When they start snickering, Mr. Dolby abruptly dismisses them. As the young lady and her male counterpart scamper out of the room, leaving only four of us, I blow out a breath.

You can do this. Pull yourself together.

Introductions are made like nothing weird just happened. I find out the agent is named Jock Sosarelli. I've actually heard high praise for him, so I shake his hand. I refrain, however, from having any contact with Mr. Oliver. He receives only a curt nod from me.

When Brent and his agent take a seat on the opposite side of the table from me and the director, I can't help but note my adversary—er, I mean new client—looks a little tired.

Good, I hope his head hurts as much as mine does.

My headache had pretty much dissipated, but it's back to pounding. It's having an effect on me too, as I suddenly realize I'm the only one still standing.

Oops.

"Sorry." I nervously smooth down the sides of my skirt as I prepare to take a seat. "Guess I should sit down now too, huh?"

Crap, I'm never all flustered like this. I'm the epitome of professionalism…usually. This damn Brent dude has me off my game.

Mr. Dolby and Jock smile at me politely. But not Brent Oliver. Oh no, there's nothing polite coming from Panty-Stealer.

No doubt recalling what he stole from me, he stares directly where my hands are smoothing down my skirt, only more centered, like directly at my crotch area.

I sit down hastily. Cocking a brow, I look directly at the epic jerk and hiss, "Really?"

Mr. Dolby clears his throat and, twisting to me, says, "Ms. Shelburne, do you foresee a problem working with Mr. Oliver?"

Yes, I foresee about a hundred problems, my internal self screams. But to Mr. Dolby, I mutter, "No, there'll be no problems." I open the file and pretend to peruse the contents. "Everything is fine. I'm just feeling a little off from the long flight out here."

"Clearly, though," he goes on, unconvinced. "It appears by your and Mr. Oliver's behavior that you two are already acquainted in some way."

I'm not sure what to say to that, except for maybe a little squeaky, *Help. Someone save me now.*

Someone does save me, someone I'd never expect. And it's Panty-Stealer, as he interjects, "We met once, sir. It was at a party at my house in Minnesota."

More like post-party, but okay, I can roll with this.

"Minnesota?" Mr. Dolby asks, clearly perplexed.

"Interesting," I hear Jock the smarmy agent murmur.

I nod and throw in, "Yes, yes, we met in Minnesota. There was a party at Mr. Oliver's house. I must say, however, that it was a very brief interaction."

Brent smirks over at me. "It would've lasted longer, our, as Ms. Shelburne puts it, *interaction.*" I glare over at him. What is he doing? "But," he goes on, flashing his million-dollar megawatt smile. "We were both very tired. Isn't that true, Ms. Shelburne?"

"Yes, yes, we were," I murmur, my cheeks flaming at the memory of Brent in his bed, his washboard abs and huge biceps on display—as well as *another* huge thing making an appearance—as he leaned back against the headboard.

"In fact," Brent goes on, "our meeting occurred under the craziest of circumstances. Ms. Shelburne here had somehow found her way to my b—"

I lift up and smack the file down on the table, making everyone jump. Well, everyone except for Brent. He's too busy chuckling, even as I state in a rather loud voice, "Okay, I think that's enough idle chit-chat. I'd like to get started on what's expected of me."

Jock and the director share a confused look, but then Mr. Dolby just shakes his head and says, "Everything is outlined in the contract you signed before Mr. Oliver got here. But the main thing is we're expecting to see a lot of one-on-one time spent between you and Mr. Oliver. I can't stress that enough."

I hear Brent mumble, in a most lascivious way, "One-on-one time sounds good to me."

I resist the urge to throw the file at him.

"Due to the extreme amount of travel involved throughout the regular season, which isn't that far off, we'll be making arrangements for you to go everywhere the team goes. You'll fly on the team plane, Ms. Shelburne, with Brent. You'll also stay at the same hotel as the team—"

"She'll have her own room, I hope," Brent interjects.

"Of course she will," Mr. Dolby replies dryly.

"Good." Brent nods, his damn whiskey-colored eyes trained on me and dancing with mischief as he adds, "I'm only thinking of Ms. Shelburne's safety. Like, what if she were to wander into one of the player's rooms? Maybe even mine, God forbid. But it could happen. She seems to have a very bad sense of direction. As I was trying to explain earlier, before I was so rudely interrupted,"—he smirks over at me— "when I first met Ms. Shelburne she had inexplicably wandered"—*I will kill you, I will kill you*, I try to convey as I glare over at him—"out to the back deck of my home."

Phew!

Jock, his Botox-ed forehead barely creasing, gives Brent a *what- the-hell-are-you-rambling-on-about* look. But Mr. Dolby doesn't appear amused.

"Mr. Oliver, I'm sure Ms. Shelburne will be fine. Hotel layouts aren't that confusing. Can we stay on topic here?"

Ha, take that, smartass.

"Sorry," Brent says, his eyes focused on me, not the director.

Wait. Is that remorse in his eyes? Is he apologizing for fucking with me at this meeting? Maybe he's not so awful after all.

Maybe.

I guess I'm about to find out.

After we review more of my duties, I'm informed that during the times the team's in Vegas—and that includes starting today—I am expected to live at Brent Oliver's property.

"What?" he says. "Like in my *house*?"

"Yes," Mr. Dolby confirms.

"You can't be serious," I chime in.

"This is crazy," Brent grumps.

"I think a hotel room of my own would be more appropriate," I add.

"Absolutely not" we are told, first by Mr. Dolby, and then by Jock.

Brent continues to bitch, and his boss says, "For Ms. Shelburne to be effective she needs to be close to you. Her living in a hotel room, miles away from you, would be of no help. We need her in your house, monitoring your drinking, watching your diet and training guidelines, keeping tabs on any drug use—"

"I don't ever do drugs," Brent snaps.

If that's true, it's one less thing to worry about.

Mr. Dolby goes on. "Okay, but there are other concerns. We don't want you distracted by women."

"She's a woman," Brent interjects in a pouty voice.

The director glares at him, and I hear Jock murmuring, "This is what the team wants, Brent. There's no use fighting it. Just keep in mind that it's not forever."

That reminds me to ask Mr. Dolby, "How long is this assignment expected to last? I was told up to possibly four months."

"Or more," he replies, to my dismay. "We have plans to revisit this discussion in December. If all's going well at that point the contract will conclude. If things aren't to our liking, there could be an extension. In the meantime, as outlined in the contract, we'll expect timely updates."

Still stuck on the fact that my last day with this asshole is sixteen long weeks away, I murmur, "December, no…"

Am I really going to be stuck with Brent Oliver till Christmas?

"Yes, Ms. Shelburne," Mr. Dolby says, "December. You're all ours till then. Is there a problem with that?"

I must be professional. I must be professional. "No, no problem at all."

I make a mental note to lock up all my panties.

The rest of the meeting passes by in a blur. I nod to questions that require an affirmative and shake my head for any nos. But mostly I sneak peeks over at Brent. He's busy doodling on the folder they gave him. Since he's paying me no heed, I have an opportunity to check him out.

Unfortunately for me, he truly is a hot specimen of raw maleness. It wasn't simply my drunken state last night or hangover mirages this morning that had me viewing him in that way.

Nope. This guy is everything I never find, but am always looking for—a perfect face, a body to die for, and a cocky attitude that I hate and love at the same time.

I did not just think that! Stop it right now. Thoughts like that will only lead to trouble, especially since you have to basically live with this guy.

I sigh, and Brent looks up, his pen stalling on a doodle. He catches my eye and smiles, like he knows what I'm thinking. Or is that just a nice smile, a truce maybe? I hope not, because that makes him even more attractive.

Living with him might pose a problem.

No, I'll be fine. I'm the pro here, and not the hooker kind he's probably acquainted with. In any case, this Oliver dude must really be a big deal. I've never been required to live right on top of one of my clients.

On top of Brent Oliver, would that really be so bad? All those muscles under little ole me. And I bet with playing all that hockey, his endurance is—

Wait! What the hell is wrong with me?

Luckily, the tortuous meeting adjourns. I quickly gather my folder and say good-bye to everyone. And then I make a beeline for the elevator.

Seems my life is becoming a series of escapes from Brent Oliver.

I stop in the ladies' room on the first floor to splash some water on my face. That delays my trip back to my waiting car with the friendly driver.

Bad move. When I arrive outside my car is waiting for me, yes, but my driver—the rabid Wolves fan—is talking animatedly with none other than my new client.

Big surprise there.

Not.

Prancing up to the car, kitten heels clicking, I announce my arrival with a very loud cough.

Brent turns and instantly offers me his water. "Here. You sound parched. Have some water."

"What? You expect me to drink from the same bottle as you?"

"Yeah, sure." He wiggles the water out in front of me. "Have a sip.

You look like you could use some cooling down."

"As if," I declare, channeling my best Cher Horowitz from *Clueless*. "I'm not, nor will I ever be thirsty enough to drink from a bottle that has touched *your* lips."

Brent shoots me a look like I'm half off my rocker. "Suit yourself," he says.

It's still stifling hot outside, and I actually am thirsty as hell. But I'll be damned if I'm drinking from his bottle. One of the "problems that need addressing" listed in the file stated that my client is a womanizer.

With this in mind, and clearly without thinking it through, I blurt out, "God knows where those lips have been and what you've picked up this summer."

Okay, it's now official—the Las Vegas heat has melted my brain *and* my filter.

The friendly driver gawks at me, surely shocked I'd say such a thing to Mr. Superstar. But it's Mr. Superstar himself who looks genuinely hurt by my comment.

"Relax. It was just a joke," I mutter.

I don't think he takes it very well, since the look he gives me shouts a clear, *Game on, bitch.*

Since I have a job to do, one that demands he respect me, I send him a message with my eyes that says right the hell back, *Go ahead and bring it, buddy. Show me your best.*

IF LOOKS COULD KILL

BRENT

was all set to be nice, willing to call a truce even. But fuck it. If Aubrey Shelburne wants to spar with me, let's do it. She's about to get more than she bargained for.

It was more than clear when Dolby informed her that she has to stay with me, to essentially "train" me to be a good boy—fuck that shit, by the way—that she wasn't digging it.

And now she has the nerve, after insulting me when I only asked if she wanted a sip of my water, to completely ignore me like I'm not still standing here.

Turning away, she strikes up a conversation with the driver.

Oh, so she thinks she can dismiss me and she'll have a nice, quiet ride to my house, just her and the limo guy.

Not gonna happen, sweetheart.

The driver is a fan, as I discovered when I first spoke with him. Well, I'm not above using it to my advantage.

Speaking right over Aubrey, which earns me a scowl from her, I say to the driver, "Hey, man. Can you do me a big favor?"

"Yes, certainly, Mr. Oliver." The driver's eager smile tells me he's more than ready to help. "Anything you want," he goes on, "you just name it."

I shoot Aubrey a smug *ah-it's-good-to-be-a-star* expression, to which she rolls her eyes. Such pretty eyes too, just like this morning. It's a shame we can't stand each other. And let me be clear. I may have been up for her challenging me, but that was before I had any clue she was about to be assigned my—insert my own eye roll here—life coach.

Back focusing on the driver, I say, "You may as well go ahead and take off since—"

"Wait, no—" Aubrey tries to interject.

"—Miss Shelburne here is headed to the same place I'm going, which happens to be my *house*." I narrow my eyes at her. "She can just ride with me."

My new life coach glares over at me. And honestly, if looks could kill I'd be a dead man.

"Sure, fine, that's cool with me, Mr. Oliver." The driver hops out and begins unloading Aubrey's bags from the trunk.

Score one for Brent Oliver.

Since I don't care to stand on the curb with Miss Life Coach—I'll be seeing enough of her in my freaking home—I offer to assist the driver with the luggage. "Hold up a sec," I call back to him. "Let me help you with those."

"Try not to steal any more of my underwear," Aubrey hisses as I stride by her.

I stop in my tracks and walk back to her. Leaning in close to the sassy vixen, I whisper in her ear, "For the record, those panties you keep accusing me of stealing were left by *you* on my bathroom floor."

Take that!

I don't add that I happened to throw the lacy undergarment in my bag, which kind of technically means I did ultimately steal them. But never mind that.

"I did what?" she gasps.

She steps back away from me, seemingly appalled by this development in the panty saga. Is that embarrassment I see on her previously smug face? I think so. Oh, I can tell already I'm going to love riling this one up. Spending time with her might end up being a blast.

"Red. Lacy?" I raise a brow. "Ring a bell?"

"Uh..."

"And I should mention that I found them to be"—I pretend like I'm holding said panties as I lift my hand to my nose—"mmm, real sweet smelling," I finish, enjoying this exchange far too much.

I'm really not this much of a pig, but it sure is fun to make her think so.

Taking the bait, she bites out, "You're disgusting."

Chuckling, I proceed to the back of the limo, where I help the driver place Aubrey's stuff on the curb. He talks a lot of hockey and mentions having a young son who's a huge fan. Before he leaves I promise to send him some signed things for his kid. We exchange info and then he drives off, happy as can be, leaving me on the curb with Aubrey, who incidentally looks as blazing hot as the sun above us. There's the slightest sheen of sweat on her brow and her cheeks are flushed. I bet that's what she looks like when she's getting fucked.

"What the hell was that all about?" she blurts out, interrupting my racy reverie.

She's fuming, but whether she's mad about my panty comment, or pissed at me for sending her ride away, I'm not entirely sure. Probably both. In any case, anger suits her.

"Are you asking me why I sent your driver away?" I jerk my thumb in the direction of the departing limo.

"Yes," she confirms.

Shrugging, I say, "Why waste gas when we're going to the same place?" Without waiting for a reply—or more likely a nasty retort—I add, "There's no reason to take two cars and add more pollution to the environment."

She bursts out laughing. "Do you honestly expect me to believe you're *that* committed to being green?"

Scoffing, I assure her, "I'm committed to a lot of things, honey." I don't add that one of them now is breaking her.

"Fine. Let's just go," she snaps.

Spinning away from me, she starts walking toward the parking garage where the players park. She knows this only because there's a sign indicating as much. Only problem is I'm not done giving her a hard time. We may as well finish this out here on the sidewalk. Maybe she'll hate me so much she'll quit before her silly life-coaching gig gets started.

"Whoa, hold up there," I call out as she prances away.

She turns, hands on her cute curvy hips, and demands to know, "What now?"

I nod down to her large collection of bags. "Don't walk away thinking I'm carrying all this shit by myself. In case you didn't notice, I'm not an octopus. You're gonna have to help, princess."

Her brow crinkles and she shakes her head in disbelief. "You can't be serious," she murmurs

"Yeah sorry, but I totally am." I lift a bag. It's a small carry-on, not one of her oversized suitcases. See, I'm not *that* much of a dick. "Here, take this one. I can probably get the rest on my own."

Huffing, she walks over to me. "Fine, give it to me."

I hand her the bag, and our eyes meet.

Shit, I'd sure like to give her more than the bag. I like the way her suit jacket is all askew, revealing her cream-colored camisole, sticking to her skin and perfectly accentuating the swell of her breasts.

Fuck, just like this morning—which now feels like a lifetime ago—my dick gets hard. I'd sure like to nail her, at least once.

But that seems unlikely as when I smile at her she returns a glare that just about lays me out.

I think Aubrey Shelburne has just made the leap from mere annoyance to outright hatred.

10

I HATE HIM, BUT MY HOOHA DISAGREES

AUBREY

I hate him. I hate him. I hate him.

This becomes my new mantra as the days pass. Brent Oliver is driving me crazy. He fights me on everything. But that's not the worst of it. The worst is when he goes up against me, I secretly love it. His obstinacy gets me all hot and bothered. And because of this I find myself doing everything I can to make him angry and rile him up.

Like right now—I'm pouring all his booze down the kitchen sink. It needs to be done, anyway—out of sight, out of mind, and all that— but he sure is going to be pissed.

No matter. I have a legitimate reason for doing what I'm doing— it's my job. My client was so hungover this morning that when his new team-appointed trainer arrived bright and early, he could barely get out of bed.

That is unacceptable.

Conclusion—he's not going to stop drinking as long as his beloved Grey Goose is around. So, here I am.

Reaching for what feels like the umpteenth bottle of booze, I let out a long sigh. Brent has so many fifths that need emptying that I'm starting to feel like I'm re-enacting the Boston Tea Party, only with Grey Goose instead of Earl Grey. Or whatever the hell kind of tea they drank back then.

I purposely chose this time of the night to complete my task. Here's where the riling him up part comes in. This is when my adversary usually heads down from his bedroom to raid the fridge. Tonight his little snack will have to be a banana, or another piece of fresh fruit, just like it was last night, courtesy of my most recent trip to the organic market.

The first night I spent in the house, Brent came down looking for potato chips. I know this because he was mumbling something about salt and vinegar as he entered the kitchen. Too bad for him I'd already found and discarded all the bags of his preferred snack.

He actually caught me as I was in the midst of changing out *all* the junk food he'd had someone—probably that smug agent—stock the fridge and pantry with. I've since replaced every bad thing with a healthy alternative. But that night I was only halfway through with the task. I heard Brent literally skid to a stop behind me, so I spun around, smile on my face and a nice healthy peach in one hand.

The sought-after salt and vinegar bags were sticking out of the top of the trash, and with his eyes glued in that direction, he asked tightly, "Why are all the potato chips in the garbage?"

It took me a full minute to formulate a coherent response. I was caught off-guard by his buff body. Seemed he'd forgotten to put on a shirt, and the baggy gray shorts he had on were doing a bang-up job of showing off how muscular his legs are.

All those bulging muscles, right there in front of me, made my head as fuzzy as the peach I was pretty much squeezing to death by then. I swear there's not an ounce of fat on that man, in spite of his junk food and vodka addictions.

Every inch of him is so firm and smooth that my hooha perked to attention immediately. I insisted she calm down, seeing as we despise Brent Oliver. She complied, after calling me out as a delusional liar *and* after I promised her some relief.

Not with Brent Oliver, just with my hand.

B-o-r-i-n-g, I imagined her spewing, along with a yawn. But then that graphic image disturbed me so greatly that I couldn't help but make a *please-bleach-my-brain-now* face.

"What's wrong with you?" Brent asked, snorting. "You're not the one whose babysitter is throwing away all the good stuff in the house."

Pointing at him, I replied, "I am not your babysitter. I'm your life coach."

He shrugged. "Semantics."

"I didn't know hockey players knew such fancy words."

"You obviously don't know much about us at all, do you?"

"Pfft," I snorted. "Let's be sure we keep it that way, Oliver."

"You got it, Shelburne."

My lady bits got all excited from the lively exchange. So much so that I completely misunderstood when he said, "You're dripping, by the way."

"Huh? What?" I wasn't *that* excited, was I? Good God, I hoped not. Because, if so, how mortifying!

I stared down at my short shorts. Could you see through them?

They were kind of thin. Could I be that freaking wet?

Brent, clearly confused, said, "What the hell are you doing?"

"I'm checking to make sure, uh..." Suddenly, I remembered the peach I was squeezing like crazy.

Oops.

"Aubrey?" He quirked a brow, like he was catching on to me.

Think fast!

"I thought I felt something on my leg," I said in a rush. "A bug, maybe." Nodding down to my sticky forearm, I hastily added, "But yes, I see what you mean. Damn peaches. They're just so overly ripe."

"Sure they are," he murmured.

When I dared to look over at him, it was clear he knew precisely what I'd originally thought—that he'd aroused me. He had, of course, but there was no need to confirm it for him. In fact, I quickly went to work on making him think I hated him.

'Cause I do, right?

Right? Right?

Crap, I don't know anymore.

Icily, I asked, "Are we done here? I'm trying to do my job, which happens to involve buying fruit for you, a food that's on your approved list by the way."

Yes, it was in his file. And since he hates the idea of a babysitter, which I sometimes kind of am, I knew that would chase him away. And so help me God, I needed him gone. He was turning me into a horny, confused mess.

Frustrated, I tossed the peach at him. He caught it easily and started to say something, but I turned away to face the sink. I was just so damn embarrassed by that point.

I heard him sigh as he left the room, and wouldn't you know it, my traitorous hooha sighed right along with him, which then made me sigh. The mood was ruined for everyone, and it was an overall crappy night.

But tonight I'm ready and prepped to spar with Brent Oliver, something that is quickly becoming a highlight of my time here. Plus, if I get all worked up now, I have a new outlet.

Smiling, I pour another bottle of Grey Goose down the drain and think about my new duo of toys and how I came to acquire them.

Lainey would be so proud.

This afternoon, Brent was off meeting with team bigwigs, which meant I had a few hours to myself. The company I work for finally got around to renting me a car, so I decided to take it out for a little spin around the area. I also needed to get out of the house for a while.

Brent's home is spacious and beautiful—it's a huge terra-cotta villa with clay roof tiles and a lovely desert garden dominating the front and extending to the back—but I was feeling closed in.

I've already explored the two separate wings of his home, which included a thorough investigation of the area I share with him. That's right. My damn bedroom is directly across from his. And all this freaking closeness is the real reason why I needed a break from Mr. Hottie's lair today.

Like it was meant to be, as I was driving along, just aimlessly making random turns, I spotted a sex shop along the side of the road.

"Yes!" I fist-pumped the air as I eased into the lot of the aptly named *Giddy-Up Adult Toys*. Okay, maybe I more than eased in. There may have been a lot of spinning tire and plumes of dust, but damn it, I was in a hurry to get in that store.

I was so pumped that I started singing, making up a little jingle. *Giddy-up, girl, go! Get your freak on in the desert at Giddy-Up Adult*

Toys.

Damn, I should do marketing on the side.

Then again, maybe not.

In any case, it was all new to me, and I was excited. I've never owned a sex toy, but my sister, as she likes to remind me, swears by them. It's high time I hop on that horse and go for a ride, that's what she's been telling me. Well, if I can't ride Brent—and I absolutely cannot—then the Giddy-Up sex toy store would have to provide the next best thing.

"Surely they'll have something for me," I told myself as I cut the ignition.

By then I was feeling a tad self-conscious after my splashy arrival, so I slid the scarf I was wearing up to cover my head. I then threw on a pair of cat-eye sunglasses, completing what was quickly becoming my fifties movie star appearance. No matter. I wanted to remain incognito and it was effective. Not that I expected to run into anyone, but with my luck it seemed a prudent move.

To my dismay, I received quite a few looks when I walked in that store. Not because I was a woman coming in to buy a sex toy—I'm sure that happened a lot—but because I kind of looked like I was about to hold up the joint.

With a nod to the scruffy surfer-looking dude manning the register, I scurried back to a wall of toys.

Damn, what I found was a dizzying array of pleasure devices, in all sorts of shapes, colors, and sizes. I peered at the packages, but it was a little hard to see with the dark glasses on.

Hastily, I grabbed two toys—one pink and one green. Yeah, color me the preppy perv. I then scampered over to the register and paid with cash, all while casting surreptitious glances left and right.

After my new purchases were placed in a bag, I grabbed the parcel and raced to the exit.

But then I heard, "Miss, you forgot your receipt."

Damn! I ignored the clerk and kept going, intent on my escape—er, I mean departure—from the store.

The damn persistent clerk was not deterred, however. He followed me out to my car. "Please, lady, would you hold up a sec," he called out as I hopped in what was no longer my car, but my getaway vehicle.

Removing my sunglasses, I threw the bag on the passenger seat and started up the engine. But by then there was no getting away. The surfer-dude had reached my open window.

He held out the slip detailing my purchases. "You forgot this," he said.

Snatching the receipt from his hand, I snapped, "Why do I need a receipt, anyway? I can't imagine you take returns."

"We don't," he confirmed. "But you can always exchange unopened merchandise."

"Well, that's good to know," I deadpanned.

Kill me now. I can't believe I'm talking sex toy return policies out in the parking lot.

I felt my face warm, especially when I placed the receipt he'd handed me in the plain brown bag containing my purchases. It was then I noticed exactly what I'd bought. One item was something called the DPMB. When I peered more closely, I horrifyingly realized the letters stood for Double Penetrator Mega Blaster.

O_O ⊠ That was me for a good solid minute.

And why wouldn't it be? Based on the size alone, the DPMB looked like it could cause some real damage. I pushed that one aside and saw the other toy I'd bought—a lime green vibrator with the weird name of Area 51.

Remembering that I was in Nevada, not far from the secret government testing area where they supposedly experiment on aliens, the name suddenly made sense. In fact, the more I peered at Area 51, the more I realized the toy did indeed resemble what one might imagine an alien's dick would look like—long and thick and florescent lime green. There was a sticker on the package that boasted that Area 51 glowed brightly when in use.

"Wow, that must be something to see," I couldn't help but blurt out.

Would it be like those glow sticks they sell at events?

Or, was it radioactive?

Yikes, was it even safe to use?

I'd forgotten for a second that I wasn't alone, and when I glanced up, still kind of perplexed about that glowing part, the sales clerk was staring at Area 51 right along with me. He proceeded to casually inform me, "That there Area 51 is a really big seller around here. The ladies seem to like it a lot." He paused and pondered, and then he added, "I'm not sure if it's popular because the real Area 51 isn't far from here, or if they buy it because Brent Oliver wears number 51."

What? No! I can't escape the damn man. "What did you just say?"

He pointed to somewhere out in the desert. "Ah, Area 51 is—"

"No, no, not that part." I shook my head vigorously. "What were you saying about Brent Oliver?"

"Oh, he's the star player for our hockey team, the Wolves."

"No, no. Not that, either." I swished my hand in the air, like maybe I could erase this whole discussion. "What were you saying about the number fifty-one?"

"Oh, that. Fifty-one is Brent Oliver's number. And you can't see it with the packaging in the way, but the toy has a fifty-one imprinted on it."

"Oh, great."

Not only had I purchased an alien dick, but the thing shared a number with Brent. Had I subconsciously grabbed this one on purpose? If so, I didn't want to even consider what grabbing the Double Penetrator Mega Blaster might mean.

As I shuddered, another disturbing aspect of the whole mindless grabbing of the toys began to bother me. It seemed I couldn't deny that Area 51 was a close approximation of the length and girth of Brent's cock. Or at least what I had discerned of it beneath the comforter that fateful morning when we'd met.

The clerk, misreading my intense staring at Area 51, jerked his chin to the package. "Another great feature of that one is that it has pulsating vibrating action *and* a temperature sensor."

I wanted to drive away, just get the hell out of there as fast as I could, but curiosity got the best of me. "Temperature sensor?" My inquiring mind wanted to know one thing: "What exactly does that mean?"

"It means the device glows brighter with body heat. You know, from your—"

I got the hell out of there then, leaving the clerk in a plume of dust. You bet your ass I had my passengers with me though—DPMB and Area 51.

So yeah, I haven't tried either of them yet—and I have a feeling DPMB might never get the chance, seeing as I like my lady bits and her backdoor neighbor just as they are—but at least I have the alien dick to satisfy me next time Brent Oliver gets me all worked up.

That could be sooner than expected. I hear his smooth voice behind me now, saying, "Hey, what are you doing with the Grey Goose? That's my special collection."

"Speak of the devil," I murmur, smiling deviously as I unscrew the cap on the next bottle of liquor doomed for the pipes. Peering over my shoulder, I then snipe, "What does it look like I'm doing, genius?"

"I don't know. That's why I'm asking."

Turning back to the bottle and dumping its contents in the sink, I reply, "The drain is thirsty. It's enjoying your 'special collection.' And better it end up here than down your throat."

"Can you at least save back a couple? Like, for a special occasion?"

"Sorry," I reply breezily, "but it all needs to go."

"What if I decide to have a party?" he throws out, like that'll work.

"No parties allowed," I say, reciting the rules in the contract. "No alcohol, no drugs, no women—"

"Fuck that last one," I hear Brent mumble.

"Hey, don't shoot the messenger. It's all in—"

"—the contract we signed," he finishes for me. "Yes, I know."

I remain facing the sink, but I can almost hear the wheels turning in his head. I sense he's preparing to come up with something to return the slam.

Sure enough, he throws out an innuendo-laden, "Are you absolutely sure you don't want to hold back a bottle or two?"

I stop what I'm doing and turn around. "Why would I do that?"

"Well, Aubrey, I think we both know how much you also enjoy throwing back a few from time to time?"

We haven't discussed the night I ended up in his bed, not once. And I don't want to bring it up now. It conjures up too many feelings—like lust, longing, and want. And there's no point in going there. Verbally sparring with Brent is one thing—like foreplay almost—but it's safe.

Too bad I can never actually be with him.

That's why I bought the toys.

Frustrated at this mess I'm in, I narrow my eyes at him and say, "*I'm* not the one with the alcohol problem, mister."

"Like I am?"

"Brent…" I sigh. "You may not be a raging alcoholic, but you don't know when to stop."

"Okay, I'll give you that," he shockingly concedes. "But I have a question for you."

Casually, he leans his shoulder against the curved entranceway that separates the kitchen from the dining room, a move that makes him look delectable. When he crosses his arms—and, of course, he's once again prancing around without a shirt—his chest muscles flex and his arms bulge enticingly.

It takes everything I have to force my gaze up to his face. Though that's not helpful either, since that part of him is just as attractive.

"What do you want to know?" I murmur as I pin my eyes to the mosaic tile floor. That way I won't stare…or drool.

"How'd you end up at a party in Minneapolis? Jock mentioned that you live in Chicago. Is that right?"

I reluctantly meet his gaze. "Yes, that's correct."

"So," he prompts, pressing for an answer. "What brought you up to Minnesota that night?"

I blow out a breath. "My sister. I was visiting her. She goes to school up there."

"Ah, got it."

He then pins me with inquisitive eyes, and I know what the next logical question is—how'd I end up at his party. Answering that will lead to the morning I was in his freaking bed.

It's best to nip this in the bud now.

Raising my hand, I shake my head. "No, no more. I think that's enough talk about that night. I'd just as soon leave it where it belongs, in the past."

He lets out a snort, and I ask, "What now?"

"It's just… You're funny, Aubrey."

I put my hands on my hips. "Oh, yeah? In what way am I funny?"

This should be good.

"You're here to help me, but you *obviously* have a few issues of your own that could use some"—he rolls his eyes—"life-coaching. One of which was crystal clear that morning in my bed."

I glare at him. We were supposed to drop this subject. Still, I can't resist asking, "What exactly are you implying? I can't wait to hear what issue of mine could be so freaking clear to *you*."

Sensing my irritation, he waves me off. "Just never mind. It's nothing."

I take a step toward him, and then another, like a challenge. "No, you brought it up. I want to hear what my big issue is."

Smirking, he says, "Okay, fine. I think you're sexually frustrated."

I stop in my tracks. "You did not just say that."

I glare into his damn whiskey-colored eyes. Whiskey is dangerous. I wished they'd stayed sunflowery.

Now it's his turn to take a step closer to me. And then another. He's faster than me and closes the gap between us in seconds.

Touch me, Brent, just do it. Make a move. Let's worry about the fall-out later.

He doesn't make a move, but he does lower his voice to a soft whisper as he says, "I did just say that, and I stand by it. Plus, I have another one for you."

"What's that?" I squeak out.

"You're also sexually repressed."

"What?"

I want to push him away, but that would mean skin-to-skin contact. We're already just about chest to chest. Mine is currently heaving under a thin tank, and his is…just so bare and in my face.

Wonder what his skin feels like? Probably all hot and—

I glance up and see the way he's looking at me. I know then that I'm not the only sexually frustrated person in the room. Brent wants *me* to make the move. I see it in his expression. He's waiting for me to do it to prove I'm not sexually repressed.

I think about going for it, but only for a few seconds. I've heard far too many stories of colleagues becoming involved with their clients, even though it's expressly forbidden. There's a reason why there's a no-fraternization clause stipulated in the contracts we sign. Relationships started under circumstances like these rarely end well.

Still, it's hard to resist. There's something undeniable between us. Something that's pushing us together, creating this friction. There's one thing that could alleviate it.

I look into his eyes, biting my lip. "Do it, Aubrey," he whispers.

His raspy voice makes my breath pick up. He's so close, close enough that I can actually *feel* the heat emanating from his body. And his masculine scent of soap and *eau de hot need* assaults my nose, making me want nothing more than to lean in and just freaking inhale him.

"I, uh…"

He raises a brow, a challenge.

But I'm afraid. "I—I can't," I murmur.

As I take a big lunge backward, a retreat, the look in his eyes tells me he views this as his victory.

"See," he says quietly, "I was right all along. You *are* sexually repressed. But it doesn't have to be this way. Maybe if we just say hell with it and fuck one time—"

"Stop," I desperately plead.

Hearing him say that word out loud, in his hot-ass voice, makes me want to give in. And he knows it.

"What's making you uncomfortable?" he whispers, baiting me. "Me saying we should fuck?"

"Yes," I practically pant.

"So let's do it, Aubrey. Let me fuck you, just once. I promise I'll make it good for you."

Before I do something really stupid, I beg him one last time, "Please, Brent, *please* just stop."

He sees I'm serious and backs off, hands in the air. "Okay. But let me say just one thing. I think you want this to happen"—he motions between us—"as much as I do."

He really wants this? It's not just a game?

I want it too, but I can't.

That's what I feel like screaming at him.

But I don't, of course.

What I do instead, the minute he's gone, is run upstairs.

I'm going to Area 51, baby. And you bet your ass I'm about to light up the sky with the glow.

11

AUBREY WILL BE THE DEATH OF ME...AND DEFINITELY THE DEATH OF MY SPERM

BRENT

This girl is going to be the one who kills me. I know it. If it isn't the fact that I can't have her that does me in, it'll be death by dehydration from jacking off so much that gets me.

Aubrey Shelburne may as well have a death warrant out on me... and my sperm.

I know that after all the womanizing I've done in the past that I deserve the slow, agonizing torture of not being able to touch this particular one. Aubrey may get on my last nerve, but our connection is as strong as it was the morning I met her. There's just something between us—a spark I keep trying to extinguish, but it keeps flaming back up—that makes me want her in ways I've never wanted anyone else.

"Fuck, fuck, fuck!" I head to my bedroom, and then straight to the ensuite bathroom. There, I strip off my clothes and step into the shower. I close my eyes and lean back against the rough stone tiles, allowing the warm water to splash over me.

I then grab the soap.

Once my hand is sufficiently lathered, I start stroking the length of my cock.

"Aubrey," I murmur as I imagine her bent over in front of me, ass high in the air.

My hand moves faster and faster, and before I know it I'm coming in long, thick strands, fantasizing the whole time that I'm shooting it over Aubrey's smooth skin. I clean up afterward, but not before jerking my dick one more time.

When I finally step out of the shower, I dry off a little and wrap a towel around my waist. My head starts to clear as my lust abates. I know it'd be a mistake to fuck my life coach. Same as starting something, like a relationship with her, would be. Not only would I probably get her fired—which, despite all my bitching, I really don't want to do—but if it didn't work out between us, it would make our situation all kinds of weird.

I can't have that. I need her too much. She's already made good progress with me. I'm eating right and working out. And after watching all that Grey Goose go down the drain, it looks like I won't be drinking anytime soon.

The team is thrilled so far, or so I've heard back from Jock. So why fuck things up? My life will become far more stressful once preseason—and then the regular season—start up.

I'm doing great, but that's partly because there's no real temptation around. It's basically just been Aubrey and me. Next week, though, Nolan is due in. And then Benny will be wrapping up with rehab and coming back to town.

Things are about to change real fast, and I need Aubrey around to keep me on track.

"So quit teasing her, jackass," I chastise myself.

I turn down the covers on my bed and sigh. I need to choose my words more carefully. All that talk of sexual frustration and sexual repression just brings up more sexual feelings. Namely, the ones we have for each other. Or so I think. I know *I* want Aubrey beneath me.

Yeah, while pounding into her.

"Fuck, stop." I'm getting hard again just thinking about her.

But what if she's not 100 percent sure she wants me. She did resist me down in the kitchen. But she sure liked me saying we should fuck. "I really wish we could."

Now I'm completely hard again just thinking about it. There's no denying I need another release before I can sleep.

Dropping the towel from around my waist, I fall back on my bed and begin stroking. All while once again fantasizing about a woman I can never really have.

12

AREA 51

AUBREY

First, I take a long, hot bath to relax my tense muscles. Brent has me so keyed up, damn him. I then slip on a short silky robe and step into my bedroom, where I proceed to light some candles.

A girl needs to set the mood for a date with some alien dick, right?

"This is so stupid," I murmur, sighing.

My lady bits don't find it dumb, though. Hell, they're urging me on. Miss Clit—she's the ringleader of the crew—is more than a tad bit curious about what the big, green fake dick can do.

I start giggling as I hold the package out in front of me. "Yes, let's see what green can do for you."

It's time to find out.

Plopping down on the edge of the bed, I remove Area 51 from the plastic casing. "I am taking the package out of the package," I say in my best robot voice.

Yeah, that does nothing to turn me on. But I can't deny the 51 emblazoned on the side reminds me of a certain someone.

Hmm, that gets me going a little.

Untying the sash on my robe, I lie back and let the silky material fall to my sides. I like the feeling of nakedness, especially when I spread my legs. It reminds me of the anticipation of sex. But this can't compare to the feelings you have when you're about to get busy with a "real" man. There's no flesh-on-flesh contact, no heated body pressed to one another in need. And, sadly, there's no kissing, not with the toy. I guess I could kiss the tip, keep in practice for when I get back to giving blow jobs. But then I'd have to suck the thing too. And I have a feeling, based on the smell, that Area 51 would taste like rubber. Or whatever the hell it is Gumby here is made of.

Nevertheless, I am undeterred. I'm going to make this good no matter what. Damn Brent Oliver and his accusations of sexual repression.

As I fire up my new toy, I remind myself, "Don't forget about the pulsating vibrating action."

And, whoa, there it is!

Within seconds of turning on that feature, I'm all like, "Hey there, hold up."

It's quite a struggle to control Area 51. He sure is a wiggly little bugger once he gets going. At one point, he almost flies out of my hands.

I quickly turn him down a notch, murmuring, "Okay, settle down, big boy."

Once I have control of the bending and twisting alien cock, I touch him lightly to my clit. "Oh, wow!"

That pulsating vibrating action is *gooood*. Kudos to whoever thought to add that.

I'm suddenly glad he moves so much. It makes Mr. 51 seem as exuberant as I. He also starts to glow a funky shade of florescent green the harder I press and the faster I go. Who cares, though? I'm starting to think this thing may be all I ever need for the rest of my life. Maybe I won't leave this room for a week. That'll show Brent. Sexually repressed, my ass.

"Mmm, Imma marry you, Mr. 51," I murmur after another minute of the pulsating vibrating action.

All the pulsating and vibrating is really intense, but so is the glow. No worries. I close my eyes and start fantasizing that my toy is really Brent. I pretend it's him sliding his big pulsing dick over my clit, and that it's his real cock that's parting my wet folds.

My fantasy works, and I start having to use both hands to keep Mr. 51—no wait, I'm renaming him Brent 51—from slipping around too much. "Yes, Brent fifty-one, right there. I like that."

I'm mainly concentrating on my clit, but when the toy dips inside me I let out a gasp. Tentatively, since it *is* kind of big, I push Brent 51 in farther and farther.

My whole hooha vibrates in response.

No, wait, that's my whole *body* vibrating.

Oh my God, now I see why this thing is so popular. I open my eyes and look down.

Brent 51 is halfway inside me and glowing like an alien ship has just docked in my vagina. Even, er, enclosed like that, the thing is still mega-bright. So bright, in fact, that my whole bedroom is glowing an odd shade of green.

I don't give a shit. I'm way too close to what I can tell is about to be an amazing orgasm. I resume my fantasy and pump my way to a release E.T. would definitely phone home about.

"God, yes, Brent fifty-one, give it to me hard. Fifty-one, fifty-one, my new favorite num—"

Just when I'm about to explode, there's a freaking knock on my bedroom door.

What the hell?

"Aubrey, are you okay?"

Fuck. It's Brent! The real Brent!

"Your room is glowing," he goes on. "Like, there's a really weird shade of green coming from under your door."

Something else was about to be coming, till you showed up.

Brent won't shut up. "It's lighting up the whole hall. I even saw it from my room. What the hell are you doing in there, anyway? Is it some kind of crazy experiment?"

If he only knew!

"Does it have something to do with life coaching?"

Pfft, he wishes!

"Ah, hold on a minute," I yell out. "Don't come in, okay?"

Of course, he doesn't listen to a word I say. The doorknob starts to turn.

Fuck me. How could I have forgotten to lock the damn door? I'm failing Masturbation 101 miserably.

I quickly pull Brent 51 from his vagina-space mission of getting me off. Not going to happen, seeing as I'm now in full Defcon-Five panic mode.

Unfortunately, out in the open Brent 51 is brighter than ever.

And the door is slowly opening...

"Aubrey?"

"Hold on," I yell to Brent.

"Turn off, you bastard!" I grind out to Brent 51.

Giving up, I fling the wiggly alien dick at the door, hoping to achieve the two-fold mission of powering the damn thing down and keeping Brent from coming in.

I fail on both counts.

Brent 51 does quit buzzing, but, damn, he's glowing brighter than ever.

Oh, and Brent the man?

Of course, he walks right into my personal masturbation den. "What the—" I hear him say as he shades his eyes from the bright glow Brent 51 is giving off.

His temporary blindness allows me to pull the comforter up to cover my nakedness.

"Oh hey, Brent, what's up?" I give a little wave and feign nonchalance, which doesn't really fly when there's a florescent-green vibrator lying on the floor, lighting up your whole damn bedroom.

Brent takes one look at me naked in the bed, and then focuses back on my glowing friend. Let's just say it doesn't take him long to figure out what's going on. If only I'd been assigned to a dumb hockey player. But noooo, I get one who's too smart for his own good. And also too snarky, meaning he'll no doubt torture me about this forever.

"Well, well, well, Aubrey. What do we have here?"

Real Brent bends down to pick up Brent 51. "I thought I heard you calling out my name. I even thought I heard mention of my number." He quirks a brow. "And then I saw the weird green glow." He nods to the vibrator and smirks over at me. "This explains the glow, but I have to wonder why you'd be calling out my name *and* my number?"

His smug grin tells me he knows exactly why.

"Just go ahead and kill me now," I say as I flop back on the bed.

I expect the worst, more teasing and taunting. But to my surprise, Brent mercifully says nothing more. He simply places Brent 51 on a table by the door. But not before pausing long enough to read the number stamped on the side.

With the hint of a smirk, he leaves.

The door closing behind him should fill me with relief, but what it actually does is scare the hell out of me. Brent knows I was getting off while thinking of him. And he's now fully aware I own a big-ass vibrator that shares a freaking number with him. He couldn't have missed the big 51 emblazoned on the side, like a goddamn tattoo.

Could it get any worse?

I cover my head with a pillow and scream. So much for professionalism. I have a feeling my life is about to become pure torture at the hands of Brent Oliver.

13

BLAME IT ON THE WEIRD GREEN GLOW

BRENT

"**F**uck me sideways." I laugh as I tiptoe back to my bedroom. "Did I really just see what I think I saw?"

Yeah, it would appear so. If I had any doubt the past five minutes were a dream, it's dispelled every time I blink. There seems to be a glowy green burned on the back of my lids.

Well, on the bright side of things—no pun intended—one thing is clear. If I wasn't 100 percent sure before that Aubrey Shelburne is attracted to me, after what I just witnessed, I am now absolutely certain.

Holy shit, she was getting herself off while thinking of *me*. I heard her calling out my name...and my number. I had no idea I had a starring role in her fantasies. Too bad I missed the main event. Instead, I was left dodging that fake green dick when I ventured into her room.

What the hell was that thing, anyway?

The shape was normal enough, so, yeah, I knew what it was. But what was with the bright glow... and the color... and the 51 on the side?

Mysteries, all of them, except for maybe the 51. I think I have that one figured out. Not only is it the same number I wear, but Aubrey was chanting it like a Benedictine monk. Wow, I wonder if she bought the sex toy *because* of the number on the side.

"Nah, that's just wishful thinking," I mutter as I crawl back into bed. "But she was definitely fantasizing about you."

I feel kind of bad for walking in on her while she was engaged in such a personal act. If I had suspected *that* was going on, I would've heeded her warning to not come in.

You're just disappointed she covered up before we could see her completely naked, my dick, coming to life, chimes in.

I ignore him. I've given him enough attention for the night.

Anyway, I never would've ventured from my room in the first place had I not noticed the strange green glow out in the hall. It was so bright it was shining in from under the door. I was almost asleep, but that shit woke me the hell up.

"What the fuck?" I mumbled. "Is there some kind of chemical spill in my house?"

You never know living out here in Nevada. There are military installations all around, and I'm sure they test all sorts of crazy things. Something could seep into the ground, or emit into the air. Hell, Area 51 is less than a hundred miles from my house.

That's when it hits me that Aubrey's toy is Area 51-themed.

Oh my God. You bet your ass I am going to have all kinds of fun with this.

Turns out, my fun with Aubrey has to be put on hold.

Claiming she's not feeling well, she holes up in her room the entire next day. I go about my usual business, which includes diligently following the new team-approved routine she has me on.

First, I eat a nice, healthy Aubrey-approved breakfast, consisting of an egg white omelet with fresh peppers, fruit and whole grain toast. I then go down to the arena to skate for a while. I'm back in time for dinner, but there's still no sign of my life coach.

I actually kind of miss her being around and giving me a hard time. I consider running out and buying some alcohol just so I can lure her out of her room to yell at me. But that'd probably be a bad idea.

I decide instead to make her some dinner, something I can take up to her. I'm not really good with anything fancy, but spaghetti is within my repertoire. After I boil some water and toss in a handful of noodles, I heat up a jar of marinara. I even grate some fresh parmesan into a little bowl. After I plate the pasta, I grab a bottle of water from the fridge and place everything on a serving tray.

"Nah, that doesn't look right."

I pour the water into a pretty crystal goblet and run outside to snip one of the more colorful desert flowers that grow in my yard. Once I have the purple bloom placed in a bud vase, I add it to the tray, satisfied that the whole presentation looks really nice.

Upstairs, and while balancing the tray in one hand, I knock on Aubrey's bedroom door. "Hey, it's me. Are you awake?"

No answer.

"I brought you some dinner."

That gets a response, but not the one I'm hoping for. "I'm not hungry, Brent. Just go away."

Not a chance. "Aw, come on," I press. "I made it myself."

Silence.

I lean my forehead against the door and try to make a joke. "I promise I didn't poison any of it."

Nothing.

"Aubrey? You have to be hungry. You've been in that room since last night when you went to bed."

I hear her groan. "Ugh, please. Can we forget last night ever happened?"

Sighing, I say quietly, but still loud enough for her to hear, "Look, I'm sorry I walked in on you. I was just worried about that...glow."

"Stop, pleeeeease!"

I try another tactic. "For the record, there's no reason to be embarrassed. Hell, I beat off all the time and—"

Wait, that's probably making things worse.

But then I hear Aubrey let out an amused snort, and I can't help but smile. Maybe I am getting through to her?

"Come on," I say. "Let me at least bring in your dinner. I'll leave right away if that's what you want."

When she mutters a barely audible, "Okay," I hurry in before she changes her mind.

First thing I notice is her "51" toy is no longer lying on the floor. I guess Aubrey put the freaky, glowing dick away. Which is good, seeing as the last thing I'd want to do is step on the thing and crush his green shaft. That would be like adding insult to injury.

"Just leave whatever you brought on the dresser," she mumbles from where she's buried under a pile of blankets.

I do as she asks, but instead of leaving I walk over to her cocoon.

"You seriously cannot be this embarrassed," I say. "Really, what happened is *not* that big of a deal."

"It is when I'm supposed to be here in a professional capacity," she says very loudly from under the covers, which kind of negates the whole "professional" aspect, more so than that sex toy.

"Yes, speaking to me while buried in blankets really gets that professionalism point across."

Oh shit. That gets the blankets off her.

Aubrey pops out from under the covers like one of those fake critters in the Whack-A-Mole arcade game. And wouldn't you know it; she's dressed in squirrel-themed pajamas. Mole, squirrel, whatever, this chick is still hot.

I resist the urge to laugh as she narrows her turquoise eyes at me from behind her glasses. It reminds me of *that* morning, and I chuckle a little.

"You know you're just making things worse, right?" she says.

Her long dark hair is a mess, in a sexy, tousled kind of way. And even though she has on no makeup and glasses—and the squirrel pj's are kind of silly—she looks really pretty.

I decide fired-up Aubrey is a good look for her.

But I better not fire her up any more. "I'm sorry," I say.

She puts her face in her hands, which I take as a cue to sit down on the edge of the bed.

"Listen, Brent," she begins, looking up and straightening her now-askew glasses. "I'm thinking of calling my firm this evening."

"Why?"

"So they can send someone out to take my place."

"Wait." I'm confused and panicked. I don't want her to go. "Why would you want to do something like that?"

She shakes her head. "How can you ever take me seriously now? You walked in on me basically fucking a sex toy. And not just any toy, but one that's florescent green, and that freaking glows."

"The glowing part is an interesting feature," I note, all nonchalant as I try to view the incident in a practical manner and hopefully put her at ease. "I have to say one thing, though. That sucker sure is bright. I bet it'd make a great flashlight if you were ever stranded somewhere."

She stares at me like I've lost my mind. "Yes, Brent, I can see where that feature would come in handy." Her tone is pure sarcasm. "Next time I'm out on some lonely road at night, and I just *have* to get myself off—because women do that on desolate roads oh-*so*-often—I'll be sure to thank my lucky stars that I happened to have on hand the only sex toy that doubles as a freaking flashlight."

I decide then and there to share something I've never told anyone. Maybe it'll quell her irritation with me.

"Hey, that needing to get-off-while-driving thing isn't all that farfetched. I can't speak for women, but men can get horny anywhere. There was this one time I was so hot and bothered that I had to pull off the road to take care of business."

She seems equal part horrified and intrigued. Intrigued wins out.

"Really?" she says. "What'd you do?"

Sheepishly, I admit, "Uh, I jacked off in some weeds." After a thoughtful pause, I add, "Come to think of it, good thing it was late at night. And really good thing there wasn't any poison ivy in those weeds."

She nods in agreement. "Definitely. That would've really sucked if there'd been any type of poisonous plant and you'd gotten too close."

"Like itch weed?" I say, going with it.

"Ooh, itch weed would've been bad, very bad. You know,"—she waves her hand at my junk—"especially down there."

I wince at the thought. And then we share a smile. "I can't believe we're seriously discussing me masturbating on the side of a road."

"Right?" she says, smiling. "Guess we can pretty much talk about anything after last night."

"It would seem so," I reply, chuckling. "So do you feel better?"

"Yes, actually I do. Thanks, Brent."

Softly, I ask, "Does this mean you won't be calling your firm? You'll stay here with me?"

After a long pause, she says, "Yes, I'll stay."

"And"—I jerk my thumb over to remind her of the tray on the dresser—"you'll eat your dinner like a good girl?"

"Hey, who's life-coaching who here?" she says with a laugh.

In a more serious tone, I say, "Sometimes all of us could use a little help, even life coaches."

"Yeah, I guess you're right."

I retrieve the tray and as I place it on her lap, I say, "How about, just for today, you let *me* take care of *you*?"

Surprisingly, she agrees. "All right. But only for today."

Aubrey begins to eat her dinner, and we talk about mundane things, like how my day went, in between bites.

At one point, she holds out a forkful of pasta for me. "This is really good," she says around a mouthful. "You should try it."

"I know what it tastes like. I made it, remember?"

"That's even more reason for you to have some." She wiggles the fork in front of my face, encouraging me to bite.

I'm planning to decline since it is the only meal she's had all day, but when a noodle comes dangerously close to hitting me in the face, I have no choice but to let her feed me the forkful of spaghetti.

After I'm done and as she's pulling away, I grab her hand. Slipping the fork from her grasp, I say softly, "It's my turn now."

I proceed to twirl spaghetti, and holding it out to her, I urge, "Be a good girl, Aubrey, and open your mouth."

With a smile she can't hide, and a bit of a blush, she lets me feed her, just like she did for me.

We take turns feeding each other, but finally I have to say, "This is supposed to be your dinner, you know."

"It doesn't matter. I like sharing it with you."

"Yeah, I kind of like you sharing it with me too."

After we're done eating, I figure it's probably time for me to leave. But when I start to stand she asks me to stay.

"You sure you're not too sleepy?" I say, cognizant that it's getting late.

She rolls her eyes. "Are you kidding? I slept all damn day."

"True."

"Hey!"

I evade a smack, as well as the plate that almost tips into my lap. Catching it and slipping the tray off her, I say, "Okay, I'll stay. But let me move this thing before we both end up covered in tomato sauce."

"Good call."

After placing the tray back on the dresser, I return to the edge of her bed. Aubrey wiggles back against the pillows, getting comfortable. "So... What should we talk about now?" she asks.

Waggling my brows, I propose, "More masturbation stories?"

She hits me with a pillow. "No way. Any more talk of itch weed and *I'm* going to break out in a rash."

"Well, we can't have that."

Sighing, she says, "Why don't you tell me about your family, Brent."

That sounds good to me, but I insist she'll have to share with me, as well.

We proceed to talk about everything. Not just families, but her days at college, and my time in juniors. She tells me about the townhouse she bought in Chicago, but explains that it's only been her home for a short while. She was born and raised in western Pennsylvania. We talk about my life growing up in Minnesota, and I share with her some of my fondest memories, like the hours I used to spend skating out on the pond at the back of our house.

"Wait. Didn't you say before that you guys had an indoor rink?"

"Yeah, we did. But I liked skating outdoors way better."

Pretending to shiver, she says, "Ugh, but winters are so brutal up there."

"They're no worse than the ones in Pennsylvania."

When she gives me a *yeah right* look, I concede, "Okay, yeah, ours are probably worse."

She tells me about her sister, Lainey, and when I hear how fun-loving and carefree she is, I say, "We should set her up with Benny. He's a let-the-good-times-roll kind of guy. They'd probably be perfect together."

"Who's Benny?" she asks.

"Benjamin Perry. He's one of my teammates."

"Oh, wait." She holds up her hand. "I read about him in the file they gave me. He's on your line. Plays left wing, right?"

"Left wing, eh?" I laugh. "Sounds like someone's been brushing up on their hockey terminology. And yes, that would be the same Benny."

We talk about hockey for a while. Hell, I could talk about hockey all night. But eventually our conversation turns to my father. I feel so comfortable with her that I end up sharing how all I've ever wanted to do in this life is make my dad proud of me.

"I'm sure he's plenty proud already," she says with a smile that tells me she thinks I'm a big deal. That makes me feel amazing.

"I'm sure he is," I reply. "But I don't think he'll ever truly be happy till I win a Cup."

"A Stanley Cup, right?"

She is too adorable.

"That would be the one."

"Wow. That's a lot of pressure, Brent," she says as her brows crease with concern.

It's sweet she's worried, but I assure her, "I'm used to pressure. I'm the captain of the team, remember?"

"I know. I meant family pressure."

I shrug. "Eh, it's always been that way. I don't have any brothers or sisters, so my parents' expectations have always fallen on me."

She eyes me warily.

"Uh-oh, what's that look for?"

"I was just thinking," she says. "Do you think maybe that's part of the reason why you sabotage yourself sometimes?"

Whoa now, hold the bus.

Bristling, I snap, "Are you life-coaching me right now?"

She shakes her head. "No, not intentionally. But it is a legitimate question. I'm asking it tonight, though, simply as your friend."

I cock my head. "Is that what we are now?"

"You tell me."

She *is* becoming my friend, it's true. Despite all our run-ins, or maybe because of them, we're growing closer and closer. Though, if I'm to be honest with myself, I kind of want more. Oh hell, there's no "kind-of" about it when it comes to any of my feelings for Aubrey.

But the friend zone is safe—and allowed—so I say, "Yes, we're friends."

She smiles. "I think so too." Pinning me down with serious turquoise eyes, she resumes her earlier line of questioning. "So back to the point, *friend*. Do you think all that pressure has made you rebel and act out?"

"Act out? You make me sound like a three-year-old."

"Some of your behavior would rival that of a three-year-old."

I let out a snort. "You *are* life-coaching me now, Miss Shelburne. Don't try to deny it."

"Maybe just a little," she admits. "But I'd really like to hear your answer, as your friend *and* as your life coach."

"Wow, okay." I run my hands through my hair. "You know, I've never thought about it like that. But it does make sense. There is an element of rebellion in most of the things I do."

Softly, and after a long pause, she says, "Maybe that's because a person has to want for themselves all the things other people are pushing them to do. You can't live your life for someone else, Brent."

"I don't." I shake my head. On this, I'm sure. "I really want those things too."

"So what's the problem?"

I hate that she makes me analyze myself like this. But I know it's for my own benefit.

Why *do* I sabotage things? I want success; I definitely want to win championships. But—and this is why her being here has been so helpful—I don't want those things all alone. Sure, there's an entire team striving for the same thing as me, but it's different. I want to share my success with someone who really cares about me, but also someone who can call me out on my bullshit.

Like Aubrey.

Hell, no. She's my life coach and my friend, nothing more.

Liar.

Getting involved with her is strictly forbidden, remember?

We could always say 'fuck it.'

Shit, this is too confusing, so I just answer her question. "To be honest…and this is hard to admit…"

"Go on."

"I think I'm the kind of guy who needs someone to share things with."

"You have your parents—"

"Not like that." I make a face. "I mean something different."

"Oh? Ohhh…" It finally dawns on her. "You mean you want to share all the good things in your life with a girlfriend, or even a wife."

I pin her with a withering look. "Let's not get crazy here. I'm not ready for marriage."

"Okay. Well, a girlfriend, then."

"Maybe someone like that," I say, hedging.

Shit, I don't want to sound like a total pussy here.

"Hey," I say in a rush, "can we talk about something else? I think my dick is turning in on itself and becoming a vagina."

She rolls her eyes at my colorful imagery. "Sure, Brent," she dryly replies. "Pick a new topic."

"How about something simple, like what's your favorite color?"

"It depends on the day," she replies.

It's my turn to roll my eyes. "Aubrey." I sigh. "And you say I'm difficult. Okay, what about food? Have any favorite dishes?"

On that, she has an immediate response. "I love anything with tomato sauce."

"Hmm, interesting. Guess I chose wisely when I was trying to decide what to cook for you tonight."

"You did. The pasta was delicious."

"My mother would kill me, though," I admit. "If she knew I used jarred sauce she'd kick my ass."

"Why's that?"

"Half Italian,"—I point to myself—"right here. My mom's 100 percent Sicilian. Someday you'll have to come to Minnesota and try her homemade sauce. She lets it simmer for hours. It's to die for, I swear."

Wait. Did I just invite her to my parents' house for dinner?

Looking down to where she's folding the edge of the comforter over and over on itself, she murmurs, "I bet her sauce *is* really good."

"Yep," I quietly reply, looking away.

There's this long, awkward moment of silence, until Aubrey clears her throat and says, "Okay, your turn. What's *your* favorite food?"

I blow out a relieved breath. "That's an easy one. I love steak."

"What about color? Have a fave?"

I grin as I throw her words back at her. "It depends on the day."

"Ass." She pushes my shoulder, but it's like she's trying to topple a stone statue. "God, you're like a damn boulder, Brent," she remarks.

I laugh. "I have to be. Otherwise, I'd get knocked off my skates every play."

Frowning, she says, "There sure is a lot of hitting in hockey. I guess it's good you're so…hard."

"Guess so," I agree.

Our eyes meet, and I suddenly blurt out, "Turquoise. You know, like sea-green."

"What the hell are you going on about?" she asks, clearly confused.

"My favorite color." I hold her gaze. "You asked what it is, right? Well, today it's turquoise."

"Brent…" She rips her gaze from mine when she realizes the color of her eyes is what I'm referring to. "We should probably wrap it up here."

"I don't want to go," I whisper.

"I don't want you to, either. But that's exactly why you should go."

Blowing out a breath, I give up…for now. "Okay, Aubrey. I'll go."

I leave her room, but all is not lost. Despite how things wrapped up—too abruptly if you ask me—I feel like the time we spent together was a win. We were real with each other, all pretenses were dropped. And because of that we now know each other a little better.

Though the more I think about it, the more I realize that getting to know each other better is a double-edged sword. 'Cause now not only does my body crave Aubrey like crazy, but my heart's starting to want her too.

14

NOLAN THROWS A WRENCH IN THE WORKS

AUBREY

I wish I could call my sister and tell her everything. I texted her when I first arrived in Las Vegas like she asked me to, and we've traded a couple of long voicemail updates back and forth since then, but she'd die if I called her now and told her the supposed baseball player who hosted that party in Minneapolis is really a hockey player who's on his way to capturing my heart.

Oh, boy!

Talking with Lainey, though, even if I were permitted to tell her everything, would so not be a good idea. It would only make things worse. My sister is a sucker for a forbidden love story. And let's face it— falling for Brent Oliver is strictly forbidden. As in, it can never happen. I'd be terminated for sure if my boss ever found out. And then I might never work again. 'Cause, really, talk about unprofessional!

Besides, I've truly been helping Brent, as demonstrated by his exemplary behavior of late. There's been no drinking, no partying, and no women in his life. He's also skating every day and working out rigorously. All of which is good since training camp starts up this week.

A creep of dread works its way up my spine, and I have to address the glaring observation that Brent staying on-course is due, in part, to his not associating with his rowdy teammates.

That's all about to change though, and real fast. The team e-mailed me something this morning—almost like a warning and a heads-up rolled into one long memo—informing me that Brent's linemates, Nolan Solvenson and Benjamin Perry, who also have the distinction of having been his summer party pals, are back in town. Nolan apparently lives in the same gated community Brent's house is in, so I suspect he'll be stopping by soon enough.

Let's hope it's not to recruit my protégé for a night of partying and puck bunnies.

Benjamin, I'm less worried about. Though the e-mail indicated he was quite the party animal this summer, he made it through rehab with flying colors. I can't imagine he'll be any trouble, except in one area—women. He could very well try to talk Brent into partaking in a hockey whore orgy or something just as sleazy.

I shudder at the images that flash through my head like a bad porn movie. With these horndog hockey players anything's possible. I have to be prepared, and so should Brent.

As I venture around the house, searching for him so we can discuss new parameters for dealing with his potentially bad influence friends, the doorbell chimes.

And chimes...

And chimes...

I'm apparently the only one around—*where the heck is Brent?*—so I have no choice but to go see who it is.

When I open the door, I come face-to-face with a handsome, dark-haired man, one who oozes coolness and sophistication. He also happens to be built like a world-class athlete, much like Brent, so I suspect right away he's a teammate.

"Hello," he says, all James Bond-like. He lowers his dark sunglasses and gives me the 'ole once-over.

"Hi," I reply, rolling my eyes at his flirtatious demeanor.

He chuckles, unaffected by my blasé attitude toward him.

Dismissing me just as summarily as I did him, he takes off his glasses and cranes his neck to peer past me. "Is Brent home?" he asks, distractedly, like I'm the help or something.

Well, I kind of am, but he doesn't know that.

"Who wants to know?" I ask as I cross my arms and try to block his view.

God, you're acting like your Brent's mother.

"I'm Nolan," he states dryly. "I play with Brent."

I'd kind of like to play with Brent too. Yikes, now I sound like I'm his girlfriend.

"No!" I exclaim, as I perish the thought.

"No, he's not home?" Nolan asks, the first crack in his cool demeanor revealing itself when he looks a tad confused.

"Uh, actually, I'm not sure," I admit.

"And who are you, exactly?" he asks, back to sounding suave and collected.

I hold out my hand. May as well make nice with the guy, right?

"I'm Aubrey, Brent's life coach."

"Ahh, yes." He shakes my hand firmly. "I heard about you."

Before I can stop myself, I blurt out, "You have? From who? Brent?"

I try like hell to tamp down the inner total-girl part of me that's secretly jumping up and down at the idea Brent may have mentioned me to this obvious friend. If he did, then that must mean something, right? Like maybe he's really into me.

Those burgeoning hopes are crushed to smithereens when Nolan responds, "No, nothing from Brent. I just heard about you through the team grapevine."

"Oh, okay."

So there's a team grapevine? Probably the same grapevine that passes around info on which puck bunny is the best lay. Or maybe who gives the best blow jobs. I hope it's not a grapevine I have to worry about with Brent. Though I suspect I probably do.

Just then the man I'm thinking of appears, saving me from any further embarrassment with Nolan.

I move out of the way quickly. That way there's no physical contact when Brent wedges his hard-bodied self in the doorway.

"Hey, man," he says to Nolan. The two linemates then do some kind of bro-hug, fist-bump ritual. "When'd you get in?"

"Last night," Nolan replies.

"Cool. Come on in."

Brent steps back to make way for Nolan.

Feeling suddenly left out, I swish my hand through the air and announce, "Well, I guess I'll get out of your hair. I have a few company reports to work on. I'm just going to head on upstairs to my lonely little room."

I point in the direction of the stairs, but I make no move to go. I'm secretly hoping Brent will stop me. I'd like an invitation to wherever they're going for two reasons. 1) I kind of want to hang out more with

Brent, and 2) I can keep an eye on him if I'm with him.

But no such luck. He nods distractedly and says, "Okay, yeah, work reports. Great. Have fun."

"Nice meeting you, Aubrey," Nolan adds, effectively sending me on my way.

"Yeah, you too," I mutter as I turn away.

So much for discussing parameters for dealing with friends. So much for invitations. Looks like Brent's on his own till I can get him alone.

Oh well. I actually do have reports to work on and turn in, both for my firm and for the team.

I work on those assignments until evening, and when I venture back downstairs I'm surprised to discover Nolan is still at the house. He and Brent are out back by the pool, grilling hamburgers, laughing, talking, and—*wait, what?*—drinking beer.

I'm out the sliding glass doors leading to the backyard in less than a minute. Picking up one of at least a dozen bottles snuggled down in a tub of ice on the red sandstone patio, I point the thing at Brent and say, "I hate to ruin your little get-together out here, but you absolutely should not be drinking."

"Uh-oh," trouble-maker Nolan chimes in, chuckling. "Looks like your life coach"—he shoots me a challenging ice-blue glare—"is on the warpath."

Brent laughs right along with him. *What?* "You're not kidding, man."

What happened to my star client? And I don't mean as in superstar, which he clearly has down pat as indicated by this out-of-the-blue display of attitude. What I want to know is where's the sweet guy who made me dinner? The great guy who talked with me late into the night?

You know, the guy I'm freaking falling for.

I scowl at both men, shooting Brent an especially disappointed look. He, at least, has the decency to turn away.

Amazed by how quickly things can change, I ask, "Where did this beer come from, anyway? I thought I dumped anything even remotely resembling alcohol down the drain?"

"You did," Brent mutters.

Nolan, still looking smug, says, "Wow. That was harsh. Good thing I thought to throw a case into a cooler and toss it in the back of my SUV."

"How very thoughtful of you," I snap, my tone dripping with sarcasm.

Nolan narrows his eyes at me and then, turning to Brent, says, "Maybe we should move this over to my house. There are no life coaches over there."

Yikes, but there could be hockey whores.

I try to stop them. "Wait, no."

Paying me no heed whatsoever, Brent downs the beer he's drinking in two seconds flat, then says to Nolan, "Sounds good to me, man. Let's go."

In that moment, I feel all my work, all the progress I've made with Brent thus far, crumbling around me.

SO MAYBE I DO LIKE HER MORE THAN I SHOULD

BRENT

I don't know why I'm acting like a dick. I don't even feel like drinking. But I also don't think a few beers will kill me. Nor will they ruin the progress I've made up to this point. I mean, come on. It's not like I'm never again going to consume alcohol.

What if we win it all someday?

Surely I'll drink champagne from the Cup.

What if Jock comes into town and wants to smoke cigars and drink whiskey in the gentlemen's club he likes to frequent?

I may pass on the cigars—and the lap dances—but I can't turn down a good Irish whiskey.

What if I take Aubrey out on a date someday and we want to share a bottle of fine wine?

Whoa, wait! What am I thinking here? No lap dances and dates with

Aubrey?

Never. Going. To. Happen.

"Dude, what's up with you?" Nolan asks. "You've been weird since we left your house."

We're on the back patio of his house now, which is four doors down from my place. I'm still drinking, but much more slowly.

Setting my beer down on an outdoor iron table in front of me, I sigh. "I don't know, man. I guess I feel kind of bad treating Aubrey the way I did."

"What?" He makes a *who-the-fuck-cares* face. "You mean the life coach chick?"

"Yeah, the life coach chick." I blow out a breath. "But she's more than that. She's a really great girl."

Nolan knows me far too well. He senses where this is leading.

"Dude," he begins, in full warning mode. "Don't even think of going there."

I play dumb. "What do you mean?"

"Oh, you know what I mean. Getting involved with that woman would be nothing but trouble. She was hired by the team to help you, which kind of makes her like your employee by default."

"An employee I'd like to bang," I admit.

"I wouldn't do that if I were you."

I glare over at him from across the patio table. "Are you kidding? Of course you would."

"Yeah, you're probably right," he concedes. "So maybe you *should* bang her. But real secretly. And just once. Get her out of your system before you fuck up your career."

When he starts staring over at me, like he has more to say on the subject, I make an attempt to change the topic. I need to end this conversation about my life coach, who I already can't get out of my goddamn mind.

In my most dickhead tone, I say, "Stop giving me your googly eyes, Solvenson. You know how it makes me all warm and fuzzy inside when you do that."

"Fuck off, Oliver," Nolan volleys back, looking away as he takes a long pull from his beer. As he lowers his bottle, he adds, "I know what you're doing, anyway."

"Oh yeah, you do? Please tell me then, great sensei, what am I doing?"

"You're deflecting. You're trying to hide from the truth."

"Which is?"

"You're falling hard for your hot little life coach."

Shit, I hate when he's right.

16

MIDNIGHT VISIT

AUBREY

At midnight, there's a knock on my bedroom door. "Aubrey? Are you up?"

"Shit, Brent!"

I'm awake, reading in my bed. Throwing down my Kindle, where I'm discovering the joys of book boyfriends, I jump to my feet.

Then I sit back down.

Then I'm up again.

Help! I don't know what to do.

"Aubrey?" Brent calls out from the other side of the door.

"Hold on a minute, okay?" I reply.

Should I let him in? I'm torn. Apart from feeling kind of pissed at him, I'm stressing over my sleepwear. I have on the new jammies I bought the other day. And that'd be all fine and good, except I never planned on them being seen by anyone outside this room, especially not Brent. Bad enough I had on my squirrel jammies the night he brought me dinner.

These are far worse, though.

It's not the top half, the rose-colored tank, that's an issue. Except for maybe that it shows off more nip than anticipated thanks to the near-sheer material. But really, I don't mind if Brent gets a little breast peek. It's the pants I'm worried about. They happen to be covered in colorful little hockey sticks and pucks.

He's going to think you bought them because they remind you of him.

"Ah, that's kind of why I did buy them," I mutter to myself.

Admit that you like little hockey sticks and pucks all over your ass and crotch. That also reminds you of him.

"All true. If it can't have Brent's big stick, then I guess I have no choice but to settle for little sticks on my pj—"

"Aubrey? Are you talking to someone in there?"

Poor Brent, he's out there waiting. And now he sounds concerned. He probably thinks I have a guy in here with me. Why else would I be talking out loud and not opening the door?

The idea he's sweating it out gives me an empowered feeling. And when you think about it, he deserves a little grief for being such an ass earlier.

But then I remember he knows about Brent 51.

Crap. What if he thinks I'm talking to my sex toy? Not that I'd be doing much talking. Probably just some moaning and—

Enough!

Rushing over to the door, I throw it open as wide as it goes. "Hey, hi," I say, out of breath.

He cocks his head, which makes him look absolutely adorable.

Adding to that, he's sexy as hell. He's half-clothed, as usual, wearing only a pair of navy blue lounge pants.

"Is everything okay in there?" he asks, looking beyond me to the interior of the room.

I shift from one bare foot to the other, feigning nonchalance. "Everything's fine. What's up?"

Maybe not the best choice of words, seeing as he's now staring at my boobs, prominently displayed in my skimpy tank.

I clear my throat and his whiskey-colored eyes snap up to mine, but only for a second. Still, it's enough to give me a tingle down my spine.

With a smirk, his gaze drops to my bottoms. "Nice," he mutters. "Pucks and hockey sticks, eh? That's cute."

Cute?

He's acting a little strange, and when our gazes once again meet I notice how bloodshot his eyes are. Letting out a disappointed huff, I exclaim, "What the hell, Brent? Are you drunk? You are, aren't you?"

That bad influence Nolan. Fuck him!

"Maybe just a little," Brent confesses.

"How much is a little?" I warily inquire.

He raises his hand and squints down to the inch of space he's trying to indicate with his index finger and his thumb. "About this much," he says.

Clearly, this is his smartass, and not very successful, attempt to indicate he's only a tiny bit drunk. I question that, however, seeing as he's here at my bedroom door.

I can't resist giving him a hard time, a little payback for the way he treated me earlier. Plus, what the hell is he thinking, getting trashed like this? A beer or two is one thing, but he's throwing weeks of progress out the damn window.

Pointing to where his hand is still hovering in the air, I nod to the teeny space between his fingers and say in my snarkiest tone, "Are you sure that's an indication of your level of drunkenness? Or is it something else. Like, is that tiny space an approximation of your, uh, you know." When I gesture to his groin area, he quickly drops his hand.

And then he scoffs, "Well, we both know that's not true. And what *exactly* are you gesturing to anyway, Aubrey? Are you too shy to say the word 'cock'?"

"No," I snap. "I can say that word just fine."

"Really?" His tone drips with doubt. "It sounds to me like your avoiding it."

Crap, does he mean the *word* cock…or *his* cock?

To prove him wrong, at least on the first count, I start chanting out, "Cock, cock, cock, cock. See? Are you happy now?"

He breaks into a grin, a very smart-alecky grin. "Wow. If you add a few *a-doodle-doo's* you'd totally sound like a rooster."

"You must really be annihilated, Brent."

"And you must really be horny, Aubrey."

"*What?*"

"You're clearly obsessed with my cock."

"I am not."

"Don't deny it. You bought a sex toy with my number on it. And don't think I didn't notice the dimensions of that weird-ass thing. I have to say, they're pretty spot-on."

"Weird-ass thing? What the hell does that mean?"

He gives me a look. "Really, Aubrey? You need me to spell it out for you? Your sex toy is bright green and glows like a—"

"You…you…" I'm so mad I can't find the right words, so I go with an old standard. "You're such a prick!"

"See, another cock reference."

I try to close the door on him then, but he puts his foot in the way. "We're not done here," he says.

"Yes, we are," I grind out.

Again, I try to shut the door, but his damn foot won't budge. "I'll smash your toes if I have to," I warn.

That makes him laugh. "Good luck with that."

I give it my all, struggling and straining to close the damn door. I don't really plan to break his toes, but I do want him out. But my efforts are all in vain, anyway. The door doesn't move. And neither does Brent.

And then something happens, something awful. Due to my vigorous attempts to close the door, a strap of my tank falls down.

And then a damn boob falls out!

"Oh, shit." Brent moves his foot immediately, adding a mumbled apology.

That just makes things worse.

Unbalanced from him releasing the door so quickly, I stumble forward, right into his arms, loose boob and all.

"Quit touching me!"

"I'm trying to help you."

"You're trying to grope me."

"I am not. That's your shoulder I'm grabbing."

"Oh my God, you have clearly touched far too many fake boobs. My tits are not hard like bone, asshole."

Brent rights me as fast as he can. Then he steps back and looks away. "Sorry," he mumbles.

I slip my wayward breast back into my tank and snap, "How about a little warning next time? You could've said something before you moved your foot and let me fall."

"I didn't mean for that to happen, I swear." His voice is full of remorse and he keeps his eyes averted, so I believe him.

Sighing, I say, "You can look now. I'm decent."

He does look at me, but then he starts to smirk. "Decency after that debacle is a debatable point."

"What's that supposed to mean?"

"Nothing." He lets out a sigh. "I'm just being an ass." Scrubbing a hand down his face, he says, "Look, I didn't come here to argue with you."

"But it's so fun," I snidely remark.

I'm trying to sound irritated, but truth be told this actually *is* kind of fun. Brent looks so hot standing there that I don't care he saw—and sort of touched—some boobage.

"It really is kind of fun, isn't it?" he says when he sees the smile I'm trying to hide.

"It is," I admit.

"And why do you think that is, Aubrey?"

He casually leans against the doorjamb, making all those damn muscles in his chest and arms pop.

Please. Don't do this to me. Not now, not after your hand was on my boob.

Brent 51 has already gotten a workout lately. And a lot of my fantasies—okay, 99.99 percent of them—involve Brent showing up at my bedroom door, maybe not drunk, but definitely looking hot like this.

Unable to make eye contact, I murmur, "I don't know why."

He takes a step closer. "Oh, I think you do."

God, he smells good. He must've showered upon returning from

Nolan's place. Come to think of it, his hair does look a little wet, especially at the ends, where it curls a little in the most adorable way.

I want to reach out and touch just one dark strand.

Oh, what the hell.

Emboldened, I do exactly that.

And he lets me.

I've never touched him before, not like this.

My fingers linger at a droplet of water at the end of the strand that's touching his neck. I press my index finger to the drop…and next thing I know I'm touching his actual neck.

His hand goes to my cheek, where he softly caresses my sensitive skin. Our eyes lock, and we both know there's so much we should say right now.

But neither one of us utters a word.

I think we're too afraid we'll sever this amazing connection we're feeling. It's more than the usual pull. This is something electric, something that's pulsing in the air.

So when he lowers his face to mine and our lips finally touch, I don't stop him.

It's just a brush, but it's filled with a promise of more.

And I want more. God, do I want more.

I'm about to go over the line with Brent, and I don't care. Still, my conscience makes one final appearance and I murmur a half-hearted, "We shouldn't do this."

"You're right," he agrees.

But neither of us stops. Instead, we start kissing, really kissing. And holy hell, it's hot. Brent Oliver is kissing me. Not all aggressively like I expected him to, but softly and tenderly, which is probably worse for my restraint.

Yeah, it is. I melt in his arms and let out a whimper. To which he becomes a little more forceful.

Passions we've been fighting are ignited. And fuck touching that one strand of hair; my hands go all up in his dark locks. His hair is damp all over, but so incredibly soft. A striking contrast to a guy who's so hard everywhere else.

Speaking of which, his substantial erection is pressing into my belly. No Brent 51 tonight. I'm going for the real thing.

I swear I hear bells ringing in my head, like a joyful jubilation that this girl is about to get laid by a massive c—

Wait, those aren't bells in my head. Someone is ringing the doorbell downstairs like a goddamn maniac.

Pulling away from Brent, I breathlessly inquire, "Who the hell rings a doorbell like that at this hour?"

His eyes, hooded with lust, scan down my body. Lowering his head to nuzzle my neck, he murmurs, "Who cares?"

Not me.

But while Brent sucks and nibbles at the sensitive skin along my collarbone, the incessant ringing continues. It's like the worst make-out soundtrack ever.

"Christ," he breathes against me. "I don't think whoever's down there is going to give up anytime soon."

I sigh. "Yeah, me neither."

Smiling, he takes my hand and says, "Come on. We can go kill 'em together."

17

COCKBLOCKED

BRENT

Benny turns out to be the nut ringing the doorbell like a maniac. And since I like my linemate, even though he pretty much just totally cockblocked me, no murder occurs.

Instead of committing a capital offense, I invite the asshole in and introduce him to Aubrey.

She stares at him like she knows him. *That's weird.*

I pass it off as nothing, especially when she shoots me a withering look as I mention to Benny that "Aubrey's my life coach."

Still aggravated with me, she shakes Benny's hand, and then excuses herself to head upstairs to change into something more appropriate than PJ's.

"Dude," Benny says once she's out of earshot. "Did I interrupt something with you and your sexy-as-fuck friend? Her clothes are a wreck, and you both look a little out of sorts."

"First off," I state, "Aubrey is not my friend."

Yes, she is, you asshole, a little voice in my head reprimands.

I'm clearly having regrets over kissing her. Not that I didn't like it—I *loved* it—but what we did is just plain stupid.

"I meant, like, the 'with benefits' variety," Benny clarifies.

He would know, as he keeps many friends with benefits on speed dial. I do too, but for some weird reason I haven't had the urge to call any of them lately.

Worried what this all could mean, I hasten to add, "I told you she's my life coach, dude. There's nothing going on between us."

He shoots me an *are-you-sure-about-that* look, but asks nothing more. I'm relieved since I have no idea what the hell is going on with me and her. What was I thinking? Kissing her was so not a good idea.

It sure was amazing, though.

Okay, yeah, it was. But I know better, I do. For her sake, and mine—hell, I don't want to lose her—I pledge right there and then that it won't happen again.

Benny and I talk some more by the door, then we go into my living room. Once we're settled in, me on the sofa and him on a chair, he informs me that he plans to hang out with me a lot. "You're the only player not partying at all," he says. *Oh, the irony.* "That makes you, my friend, an integral part of my temptation-avoidance plan."

Too bad I fail at staying on course when it comes to Aubrey. Though this transgression tonight was probably due to all the beer I consumed earlier with Nolan. I feel pretty sober now, however, so Benny doesn't need to know I partied a little tonight. He just said he needed me, so I'll be there to help him with his no-drinking, no-drugs thing. I was never one for illegal substances anyway, so we're solid there. As for drinking, tonight was an anomaly. I won't be having a drop anytime soon. Not after this debacle with Aubrey.

Benny and I are in the midst of shooting the breeze about the upcoming season when Aubrey reappears. I notice immediately that though she's ditched the cute hockey-themed pj bottoms, she still has on the thin tank top. It looks like she's paired it with some tight jeans, making her look hotter than ever.

Did she do this to torture me?

Maybe, 'cause I can't help but feel a surge of possessiveness when Benny casts an appreciative once-over down her lithe form. I then practically growl at him when he mutters under his breath, "Damn, Oliver. You sure you don't want to rethink that 'there's nothing going on between us' stance?"

"Shut up, Perry," I snap.

Aubrey sits down about a foot away from me on the sofa, and although she and I share a few meaningful glances, we act as if nothing happened in her room. Still, it's tense at first.

Eventually, however, the atmosphere relaxes.

It's amazing how well Aubrey gets along with Benny. It's like they've known each other forever. Nolan may have had an issue with her— only because she was trying to derail our drink-fest—but my other linemate clearly thinks she's cool. He gets into a huge discussion with her about hockey. But it's more like a lesson, which is fine with me. I want Aubrey to understand the game I love and play. Problem with me explaining it to her—apart from her distracting me with how attracted I am to her—is that so much of the game is inherent to me. It's hard for me to break it down to basics for someone who has virtually no knowledge of the sport.

But Benny thrives on that crap. I guess that's why the team's always sending him out to schools to speak.

"No, a player can't just skate into the other team's offensive zone and wait for one of his guys to pass him the puck," he tells her when she wants to know why everyone waits for the guy who has the puck to cross over the blue line and into the opponent's zone first.

I let out a laugh. "Yeah, we'd be called for being 'offside' in a heartbeat. Although I wish we could just skate on over to the opponent's net and wait for the player with the puck to pass it to us from the neutral zone."

"Imagine the resulting scorefest." Benny laughs.

I nod wistfully. "We'd have, like, twelve-goal games all the time."

"Probably more like twenty-goalers," Benny replies.

I feel Aubrey's gaze on me, so I turn to her and ask, "Do rules like those make more sense to you now?"

"Yes." She nods. "They're starting to."

Those eyes, those beautiful sea-green depths, remain focused on me, like she has another question. "What else is on your mind?" I inquire.

She smiles, and for a minute it's like we're back upstairs. I don't care about my new rule to leave her be. I want to kick Benny out and crawl over to her so I can take her in my arms and pick up where we left off.

But wait, no, we can't.

I think she senses all the back-and-forth confusion going on in my head, as she quickly looks away.

Benny clears his throat. "Hey, maybe I should get going."

"No!" Aubrey and I cry out at the exact same time.

He looks at us strangely. "Okaaay."

Shit, this is going to be a problem. I need to steer clear of Aubrey unless someone is around.

'Cause the minute I'm left alone with her...

Let's just say, like they do in this gambling town, that if that ever happens, all bets on us not touching each other again are off.

THE SEASON STARTS OFF WITH A BANG, THOUGH NOT THE KIND I'D LIKE

AUBREY

Who knew Thor from the party would turn out to be one of Brent's teammates?

When I return to my bedroom I take out the file the team provided on Benjamin Perry. Just as I remembered, and like in Brent's folder, there are no pictures.

What do they think, that everyone on the planet loves hockey and knows these guys?

Well, you're starting to do both.

"Good point."

I want nothing more than to call my sister and share with her all the events of late. First off, I'd tell her about Benjamin Perry. She'd die if she knew Thor—ah, I mean Benny—is my client's friend. But then again, maybe it's for the best that Lainey not be involved. Though

Benny is supposedly clean and sober, his manwhoring ways are well-documented in the file. I seriously doubt *that* behavior was addressed in rehab. He's probably still a player.

Crap, I feel bad thinking about him like that. He's actually a really nice, likable guy. That's also going to make it hard to keep in mind that I need to watch Brent around him. One of the things the team wants reined in is Brent's womanizing. Not a problem thus far, but hanging with Benny could lead to that kind of bad behavior starting back up.

I'm thankful I haven't seen that side of Brent. I would've simply been annoyed early on, but with my burgeoning feelings for him now in play, I'd be livid if he started whoring around. I'd also be insanely jealous. Eye-gouging might occur, and maybe even some hair-pulling. Not that I'd have any right, as I have no claim on the guy. But damn it all to hell! I do have feelings for him, strong feelings.

That's why what happened in my room can *never* happen again. No matter how much I want it to. My job isn't to seduce the guy, though how much fun would that be? My job is to keep him on track. And that means keeping my own damn self under control when it comes to the lust department.

That becomes supremely difficult when a couple weeks later I attend the home opener, a game kicking off the new season.

Sweet baby Jesus!

Who knew Brent Oliver would be so breathtakingly beautiful on the ice? Not only is he a pretty skater, all fluid-like and graceful, but he's fast as hell and his skills are off the charts.

I ask you, what's more appealing than a man who's good at what he does?

Nothing, I say.

Hell, I should've gotten into hockey sooner. I'm into it now thanks in large part to Benny. He's still diligently continuing with my hockey lessons, and there's been a lot more of them since that night in Brent's living room.

Benjamin Perry's commitment to teach me all I need to know about hockey, so I'll be ready for the regular season, is paying off. When I say it's with a whole new appreciation that I watch Brent play, I'm not kidding.

And he is nothing short of mesmerizing.

In the stands, I watch the home opener with rapt attention. When Brent makes a spot-on drop pass to Nolan, resulting in a goal within the first five minutes of play, I go nuts. The crowd goes crazy right along with me. It's like we're all in this together.

"I love hockey!" I yell out as I'm caught up in the moment.

In the second period, just as an opponent is blatantly hooking him, Brent scores a beautiful goal of his own, making the score 2-0. I'm excited he scored, but I'm mad at the refs for not calling an obvious penalty. What if that player's stick had hit Brent in the face?

Perish the thought!

Rising to my feet, I scream, "Hey, Ref, are you blind? That was a hooking infraction."

The official doesn't hear me. No one does. People are too busy celebrating that we scored. They're all chanting, "OPS, OPS," in recognition of Brent's line.

I cheer too when I give up on having the penalty get called. Some even more enthusiastic fans than me are pounding on the Plexiglas, celebrating the goal. We're all in the front row, so when Brent looks over I give him a thumbs-up that makes him smile.

God, his smile. I am so putting Brent 51 to use tonight. I may have vowed not to get physical with the real man, but that doesn't mean

I can't think about him in that way. I do all the time anyway, and it makes my moments spent with his namesake that much more fun.

The next couple of games are just as amazing as the first. I attend both and cheer like the lunatic fan I'm fast becoming. When we finish up with our home stint I'm called in for a progress meeting with Coach Townsend and Mr. Dolby.

Everyone is pleased I'm keeping Brent sober, away from women, and fully focused on hockey.

"Whatever you're doing," Mr. Dolby says to me with a rare smile, "keep it up."

"My being in Brent's life is definitely making a difference," I candidly agree. "He's been a wonderful client, so far. And I'm happy to report we've really clicked."

Oh, if they only knew to what extent those words ring true.

"Well, if that's the case," the coach chimes in, "maybe we should think about extending your contract beyond December."

"Uh..."

I'm torn, so I do my best to hide my emotion. They can't know my real thoughts. Extending the contract guarantees I'll spend more time with Brent—and that would be great—but the no-fraternization clause would remain in full effect. If I'm done with Brent in December, as originally planned, then he and I would be free to explore our feelings. And I'd definitely like to do that.

Lucky for me, Mr. Dolby, a much more cautious man by nature, balks at the idea of a contract extension.

I breathe a sigh of relief when he says, "Let's see how things go the next month or two. We've seen this pattern with Brent for the past three seasons. He starts out strong, but it never seems to last." He eyes me pointedly. "Remember to keep on him about staying focused. The last thing he needs is a distraction."

Like me?

Clearing my throat, I say, "Yes, sir."

"Are you still having daily meetings with him?" Mr. Dolby asks.

Hmm, this is where it's going to get tricky.

"Um," I begin, "well, he's been really busy lately with the start of the season. But we try to make time to talk."

Not true.

It's a small fib to protect us both. The truth is Brent and I speak one-on-one only if other people are around. That means our private meetings have dwindled to none. I just can't trust myself around him, and I think he feels the same way.

"Going forward, I'd like for you to spend as much time as you can with your client, Ms. Shelburne." Mr. Dolby stands, signaling an end to the meeting. "You seem to be exceptionally good for him."

Yeah, that's the problem.

We know there could be something "exceptionally good" between us, but not in the way the team wants. And that's why we can't be alone together. Not being allowed to give this thing a try makes us want it all the more. There are days I *crave* Brent Oliver. I long for him to touch me. And I sure as hell want him to kiss me again.

But no, none of that can happen.

That's why when we're in his house, we're never alone. Not only does Brent invite Benny and Nolan over all the time, along with a bunch of other players I'm getting to know, but a day after our encounter in my bedroom he hired two live-in employees. There's now a housekeeper and a cook on the premises, though their accommodations are located on the first floor.

Nevertheless, we take steps to avoid running into each other in the upstairs hallway that separates our bedrooms. I always stick my head outside my door before leaving my room to make sure the coast is clear. I suspect Brent does the same since there've been no slipups on either of our parts.

A day after the meeting with Mr. Dolby and the coach, it's time to hit the road for upcoming games in Detroit and Chicago. I pack my bags and head to the airport by myself. When I arrive, I notice Brent's already there. We share a nod and a smile, and then busy ourselves with talking with other people.

All the guys look so damn good in their finely tailored suits, but Brent especially does. When we all start boarding the team plane, I make sure he's in front of me so I can check out the view.

Wow, what an ass!

I suddenly wish we were flying off to some exotic locale, sans the team.

How romantic would that be?

Stop it, Aubrey!

I sit far away from Brent on the plane and continue to avoid him in the hotel we're staying in. I hole up in my room, waiting for the game against Detroit.

That game turns out to be another great one. Brent racks up four points, two goals and two assists, and the OPS line is firing on all cylinders. In addition, and giving my libido a mighty boost, Brent gets into a fight late in the third period.

Shit, seeing him all riled up gets *me* all riled.

I squirm in my seat as I watch him throw a mean right hook that knocks the other player off his skates. When the player gets up, they go at it again and have to be broken up by the linesmen. Since it's so late in the game, Brent gets kicked out for fighting. I'm fine with that.

It gives me a perfect opportunity to watch him as he skates off the ice, all sweaty and fired up. I allow myself an indulgent moment to imagine what it'd be like to meet up with this angry version of Brent in the locker room. He'd have *all* that aggression to work out.

"Oh my," I squeak out, making the people around me look at me strangely.

Time to go.

But not to the locker room.

I beeline instead to the bus that will be taking us all to the airport, after all the players are showered and locker room interviews are concluded.

On the plane to Chicago, I sit next to Benny. He's seated by the window and out like a light. When Brent boards, he chooses the seat across the aisle from me.

"Hey, Aubrey," he says as he gets comfortable.

I give him a little wave. "Hey, Brent. Great game, by the way."

"Thanks," he replies, smiling.

I notice he has a split lip, a tiny reminder of the fight. "Does it hurt?" I quietly ask.

He shakes his head, chuckling as he does. "No, it doesn't hurt at all. Thanks for asking, though."

"Yeah, sure." His eyes meet mine and we share a bittersweet smile. "I'm just glad you're okay," I whisper.

We can't tear our gazes away from one another. "That's sweet of you to worry," he says.

I stare into those whiskey-shaded orbs longer than I should. He makes no move to turn away, either.

I hate that I can't be alone with you, I try to convey.

All I want is to be alone with you, I think he says back.

What are we going to do?

Our silent communication is unfortunately interrupted when Nolan makes his way to the seat behind Brent's. "You two seriously need to get a room," he mutters.

"Fuck off," Brent snaps.

"Shut up, Solvenson," I add.

Nolan laughs at us as he sits down.

Our sniping wakes up Benny. "Hey, what'd I miss?" he asks, yawning.

"Just more eye-fucking," Nolan mutters.

Benny turns to me. "What's he talking about?"

"Nothing," I say.

When he raises his brows, waiting for elaboration, I shake my head, a plea for him to drop it. Benny, nice guy that he is, does drop it, just as I catch Brent twisting in his seat to shoot Nolan a warning glare.

"Nolan's such a dick," I mumble under my breath to Brent.

"Don't let him get under your skin," he quietly replies as he turns back around to face the front of the plane.

I don't think the team as a whole realizes what's going on between Brent and me. They seem rather oblivious, in fact. Looking around, I notice most of the guys are playing cards with each other or computer games on their phones. Some are simply sleeping. Nolan and Benny know what's happening, though. They're too good of friends with Brent to not see what's up.

Benny has been cool about our predicament, supportive even. I think he secretly wants us to end up together. He's such a rough and tumble guy, but he's a true romantic at heart. He really might be great with Lainey. But that's another relationship that can never happen. I talk to my sister all the time, but still have to be careful to keep all work-related stuff secret.

I sigh and glance back at Nolan. He rolls his eyes at me, so I turn back around.

The whole reason we can't get along is because of Brent. Nolan views the whole situation with his cool, logical mind. He believes what Brent and I are fighting is simply a lust thing. He thinks if we have sex once and get it out of our systems, we'll be fine.

He is so wrong. What Brent and I are fighting is much more than that.

Benny, noticing the sad expression on my face, nudges my shoulder. "Hey, are you all right?"

"Yeah," I say on a sigh. "I'm fine."

Sensing I need a distraction, he says, "Did you watch the whole game?"

"Of course," I reply, livening up. "I was seated in the front row, like always."

He nods approvingly. "Good. Then you saw all the plays down on your end, right?"

"Sure did," I confirm.

Benny proceeds to whip out a dry-erase board that's marked with the configuration on the ice. I notice it's the same kind of board Coach T uses when he's drawing up plays behind the bench.

Brent, glancing over at us, says to Benny, "Hey, where'd you get that?"

In a hushed tone, Benny says, "Don't say anything, but I kind of 'borrowed' it from Coach. He must have a hundred, so I figured he could spare one."

Brent laughs. "Don't worry, man. My lips are sealed."

And still looking like they'd benefit greatly from a healing Aubrey kiss, I note.

Cut it out! You're making things worse.

Thankfully, Benny pulls out a marker and that garners my attention. "Okay, Aubrey," he says, pointing the thing at me. "It's time to listen up."

"Okay." I laugh. "But why do we need the board?"

"You, my little life coach friend, are ready for phase two of your lessons."

"Which involves what?"

"Drawing up plays on this board to show you how our awesome OPS line really works."

I smile. "Sounds good to me."

"So," Benny continues, "did you happen to see my replay-worthy goal tonight?"

I nod. "Yep, I sure did. It was nice."

"It was more than *nice*," he scoffs. "But let me explain to you why. Did you pick up on how Brent and Nolan set me up for that goal?"

He cocks a brow my way as he marks a LW, a RW, and a C on one side of the ice, indicating his, Nolan's, and Brent's left wing, right wing, and center positions at the time of the goal.

"Yes." I point to the C. "Brent shot the puck over to"—I tap on the RW—"Nolan."

"Yeah, he did. And then Nolan shot it back to Brent." Benny draws a line from RW to C. "But if you recall, Brent had no clear lane to the net. There were too many defenders in the way."

I nod once. "So that's why he passed the puck over to you."

"A rather sweet-ass pass it was too," I hear Brent murmur from across the aisle.

"Dude, let's not take all the credit." Benny leans forward to narrow his eyes over at him, but it's all in good fun. "That puck was on edge when you sent it my way. I'm the one who settled it down and got it in the net." Leaning back, he smugly adds, "And that, my friend, was clearly *my* fine skills on display."

"Pfft, I scored five minutes later, anyway," Brent counters.

"About the only scoring you've been doing lately," Nolan chimes in.

Brent, ignoring him, reaches down to his bag for his earbuds. That's when I notice he's kind of blushing. *How cute!*

"I think I've heard enough," he mumbles as he sets up his phone to play music and pops the buds in his ears.

The bantering never stops with these guys, and half the time I tune it out. But hell, I'm more than thrilled that I didn't miss that one. Brent "not scoring" lately confirms what I've been hoping was true all along—he's not sleeping with anyone. I didn't think he was, but I'm not there to monitor him constantly like I could do before the season started.

I want to get up and dance in the aisles to celebrate. But that would be unwise. Nolan would surely notice and have a smartass remark. As it is, I hear him grumbling now about losing his strip club bud, meaning Brent.

I twist around and, in my iciest tone, snap, "You know what your problem is, Solvenson?"

"Oh, pray tell, great life coach,"—he crosses his arms and tries to unnerve me with that damn cool blue gaze—"what's my problem?"

Standing my ground, I say as evenly as I can, "For someone who's supposed to be so freaking smart, you're dumb as a stump when it comes to women."

"Ooh, burn," Benny interjects.

That's right. I can banter with the best of them. I'm quickly becoming one of the guys, though hopefully not to the one I care about the most.

I sneak a peek over at Brent and see he's trying not to smile. He definitely heard me, which means he's either not listening to music or the volume's turned real low.

Nolan, of course, is quick to fire back. "Well, Aubrey, for someone who's supposed to be such an insightful life coach, you sure are blind when it comes to your own affairs."

"What's that supposed to mean?" I reply.

He nods to Brent. "You think you have a handle on a certain… shall we say, situation. But from where I stand it's becoming clearer and clearer that it's doomed to blow up in your face. And you know what? I don't care anymore. It's your life to fuck up, Miss Life Coach."

I stare back at him, mouth hanging open. He sure is in a rotten mood today.

"Dude," Benny murmurs, "that wasn't cool."

Benny is calm in his response, but Brent sure isn't. Jumping up from his seat, he glowers down at Nolan. "You need to tone it down right the fuck now, Solvenson," he says in this real low, kind of scary voice.

Damn, Brent's ready to throw down with his friend over me.

Though a formidable force himself, Nolan appears concerned. "Chill out, Oliver," he says, albeit a little shakily. "Aubrey and I are just giving each other a hard time, like always. Isn't that right, Aubs?"

He nods to me, and I say, "Yeah, sure, giving each other a hard time…" I smile weakly at the few players seated near us who have taken notice of our little scuffle. "…it's what we always do. You all know me and Nolan like to fight, fight, fight."

The players shrug and go back to what they were doing. Once no one is looking anymore, except for Nolan and Benny, I reach out and touch Brent's forearm. His muscles are corded and taut, until I give him a light squeeze. He then softens.

Blowing out a breath, he says to Nolan, "Hey, sorry, man. I guess I'm still wired from the fight."

"Yeah, I'm sure that's it," Nolan replies dryly.

We all pretend it's the truth, but we know it's not. Brent standing up for me is as good as him declaring me his. Like a girlfriend, someone he cares about. I'm not to be fucked with is the message.

Too bad we're both fucked by a contract that forbids me from being more than a life coach to him. A life coach who can't even see the wall right in front of her, the one she's about to crash headfirst into.

19

WHO THE FUCK IS AL?

BRENT

The game against the Hawks isn't till the next night. That means we have an entire day to do whatever we want.

A bunch of the guys plan a golf outing. Since it's a beautiful October day, all crisp and cool and perfect for a few hours spent on the greens, I decide at the last minute to join them.

I meet up with Benny and Nolan down in the lobby of the hotel we're staying in. They inform me there are rented SUVs, running about every ten minutes, shuttling players over to the course. I have every intention of catching the next one with the boys, so I plop down on an easy chair next to Nolan and Benny.

It's then I notice Aubrey is seated on the sofa behind us, talking on her cell.

I listen in. Yeah, I'm jealous it may be a guy she's chatting with. I breathe out a sigh of relief when I figure out she's talking with her sister.

"Yeah, sure, Lainey," I hear her say. "I can do that. After we hang up I'll grab a cab and head over to my townhouse. I need to stop in there, anyway. I could use some different outfits to wear out in Vegas."

I shouldn't keep on eavesdropping, but I can't help myself. Benny and Nolan are preoccupied with their phones, so I take mine out too. But instead of looking shit up or checking messages, I listen in some more on Aubrey.

And this is what I learn…

She's definitely heading over to her place today. I'd almost forgotten she lives in Chicago. She's been staying at my house going on two months now, and that makes it sometimes hard to remember she has a whole life outside of me. A whole life she'll eventually return to.

God, why does that hurt so much?

It hurts because that'll be the end—the end of us being friends, the end of me feeding her spaghetti, the end of long talks in the night, and certainly the end of us ever having a chance to become something more.

With that dismal thought in mind, I freeze in horror when I overhear her giggling like a schoolgirl. "Of course, Lainey. I'll be sure to tell Al you said hello."

Who the fuck is Al?

It only gets worse from there.

"Right, sure, I can take a picture of him for you. He likes getting photographed." And there's that giggle again when she adds softly, "I'll give him a kiss from you too. But remember, he's all mine as long as he's staying at my place."

What the ever-loving hell?

Do Aubrey and her sister *share* some guy? That's some crazy shit right there. Though I shouldn't be shocked by such an arrangement. A lot of the players sleep with a rotating stable of girls. I suppose women do the same thing with guys? Or, in this case, with just one guy, a guy named Al.

I want to kill him already.

He sure must be something special if he keeps both Aubrey *and* her sister satisfied. I guess he does though, since Aubrey sure sounds happy she's going to be seeing him at her freaking house. Giving him a kiss, even. And taking pictures to send to her polygamist-in-training sister. What kind of free-loving family do they come from?

"Shuttle's here," Benny says, breaking me from my thought train of terror.

He and Nolan stand, but I remain seated. "Hey," I say, "I think I'm going to stay here, after all."

Nolan shrugs. "Suit yourself, Oliver."

Benny adds, "Cool. We'll catch up with you later."

And then they're gone.

Guys are so much easier than girls. There are no questions, no third degrees.

Aubrey finishes with her call, and I position my chair so she'll see me when she gets up. Sure enough, when she stands and peers over at the concierge, where she'll probably be calling for that taxi to take her to Al the Stud, she catches sight of me.

"Oh, Brent… Hey." She casts a glance around the lobby, looking for other players. When she sees the guys are all gone, she says, "Aren't you going golfing with the team?"

I shrug. "Eh, I was thinking about it. But I missed the last shuttle."

She cocks her head and purses her lips. "Hmm, you look a little upset. Is everything okay?"

"No, no." I smile tightly. "Everything is just fucking outstanding."

"Okaaay."

Aubrey doesn't seem convinced, and I'm not surprised. I sound a little psycho.

Folding her arms across her chest, a move that makes her luscious tits just about spill out over the top of her low-cut shirt, she says, "So, if you're not golfing what are you planning to do all day?"

"Actually…" I tamp down my ire and turn up the charm. Shooting her my most-winning smile, the one I reserve exclusively for getting my way, I say, "I was thinking maybe I could tag along with you to wherever you're going." I pause. "That is, if that's okay. I mean, I wouldn't want to cramp your style or anything."

Yeah, or interrupt any romantic interludes planned with fucking Al.

A little flustered, but cute as hell, she replies, "Uh, I guess that'd be okay." Biting her lip in a sexy way that makes me have to look away for a few seconds, she adds, "Maybe not for the whole day, though."

Is her hesitancy because she doesn't want us to be alone? Or is it because of Al?

"Why's that?" I question, raising a challenging brow.

"Brent," she sighs.

"What? Do you have plans with someone else?"

"No, yeah… I mean, I don't know."

Shit, she does have a date with this Al. And he's already at her place. Just the mere thought of her with another man makes something in my chest tighten. Shit, I think it might be my heart.

"Brent?"

"Yeah?"

I'm sure I sound as dejected as I feel.

Her gaze softens, and releasing a breath, she says, "Let's just see how it goes, okay?"

I nod. "Sure, yeah, whatever you say."

I may sound all compliant, but you bet your ass I'm not. My mission is now to spend not only the entire day with Aubrey, but most of the night too. Whatever it takes to keep her far, far away from this Al, I'm willing to do.

20

DIDN'T THAT HURT?

AUBREY

'm stuck with Brent for the day. Don't think because I'm phrasing it that way that I'm not secretly rejoicing.

Truthfully, though, I'm worried I may slip up and jump him or something.

No, no, no. Be strong.

That's right. I can do this as long as I keep my emotions in check. And as long as we pretty much hang out only in public places. Of course, when we stop by my place we'll be alone.

That stop will have to be a super quick one.

As we hop into a cab outside the hotel, I start to feel happier and happier to have Brent accompanying me. It's been so long since we've simply hung out. And I kind of want to get back to sharing things with him, starting with where I live.

I give the cabbie the address of my townhouse in Wicker Park—a chic, urban area in Chicago—and then we're on our way.

Brent and I don't speak much on the drive there. He seems preoccupied with something, so I leave him be. Still, all the silence in the world can't quell the magnetic pull between us. Even with the cab driver in the car with us, it's like we're all alone. My pulse quickens, and I can't stop myself from stealing glances every few seconds his way. When I catch a smile playing at his lips, I know he's onto me.

Oops, busted.

Speaking of busted and lips, his split one is healing nicely. It's still a little swollen, but that just makes his highly kissable mouth all the more attractive.

As he lets his hand rest on the seat between us, I yearn to reach down and lock our fingers together. If I can't kiss Brent, I'd at least like to touch him.

When he sees me staring down at his hand, he says, "Is everything okay, Aubrey?"

I jerk my eyes up to his. "Uh, yes, everything's fine."

We can't break our locked gazes till the cabbie clears his throat. "We're at your destination," he says as he stares at us in the rearview mirror, clearly uncomfortable.

"Ooh, oh," I blubber to the driver. "Sorry." I grab my purse. "How much do I owe you?"

While the cabbie replies with the amount of the fare, I dig around for my wallet.

But Brent beats me to it.

"Here." He fishes some bills from the back pocket of his dark-wash jeans. "I got this."

Once the cab driver is paid, we exit the car.

Pointing over to a red brick building across the street from us, the house number clearly displayed out in the front, Brent says, "That one's yours, right? I heard the number when you told the driver your address."

"Yes," I reply, "that one is mine."

"Great." He squares up his shoulders and sucks in a breath, like he's preparing for a fight or something. "We should go in."

Damn, he looks hot.

Stop it, Aubrey!

While I struggle to get my libido under control, Brent says again, "Let's go, Aubrey. What are we waiting for?"

What is up with him? He sure seems determined to get in my house. Why? If his game is to get me inside so he can seduce me, with the way I'm feeling right now it just may work.

But we can't have that, now can we?

We sure can, my lady bits chime in.

"No way," I mutter, though it's not with much conviction.

"No way, what?" Brent wants to know.

Like I'm going to share that with him?

"Nothing. It's nothing." I wave my hand around, hoping he'll drop it.

Thankfully, he does. But I'm still not quite under control. So, injecting a massive dose of enthusiasm in my voice, I throw out, "Maybe we should take a walk around the neighborhood before going up to my house. It's such a pretty autumn day." I hasten to add, "And I'd love to show you around."

It *is* a perfect day for an autumn walk, so that's not a lie. Plus, the neighborhood I live in is pretty cool. It's hip and trendy, making it fun to stroll around in. There are tree-lined streets and little boutiques and cafes around every corner. But, of course, my real reason for suggesting the detour is to keep me from losing control with Brent. The bed up in my bedroom is really big and comfy, and it hasn't seen any action in, well, ages.

Brent seems to suspect something nefarious is afoot. Narrowing his eyes at me, he asks, "Is there some reason why you don't want me in your house, Aubrey?"

Jeez, he acts like I have a secret guy I'm hiding up there.

But lest he catch on to the real reason—my inability to fight my own urges—I shake my head, rather violently and giving me a dizzying head rush. "Ow," I mutter as I waver on my feet.

Good thing I have on ballet flats, not heels, or I'd be doing my best face-plant onto the sidewalk. How attractive would that be?

Brent, looking concerned, reaches out to steady me. "Are you all right?" he asks, one strong hand on my elbow.

I nod, just once this time so as not to induce another blood rush. "Yes. Thank you."

"Hey." His voice softens. "I didn't mean to give you a hard time. I'm fine with a walk."

"Okay."

I'm tense as we start down the road. Brent seems on edge as well, though I'm not sure what reason he has to be so wound up. Thankfully, the longer we walk along the tree-lined streets, the more we relax.

Under the golden leaves of a particularly vibrant tree, Brent buys me an iced latte from a street vendor. I end up sharing it with him a few minutes later when we find an antiques store we both really want to go in. The *Absolutely No Drinks Allowed* sign on the door requires us to down the latte quickly.

"We can't let this go to waste," I say as I hand the iced beverage to

Brent for his turn. "It's way too good."

He nods in agreement as he takes a pull from the straw.

Once he hands it back to me, I take another sip and then announce, "I think the caffeine is really hitting my system. I feel so energetic suddenly."

"Me too," he agrees, laughing as he takes the cup from me.

But when he's done, instead of passing the drink back to me to finish it off, he angles the cup my way. "Here," he says softly, "let me hold it for you. Go ahead and drink the rest."

I bend down and wrap my lips around the straw, peering up at him in what can only be described as a suggestive manner. I just can't help myself.

"Aubrey, don't." His voice is raspy and his nostrils flare.

I like playing with fire. Brent's fire, especially.

"What?" I ask all innocently as I let go of the straw.

Pressing his lips together in a tight line, he mumbles, "Let's just go in the store."

Following a wrought-with-sexual-tension stroll through the antiques store, we start back to my place. To de-charge the atmosphere I purposely choose a longer route. We both need more time to cool down before we find ourselves alone in my place.

"Are we walking around in circles?" Brent asks as he stops cold. Nodding to a small grocer storefront, he says, "This is the third time we walked by that little market."

"Uh, I may have lengthened our route," I sheepishly admit.

"Why?" he asks. And then, "Aubrey, what's going on here?"

Uh-oh, he's back to eyeing me suspiciously.

Sighing, I give up on delaying the inevitable. We have to go to my place eventually, right?

"Come on." I motion to a side alley. "This way is a shortcut."

We turn down the narrow passageway and it feels like the clock is ticking on our time bomb of lust. We have about five minutes before we reach my place, and I really need to get a hold of myself by then. Fortunately, I'm given a few extra minutes' reprieve when a tattoo shop along the way catches Brent's attention.

Stopping in front of the store, he suddenly asks, "Do you have any?"

Peering in at the colorful display of artwork available to be inked anywhere a person desires, I clarify, "Do I have any what? Tattoos?"

"Yes, Aubrey. Do you have any tattoos?"

Shaking my head, I admit, "No. But it's only because I'm a really big sissy when it comes to needles."

Brent smiles over at me. "You shouldn't let that stop you. It's really not all that painful."

"Says the hockey player who's immune to pain."

He laughs.

This is a very interesting development, however. Not the pain part. As noted, Brent has a high tolerance for discomfort. I'm sure needles don't faze him. It's the ink thing that has my curiosity piqued.

I've never noticed any tattoos anywhere on his body. Not like with Benny, who has loads of them. With the way Brent runs around the house, though—semi clothed half the time—you'd think I'd have seen a tattoo somewhere, right?

Yet, I haven't seen *any* ink on him. And that begs the question, "Do *you* have any tattoos?"

"Yeah," he replies with a smug smile, "actually I do."

"Do you have many?" I'm insanely curious as to where all this ink could be hidden.

But then I understand better when he says, "Nah, I only have one. It's not very big, either. I'd like to get more eventually. Something more detailed, for sure."

Cocking my head and staring at him curiously, I ask, "So where is this secret tattoo? I've never seen it."

He looks at me pointedly. "You've not seen *all* of me, now have you?"

"Just about," I blurt out before I realize how that sounds.

While Brent chuckles amusedly, my cheeks warm. He's right, though. I've not seen *all* of him. He always has on shorts... or a towel... or a comforter covering the goods. Like that morning when he was hard as steel.

Clearing my throat—and my head of deliciously obscene images—I ask, "What is it of? Your tattoo, that is."

His gaze never leaves me as he says, "My number."

Say, what? "You have a tattoo of your number?"

He smiles at me, like he knows just where my thoughts are headed. "Uh-huh. I have the number fifty-one tattooed on me. You know, Aubrey, kind of like the number that's inked on your green"—he coughs—"friend."

It's all I can do to keep my eyes from popping out of my head. And then all my filters fail and I blurt out, "You really have your number tattooed on your *dick*?"

"I prefer to call it a cock," he coolly replies.

Holy crap! Real Brent is just like Brent 51. Only his, er, appendage is attached to a real man, with real skin, not some cheap imitation with a green plastic cover.

But still, a tattoo on his penis? I have to ask, "Wow, Brent. Didn't that hurt like hell?"

He laughs. "I didn't say my tattoo was *there*."

"You didn't say it wasn't, either," I counter.

"True."

"So which is it?"

Brent Oliver then has the nerve to say to me, "Guess someday you'll just have to find out for yourself, Aubrey."

21

I'M DONE HOLDING BACK

BRENT

Okay, so the number 51 is not on my cock. But I let Aubrey think it might be. I gotta give her *something* to think about, especially for when I get in that damn townhouse of hers and get busy kicking Al's ass.

I've been so damn patient. And she's such a tease. That little maneuver she did when I held out the latte for her, like she didn't plan for me to imagine her lips wrapped around my cock when she did that thing with the straw. Of course, she'd need to open her mouth a whole lot wider if it were me.

I snicker and she looks over at me. "What's so funny?" she asks as she unlocks the door to her townhouse.

"Nothing," I reply.

It's true. Any humor seeps out of me at the prospect of meeting this other guy in her life. But something is weird. When we walk into her high-ceiling, open-space home I don't notice any signs of someone living here. It's empty and quiet, and has a closed-up feel.

Still, she clearly mentioned an "Al" to her sister. And he's supposed to be here.

Done messing around, I flat-out ask, "Where is he, Aubrey?"

She looks totally confused, and I don't think it's an act. "Who are you talking about?"

"Al."

Aubrey gives me a look like I've just lost my mind. And then she starts laughing, like hysterically. "Oh my God, you were totally listening in on me when I was talking to my sister. This is too funny."

How can she find this amusing? It's definitely not.

Instead of pretending I wasn't eavesdropping, I admit everything.

"Yeah, okay. I was listening in. And yes, I heard you mentioning some dude named Al. You told your sister you'd take a picture of the guy. And give him a fucking *kiss*." I make a face of disdain. "Really, Aubrey, you have no room to ever judge *my* past exploits." I let out a snort. "You and your sister sharing some dude and keeping him at your house like he's a piece of meat has to be one of the most crossing-the-line, taboo-sick-shit things I've ever heard of. And trust me, I've heard *and* seen a lot!"

Aubrey is doubled over with laughter before I even finish my diatribe. I'm dumbfounded that she finds this so amusing.

But she does.

Laughing so hard that she's bending over and holding onto her black legging-covered thighs for support, she snorts out, "Oh, Brent. You're killing me here."

"I'm not trying to kill you, Aubrey," I say dryly as I scan around for signs of this Al dude. "But someone may die tonight."

She can't respond due to the convulsing chortling fit that comes over her next. "Oh my God, Brent. You have to stop. My sides are hurting."

Sarcastically, I mutter, "It's really nice you find this all so amusing. 'Cause I sure as hell don't." I take a breath, square up. "Where is this guy, anyway? You may as well tell me now. There's no point in hiding him. I *will* find this dickhead and deal with him."

"Come on." Finally calm, she takes my hand. If I weren't so pumped to lay this Al motherfucker out, I'd find her move endearing.

I let her lead me up the stairs, all the while wondering if she's taking me up to engage in a threesome with this Al guy. Why else would she so willingly lead me to him? Has she mistaken my anger for lust? We've already established that she and her sister are little freaks.

Sorry, but kinky as I can be, I am not sharing Aubrey with anyone. When I get to have her, *if* I ever get to have her, it's going to be strictly one-on-one action. The things I have planned for her don't need an audience. And she certainly won't have energy to spare on someone else.

Just the thought that there could be someone else gets my blood boiling. When we reach a closed door, I stop and disengage my hand from hers.

"Hey, I think I should go in alone to talk to this guy, okay?" That makes her snicker. "It's not funny, Aubrey," I add, seeing red.

"Brent, calm down."

"I don't want to calm down."

She pushes on the door and I press my lips together. I make a fist with my right hand as I follow her into what is clearly her bedroom. She asks me to stay put as she heads over to a large walk-in closet.

She goes in for a few seconds and then comes out with a fuzzy green, floppy-limbed two-foot-high alligator in her hand.

Tossing the stuffed animal my way, she says, "Brent, meet Al, as in Al the Alligator."

I catch the thing.

And then I start laughing.

God, what was I thinking? Clearly, Aubrey Shelburne owns my ass. She makes me fucking nuts. I can't even think straight. Despite every attempt I've made to rein in my feelings for her, they exist, indisputable, undeniable.

And, frankly, I'm sick of fighting what I feel for her. Fuck everything. I'm done holding back.

I want to go to her and kiss the hell out of her.

But, whoa, she looks pissed.

Hands on her hips, she informs me, "For the record, Lainey and I have never fucked Al the Alligator. That would just be…sick."

"Hmm, I can also see where that might be a problem." I turn the stuffed alligator over to check out his junk, or lack thereof. "Impossible, it would seem," I add.

Aubrey lets out a snort of amusement. Thank God she's not too mad. Since I can't help but like her even more when she's fired up, I'm quick to add, "Although…"

"What now, Brent?"

I pin her with a challenging stare. "Al is green. And we all know how much you like inanimate objects that are *green*."

"You are such an ass!" She throws something at me—a pillow, I think, from her bed. I duck, and she adds, "I can't believe you'd bring that up!"

"Oh, I think enough time has passed." I take a step toward her.

"Besides, it wasn't anything to be ashamed of. We talked about it that night, remember?"

Shifting from one foot to the other, she says, "Yeah, I do."

In a husky voice, I go on. "It was actually really hot, Aubrey. I only wish I'd walked in on you sooner and caught you in the act."

She takes a step back. "Uh, maybe we should talk about something else."

"Why?"

She shrugs. "I don't know. I guess just because." Clearly trying to change the subject, she says, "Hey, can you toss Al over to me? I should put him away."

I'm making her nervous. She doesn't trust herself alone like this with me. Well, we're even on that count. I've officially lost all control around her.

I take another step closer. "Aubrey, we should talk."

Ignoring what I'm saying, she remains focused on the stupid green alligator. "Did you know Al is Lainey's prized possession from childhood?" she tells me. "No, how could you know that? Well, anyway, he is. He's kind of like a good luck charm to her." *Hmm, maybe he'll work for me too and I'll get lucky.* "She forgot him here last time she stayed with me. We've been goofing around about him ever since."

"You're rambling," I say quietly.

Aubrey sighs. "We should go back downstairs."

"Like that sounds convincing," I murmur.

Another step closer and I can see in her eyes that she wants me as much as I want her. Despite the fact that she's been backing away from me the whole time I've been approaching, her body language tells a different story. It's a story that says, *Come and get me, Brent.*

So I do.

The bed is behind her and there's nowhere to go. So, taking the final step to close the gap completely, I give her a choice. "We can go back downstairs if you really want. Or we can stay right here. Either way, Aubrey, here or there, I *am* going to kiss you. And then I'm going to do what I've wanted to do for a long time."

"What's that?" she rasps, swallowing hard.

"Make you come so hard you scream out my name and beg me for more. I want you so dizzy with me that you can't even think."

"Brent," she breathes out.

Cocking a brow, I ask, "So, Aubrey, what's it going to be?"

Flustered, she asks, "What was the question again?"

I toss Al onto the bed. "Do you want it here…or do you want it downstairs?"

"I want it here," she whispers.

Her arms slide up around my neck and I feel her giving in, relinquishing control over to me. "I want you, Brent. I have for so long now. We shouldn't do this, but I'm done fighting what I feel."

"I'm done fighting it too," I say.

And then my lips crash into hers.

GIVING IN NEVER FELT SO GOOD

AUBREY

This kiss is better than the one before.

That time was amazing, yes, but this is out-of-this-world good. First, Brent isn't drunk this time around. And secondly, there are no doorbells ringing.

Plus, I think I might be in love with Brent Oliver.

Oh my God, am I?

I can't think about that right now.

He lays me back gently on my bed, his lips never leaving mine. "I've wanted to do this for so long," he murmurs when we finally come up for air.

"Me too," I breathe out.

And then we're done talking. Lips meet again, mouths open, and tongues intertwine. With our bodies pressed together, he slides his hand between us and up under my shirt.

When he grazes a nipple through the sheer bra I'm wearing, I moan out a totally wanton, "Mmm, Brent."

He feels so good, even with just this little bit of foreplay. What will more feel like?

Peering down into my eyes as I wonder, he mistakes my contemplation as hesitation. "Should I stop?" he asks.

That question is easy to answer. "You better not."

"Just checking," he says, chuckling.

He lifts my shirt to just above my breasts, and then he unsnaps my bra. Rocking back on his heels, he lifts up the hem of his own tee.

God, his washboard abs are totally lickable.

It's like watching the sexiest slo-mo commercial ever when Brent pulls his shirt over his head. When he's done, he leans forward and tugs my leggings down. Low, low, lower, my panties go along for the ride. I try to kick them away, along with my shoes, but while my sneakers slip off successfully and drop to the floor, Brent stops me before I can make short work of the leggings and undies.

With the garments wrapped around my calf, and my shirt still pulled up to just above my breasts, he rasps, "No, leave your clothes like that. I want you like this for now. Not completely naked, but half dressed. You look vulnerable, Aubrey. I never see that side of you. Not really, not like this."

Ooh, I can be vulnerable for him. I'm open to whatever he wants. As long as I get what I want too—him naked.

"I'll leave my clothes half on, Brent. But I want all of yours off."

His clothes are discarded in no time at all, and when his cock springs free from his boxers, I can't help but blurt out, "Wow! Your dick is *way* bigger than I thought."

Did I really just say that? By the smug look on his face, I must have.

I want him on top of me so I can feel his muscles and his strength, so I stretch out invitingly and crook a finger for him to get to sexing me up.

Brent lowers his body to mine. It's sweet how careful he is to distribute his heavily muscled body in such a way that he doesn't crush me.

Damn, his skin feels electric against mine.

And he's so freaking built.

"I like your muscles," I say as I run my hands up his arms, then around to his strong back.

"I like your, well, everything," he replies as he slides his hand down over a breast and along my side.

The lust in his voice makes me want the rest of my clothes off. "I want to be naked with you," I whisper.

Together, we work to rid me of my bra, shirt, and the leggings and undies still wrapped around my calf. When I'm as naked as he is, Brent leans down and sucks a nipple into his mouth.

"Mmm, yeah, I like that," I whisper to him as he devours one breast, then the other, with his hot mouth.

When his hand starts to trail down my stomach, all I can think is, *Yes, please. I need more of what he has to give me.*

"I'm so wet for you, Brent," I tell him, which makes him release a raspy moan from around my nipple.

Gently, he parts my folds and begins a steady back-and-forth gliding motion over my clit.

He quickly establishes a rhythm that leaves me begging for more. *God, he's good.* "I want to feel you inside," I murmur.

"Like this?" he asks as he dips a finger into me, but only just a touch.

"You're such a tease," I moan as I arch up, encouraging him to push in farther, to fill me, to pump in and out of me.

He pushes in a tiny bit more, stretching me, but not enough. "What about now?" he taunts.

"Better," I groan, "but not enough."

Adding another finger, he plunges in, working me and leaving his hand covered in how much I want him. When he twists his hand a certain way, he hits the magic spot. "Oh, God, Brent. Don't stop doing that." At the brink, I gasp, "I want *you* inside me, Brent. Please, Brent, please. I need *all* of you."

"What part of 'all' of me do you want?" he asks, smirking as he props up on one elbow and peers down at me, his fingers still working my pussy like a fine instrument.

"*All* of you, Brent," I whisper.

"How 'bout we start with this?"

Before I can ask, "Start with what?" he shimmies down my body and sucks my clit into his warm mouth.

Holy fuck!

A few minutes of his *even-more-talented-than-his-fingers* tongue and I explode in an orgasm that has me crying out in pleasure and grinding down onto Brent's fingers and face.

He loves it. Or so he tells me when he stops licking long enough to rasp out a commanding, "Keep coming for me, Aubrey. Come for me again and again. I want you all over me."

I do as he asks, exploding over and over again. And every time I do I think I'm spent. But then Brent does something different—twists his finger up inside me just so, flicks my clit with his tongue—and I start pulsing all over again.

"I think I might pass out," I say at one point.

He chuckles, amused. "You're not going to pass out."

"I may."

He crawls up my body and presses his muscular self down onto me. "You won't," he assures me.

"How can you be so sure?"

He kisses me, softly, gently. More melting occurs, which is really saying something since my limbs are already so gooey. But I perk up rather quickly—in a good, anticipating way—when I feel Brent's hard cock pressing up against my folds.

This is it; this is for real. There will be no going back from here.

I lift up my hips, allowing his heavy shaft to stroke me. From the feel of it, it's clear he's put on a condom.

Hmm, he must have taken care of that while I was in my state of melty bliss.

"This is why I know you won't pass out," Brent says, snapping me back to the here and now as he moves his hips slowly, pushing in, giving me the tip. Even with just that, I feel stretched and opened, in the best sort of way.

"You're right," I breathe out. "I won't pass out. I wouldn't want to miss a second of this."

He circles his hips, filling me more completely. "No, you sure don't," he replies.

I pause, raise a brow. "Cocky much?"

Chuckling, he says. "You're about to find out I have every right to feel that way."

I push at his hard chest, but he's not going anywhere. Not that I want him to. "You're so smug," I say.

"Let me show you why," he whispers in my ear.

And then he shows me, with one smooth, fluid thrust.

Brent Oliver then gets down to fucking me. *And holy hell!* I find out real fast he has every right to be so damn smug. For the record, the real man is so much better than Brent 51. Who needs pulsating vibrating action when you've got real-life *variable* action? That's right—Brent can fuck hard, and he can fuck fast. But he can also give it to you slowly and sweetly.

And that's what he does, he gives me everything.

At one point, he pulls out almost all the way and then hesitates so I can feel him stretching me, filling me once more. "Ooh, I really like that," I murmur.

He kisses up my neck. "Do you like this too?"

"Mm-hmm."

"You want me to kiss you and fuck you like this for the next half hour?"

I let out a little laugh. "You'll never make it *that* long. This is our first time together, and the sex is just way too hot."

"It is pretty hot," he agrees, pulling out all the way.

I whimper at the loss.

"I can do it, though," he assures me as he s-l-o-w-l-y slides back in, making me sigh. "I like a good challenge. And when we're done we can take a break, and then start back up all over again."

"Oh God, Brent, what are you trying to do to me?"

He stops, buried deep inside me. Our eyes meet and he says, "Maybe I'm trying to make you fall for me?"

What if I already have?

23

BLISS

BRENT

Nothing matters in her bedroom. It's just me and her, one woman and one man, and everything stretching before us of what we could be.

Do I love Aubrey?

I don't know, but I think I could if I let myself.

And I want to do exactly that. Fuck the rules. Love breaks them all the time, anyway, right?

I make it the thirty minutes I promised her, and then some. While we rest in her bed afterward—me playing absently with her shiny hair, and her with her cheek pressed to my chest—I think about how we got to this point.

"I sure am glad I was so insanely jealous over Al," I muse out loud.

I feel her lips turn up into a smile against my skin. "I can't believe you thought my sister and I kept a man at my house that we shared for sex. That's just gross, Brent."

I smack her bare ass, to which she lets out a little yelp. "You are a little wild in the sack," I say. "So it could've been true."

She reaches down and pinches my thigh. "Ow," I mutter. "That hurts."

"This, from the big, bad hockey player," she says.

"Ha-ha."

"Anyway," she goes on, "it serves you right. I'd never divide up my time with a guy with Lainey. I don't like sharing." She peers up at me meaningfully with those sea-green eyes.

I would normally feel indignant. Like, *you don't own me. I'll do whatever the hell I want.* But that was the old me. I haven't felt the urge to touch another woman since Aubrey entered my life. Why would anything change now that we've had sex?

I smooth her messy hair away from her face and assure her, "You have nothing to worry about with me."

"What about all your other women?"

"What other women?" I snort.

"Oh, let's see." She ticks off the following: "There are puck bunnies, ladies at the strip clubs, regular booty calls."

"First off, the women at the strip clubs are generally not ladies. Plus, that's more Nolan's scene. As for puck bunnies, I haven't touched one of them in ages, not since the summer. You know that."

"You didn't address the regular booty calls," she reminds me.

"I'm hoping you'll become that," I say.

She bites her lip.

"What's wrong?"

"Is that all we are?"

I raise a brow. "Do *you* want more?"

I want us to become a couple, but this is her call. Her ass is more on the line than mine if this relationship is discovered. That means if she does want this, we'll need to keep it on the strictest down-low.

"Aubrey?" I prompt when there's no answer forthcoming.

"Yes," she blurts out. "I guess we are more than friends now, right? I mean, after what just occurred." She gestures to the rumpled sheets we're lying on, to our naked bodies, limbs entwined.

But, wait. Does this mean she *doesn't* want more? Maybe all she wanted all along was some cock. And we now know she could never get that from Al the Cockless Alligator.

Bristling—I don't like feeling used, not by her—I say, "Us fucking doesn't have to mean anything if you don't want it to, Aubrey."

Sitting up abruptly, she wraps the sheet around her body. "What we did felt like more than some random fuck, Brent."

I sit up next to her and fold my arms across my chest. "That's what I'm trying to find out. Was it? For you, I mean."

Her eyes search mine, and when she sees what I guess she needs from me, she says, "Yes. And I think it was for you too."

"It was," I admit.

Shit, feeling vulnerable sucks. But I better get used to it if we're hitting relationship territory here. I haven't had one of those since juniors, so this should be interesting.

I'm all set to travel down this new road of emotional intimacy, but then I notice Aubrey is staring at my dick.

I reach down and stroke it a little to give it some life. "See something you like?" I ask.

She leans in closer, her face right above my junk. It's a good look for her.

"I'm just looking for the tattoo," she says. "The fifty-one. Where is it?"

"Clearly not on my cock," I reply, amused.

"You said it was there, though."

She continues to hover over my dick, and well, he and I both like that. Aubrey's mouth that close gets us all excited, making me spring to full mast.

"I never said that," I say, at last. "I just implied it. Remember, I told you you'd have to find out for yourself."

Shaking her head, and making her soft hair stroke my shaft in an enticing way, she says, "You're such an ass, Brent."

Funny how, despite her supposed irritation with me, she can't keep her eyes off my erection. But she asked about my tattoo, so that's what I plan to show her. We can get to more sexing after that.

I move the edge of the sheet that's covering my right hip. Nodding down to a small inked 51, I say, "My tattoo is over here, sweetheart."

"Oh? Ohhh, okay."

Aubrey lies down on my leg, her tits smooshing into my thigh as she frames her hands around the number. "I like it," she says. "It looks good in that spot. Subtle, but sexy."

"If you really want to see sexy, you should check things out a little to your right," I encourage.

Aubrey feigns nonchalance, but she knows what I'm gunning for. Thankfully, she doesn't torture me for long. Within a minute, she's wrapping her hand around my hard cock and smiling up at me. "Is this what you want?"

I was kind of hoping for a blow job, but her soft little hand feels pretty damn good. "Uh-huh," I murmur.

She then asks, "Do you like how I play with this huge thing?"

What I do like is how she keeps referring to my cock as huge. A little positive reinforcement never hurt anyone, right?

She pumps once, twice. *Shit, that feels good.* "Yeah, don't stop," I murmur.

She doesn't stop, and I lie back, resting an arm over my eyes. I'm all set for this hand action, but then I feel her mouth closing around me.

I look down and… "Fuuuck."

Aubrey proceeds to work my shaft like a pro. I don't think I want to know how she got so good at this. Maybe she's a natural, like me with hockey. Or maybe she practiced a lot on cucumbers or something. After all, we all know how much she likes green—

"Holy hell, where'd you learn that," I blurt out when she does some swirly thing with her tongue.

She doesn't answer, and I don't want her to. I want her to keep sucking and licking and swirling and… "Shit, babe, I'm gonna come."

I nudge her head to warn her that the inevitable is about to happen, right in her mouth if she doesn't move. Nonetheless, she keeps on keeping on, and next thing I know I explode down her throat.

"I wanted you to do that," she informs me once she swallows.

"Shit, woman, I think it's my turn to pass out," I mutter.

We rest for a while, lying in each other's arms. God, I could get used to this. I doze off for a bit, but then she wakes me when I feel her moving around.

When I open my eyes, I'm afforded a hot view of Aubrey ripping open a condom wrapper with her freaking teeth. What a glorious sight. Guess she found the other Trojan I had in my wallet.

I didn't realize I was hard again, but hell, since I'm ready I help Aubrey roll the latex down my shaft.

Positioning her hot little self above me, she says, "Think of this as the second period of a hockey game."

"What was the blow job?" I ask.

"Intermission. Like when they're out Zamboni-ing the ice."

I can't help but laugh. "I will forever now think of blow jobs as 'Zamboni-ing the ice.'"

"As long as they're only from me, that's fine," she tells me.

"I only want them from you," I quietly admit. "And for the record, I want only you in every other way too."

She leans down and kisses me. "I feel the same way, Brent."

"Enough talk." Grabbing her ass, I shove her down on my hard shaft.

Fuck, I need to be inside her as much, and as often, as I can.

She gasps when I grab hold of her hair. But when I start pulling back her head, I worry it's too much. Better rein it in.

Releasing her, I ask, "Was that too aggressive? Pulling on your hair like that?"

"Hell no," she breathes out as she slides up along my length. She lowers back down slowly. "I might call you for 'roughing,' though," she gasps, circling her hips. "But it's only 'cause I want you to spend as much time as possible in the 'box.'"

Shit, I need to fist-bump Benny next time I see him. I love it more than ever that he's taught Aubrey enough hockey terms that she can incorporate them into something hot as hell.

I grab onto her hair again and warn her this time to, "Hold the fuck on, sweetheart."

24

DPMB

AUBREY

O ver the next couple weeks, I discover that dating Brent is really fun. It's even more fun since it's on the sly. He's so damn good at sneaking around. But the one place we can be ourselves is at his house in Las Vegas.

The day we get back from Chicago he reduces the hours of his housekeeper and fires his cook.

"I didn't like his crappy cooking anyway," he tells me in the kitchen.

We then do it on the counter next to the stove.

I move a bunch of my things over from my bedroom to Brent's room, and I sleep there every night. We're in the midst of a home game stint, with a few days off in between, so I have ample opportunity to get comfortable with our new living arrangement. I also get quite comfortable with having sex all the time.

Brent's kind of insatiable, but you won't hear me complaining.

Still, it's not all sex and bedroom times with him. He and I take walks around his property at night, talking and making out under the stars. We also play pool in his basement, and some evenings we simply pop popcorn and watch movies in the living room.

He introduces me to *Slapshot*, a classic hockey flick according to him.

I search around for a hockey-themed movie and come up with *The Cutting Edge*. I'm excited when I hear he's never seen it.

"Hmm, I don't know about this one," he muses as he reads the summary on the back of the DVD box.

I curl up with him on the sofa. "Oh, come on now. Give it a chance."

When we cue up the movie and hit Play, it starts out promising enough. Hockey at the Olympics, that's a plus, right?

"See," I say. "I told you this would be good."

Brent isn't so sure. "We'll see about that. If this is a total chick flick, Aubrey, I swear I'll—"

"What?" I taunt, peering up at him. "What will you do to me if it *is* a total chick flick?"

Looking down at me with lust in his gaze, he murmurs, "Hmm, well, I guess I'll need to think of a suitable punishment."

It's then I remember the Double Penetrator Mega Blaster. Am I brave enough to show it to him? It'd certainly be punishing, in a possibly good kind of way. Wow, seems I'm up for anything if it involves Brent. Since I trust he'll go easy on me if we do put it into play, I start hoping and praying this movie is this chickiest chick flick ever.

A few more minutes and I'm pretty sure my wish is about to come true, seeing as the lead male character, the hockey player, is hurt and considering taking up doubles figure skating.

"What the fuck is this shit?" Brent blurts out, complete with an *I-knew-this-would-suck* groan.

"You promised you'd watch the whole thing," I remind him, snickering when I think of the DPMB and how surprised he'll be when I show it to him. "Besides," I go on, "I didn't get half the jokes in *Slapshot*, but I stuck it out till the end."

That earns me a disappointed shake of the head. "I'm going to pretend I did not just hear you diss a classic hockey movie."

"I did, though, Brent. I totally did. That's bad, huh?"

"Sure is." And then he wants to know, "What are you up to, Aubrey?"

"Hmm"—I wink over at him—"I'm just thinking maybe you can add to that ever-growing list of things you're going to need to punish me for."

He raises a brow. "It sounds like you actually *want* to be punished."

"Maybe I do. But only by you."

Chuckling and pulling me in closer to him, he murmurs, "You're in rare form tonight, babe."

Distracted by what's on the TV screen, I point to a scene and say, "Oh look, the hockey player dude's going back home to tell his family what he's been up to."

"Poor bastard." Brent laughs. "I'm sure they're going to be oh-so proud."

"You're such a downer."

"Just watch," he says. "I bet I'm right."

He is right—the lead male character receives a less-than-warm reception from his hometown hockey-loving peeps. But oddly enough, as the movie plays on Brent starts really getting into it.

I knew he was a romantic at heart.

Still, he remembers my transgressions of the night, and when we reach the bedroom I'm ordered to disrobe and, "Assume the position."

With my hands on the bed and my ass in the air, Brent comes up behind me. "You were very naughty tonight, Aubrey."

He leans over me and deposits a flurry of soft little kisses down my bare back, making me shiver with the anticipation of what's to come. It won't be soft and little, like the kisses, that's for sure.

"Making me watch a total chick flick—"

"You loved it," I interject.

Whack! He smacks me on the right butt cheek. "Did I say you could talk?"

I yelp and shake my head.

"That's right." He gathers my hair and yanks back my head. "Now what should I do to you first?"

Leaning farther over my back, engulfing me, he trails his nose down the side of my neck. It's like he's inhaling me, making me his. Damn, I love being dominated by this über alpha male. He's so sweet to me these days outside of the bedroom that I kind of need him a little rough in here.

I'm putty in his hands already by the time he reaches down to stroke my clit. "Oh, Aubrey," he rasps in my ear. "So wet for me already?"

"Always," I say, since it's true.

That earns me a yank on the hair and a finger rammed up my pussy. "Talking out of turn again, eh?"

I rock back against his hand and he adds another finger. "You like this, don't you?"

Assuming that's my cue to speak, I mutter a low and throaty, "Uh-huh."

Brent fingers me till I spasm around him. "Come for me, Aubrey," he whispers as I ride out an orgasm that feels like it has no end.

Spent, I collapse onto the bed.

It takes all my energy, but as Brent undresses I wave my hand to a dresser he designated as mine when I moved into his room. "Look in the bottom drawer," I say slyly.

Naked and glorious, Brent pads over to the dresser and opens the drawer where DPMB sits in all his glory on top of my lingerie.

"Holy shit, Aubrey!"

He picks up the sex toy and turns to me, wielding it like a weapon of mass pussy destruction. "You really *are* a bad girl, aren't you?"

Assuming the no-talking rule is off for now, I prop up on my elbows and say, "I've never used it. I was actually planning to send it to my sister, seeing as she's a pro when it comes to those things—"

"Wow," he interjects, clearly astonished. "Forget Benny. We should set her up with Nolan. He's a sex toy aficionado. She sounds like his dream girl."

"I don't even want to know what that means," I reply. "But I can tell you now, I don't want Nolan anywhere near my sister."

Brent just laughs.

I continue, dismissing any thoughts of my nemesis, Nolan. "Anyway, I was thinking since I never got rid of the crazy thing that maybe you and I could give it a whirl."

"Give it a whirl?" He sounds stunned. Raising a brow, he asks, "You really want me to use *this* thing on you?"

He may act all shocked, but I sense it's for my sake, an opening for me to back out graciously. But I can see he's already hard just thinking about it. And God knows I'm dripping. Hell with backing out graciously. The only place I'm backing to is maybe onto this thing. Er, maybe.

"It looks more intimidating than I remember," I confess. "But yeah, I think I want you to use it on me. Just be gentle, okay."

He gives me a look, like that's a given. "Aubrey, of course. It has to be fun for both of us, or there's no point." He sighs. "You sure you don't want me to just put it away?"

I shake my head. "No. Let's try it."

Brent starts toward me with DPMB, and I sit up and pull my knees up to my chest.

"Changing your mind?" he asks.

"Nope. Just mentally preparing."

He reaches me and nudges my legs apart. I scoot to the edge of the bed, and he asks, "You ready?"

"Uh-huh."

He doesn't use DPMB on me immediately. First, he gets me readier than ever with his tongue. Then he fingers me. We also talk about how far and how much I want. DPMB comes with lube, which is essential for the double part.

When we get to that, Brent keeps his promise and uses the toy on me gently and carefully. It's weird and it's different, but the kink factor of Brent using the thing on me makes the whole experience hot.

When I'm so worked up I think I might die, he tosses it off to the side and straight-up fucks me.

I come so many times I lose count.

When Brent finishes, he collapses onto me. "God, that was amazing," he says.

Just wait till we play with your namesake, Brent 51, I think.

I sense the opportunity might come—no pun intended—the very next night.

Brent, back in sweet and romantic mode, drives me out to the desert in his newest car, a late model Jaguar, so we can see the many nighttime stars that blanket the desert sky.

Once we're parked in the middle of nowhere, Brent and I get out. He rests his ass against the front of the car, so I wedge between his arms and lean my back against him.

"Oh my God," I gush, looking up at the sky. "It's so freaking pretty. I can't believe how many stars are actually up there."

"And to think they're there all the time. We just can't see them in the city with all the bright lights."

"Well, they sure stand out here in the desert," I murmur. "It kind of makes you feel grounded, reminds you of what's important."

"It does," he agrees. "Life's not all about bright lights and big cities."

He kisses the top of my head, and I know *bright lights and big cities* is a metaphor for the glitz and glamour of celebrity life.

"I'm glad you brought me out here," I murmur.

"I wanted to share it with you. This is my spot to come and think about things, important things."

"So, this place is special to you?"

"It is."

"Do you come out here a lot?" I inquire. I'm thirsty to learn all I can about Brent.

I feel him shrug. "From time to time."

It's totally quiet in the desert, silence reigns, so we stop talking and just enjoy the peacefulness for a few minutes.

Finally, I break the silence when I bring up something we've not yet addressed, not directly. "Brent, what are we going to do if we're found out?"

"We won't be discovered," he assures me.

I turn in his arms to face him. "Still, we have to be extra careful when you go on the road next week." I sigh. "I love being at your house. It's a great hideaway. But how are we going to manage to keep our relationship a secret in a hotel when the team's staying mere feet awa—"

He silences my concern with a kiss.

"We'll just have to be overly cautious," he says when we break apart.

When a star suddenly shoots across the sky, I make a wish, hoping he's right and we'll be fine.

Sighing, he says, "I can't wait for when you're no longer working for the team." He kisses my forehead. "Then we won't have to worry anymore about sneaking around."

We've already discussed the next six weeks, the time remaining on my contract. We've decided to give our relationship a real shot out in the real world once I'm free from any contract restrictions.

I love Brent, and I'm pretty sure he loves me. We haven't said *the words* yet, but I suspect it's only because we're both waiting for the perfect time.

"Yeah," I say, agreeing that I can't wait for my contract to end too. "I'll have a couple months off afterward for sure. I can stay here in Vegas with you until my next assignment. And until I have to leave, I can still travel with you to your away games."

Once I'm no longer under contract with the Wolves, I can do whatever I want. *We* can do whatever *we* want.

"That sounds perfect." He closes his eyes and adds, "December can't get here soon enough, Aubrey."

"It's just a few weeks away," I remind him.

On the way back home, we take a different route and spot a diner on the side of the road. A big neon sign on a pole out front informs us it's the *Area 51 Café.*

"Oh hell, Aubrey." Brent starts to laugh. "Check out that sign. We totally have to take a picture of you next to it."

I reach over and whack him in the arm. "That's so not funny."

I'm not really mad, I'm just playing. It is actually kind of funny.

When Brent sees I'm not upset in the least, he pulls into the lot. "Uh, out of curiosity, do you still have that Area 51 toy?"

Ooh, opportunity!

"Why do you want to know?" I coquettishly ask.

"Well, we had so much fun with that double-penetrating thing last night that I thought maybe we could invite your green friend to join us later tonight."

"My green friend, huh?" I laugh. "He has a name, by the way."

"He does? You're shitting me. What is it?"

"Um, it may be Brent 51."

"It may be, or it is?"

"Okay, it is." Clearing my throat, I confess, "I obviously named him after you."

After a long pause, he says, "I don't know if I should be happy about this or offended, seeing as that thing's a pretty weird shade of green. Not to mention, it freaking *glows* in the dark."

"Not always. I found a switch where you can turn off that feature."

"Ah, that's why my upstairs hallway no longer lights up like a toxic swamp."

That earns him another whack. "Brent, be serious."

He laughs, and God, I love how happy he sounds. Placing my hand on his hard thigh, I assure him, "You should feel happy I named my toy after you. He's what I use when I fantasize about you and me together."

"You pretend that thing is me?"

"Yep."

"What about DPMB?" he asks, though it's clear he's now teasing. "Who do you pretend it is?"

"No one." I make a face. "I told you I never used it before last night. That one used to scare me."

"Does it still?"

"Not as much. But it is…a lot to handle."

"Maybe we should reserve it for special occasions, then?"

"Like once in a blue moon?" I joke. "Get it, Brent? Moon?"

When Brent doesn't fall into hysterics at my joke, like he damn well should, I sense something is wrong. "Hey, what's up?"

In a *worried-he's-not-pleasing-me* tone, he says, "Do you still use Brent 51, like, often?"

"Aw, don't worry, stud." I pat his leg, inching up closer to a part of him that's near and dear to my heart. And near and dear to *other* parts of me, as well. "I haven't taken Brent 51 out for a long time. He's been sleeping peacefully since we hooked up."

He shoots me a mischievous grin. "Well, then, I say we wake him up, for sure. Damn, the things I could do to you with that thing, Aubrey. You do realize it's *much* more maneuverable than the DPMB."

"Shit, Brent. Forget about taking a picture with that stupid sign. Hit the gas and get us home as fast as you can."

Laughing, he says, "You got it, babe."

Damn, Brent Oliver is turning me into a toy-loving sex fiend.

25

A BAD, BAD DECISION

BRENT

Aubrey likes all the things I do to her with her green toy. But not before I make certain the switch to keep that weird green glow feature is indeed turned off. The last thing I need is for my neighbors to think I'm conducting bizarre experiments over here. I think the team would be more freaked out over that— imagine the press!—than if they found out about Aubrey and me.

Then again, maybe not.

The day after our drive out to the desert, I have one more home game. And then the team goes on the road. I decide to drive to the arena separate from Aubrey to maintain appearances. And though I don't blatantly look for her in the stands, I know she's there, cheering me on.

Damn, I can't wait for December to get here.

Fueled by feelings I've never felt before, like an intense sort of joy, I come out flying on the ice. Three minutes in and our goaltender, a Russian guy named Ruslan Brezzenov—we call him Breeze—sends the puck to my stick when he's clearing his net and sees there's no defensemen around me.

The other team is in the midst of a personnel change so I skate down the ice mostly unimpeded. One of their defensemen finally notices me and comes in for a hard check.

I outmaneuver him and shoot the puck at the net.

Their goalie never sees it coming, and the light behind the net goes on. Sirens erupt and the crowd goes crazy. Our team is doing so well, in large part because of me. I'm playing better than I ever have in my career, and it's all due to Aubrey.

I realize right then and there, on the ice, as my teammates are congratulating me on my goal, I'm in love with her.

Shit, I've never been in love. Not like this.

I go on to score another goal and two assists. It's a great game and we end up leading 6-2 with only two minutes left to play. But then Benny gets hurt. After he goes down hard against the boards on a wicked check, he has to leave the ice.

We still win, and word from the team doctor is Benny will be okay.

That night, after interviews conclude in the locker room, and after I take a quick shower, I join the guys for a late dinner. I text Aubrey that I'll be home in a bit, and she messages me back to *have fun*.

We go to a fancy steakhouse in downtown Las Vegas. The food is great, but I'm not too thrilled that there's a strip club next door. I have a feeling the guys will want to stop in after we eat. If Benny were here with us, I could take off with him. He avoids all drinking situations. Unfortunately, he had to stay behind for X-rays.

Sure enough, dinner ends and Nolan suggests we stop in at the strip joint.

"Come on, Oliver," he says when I attempt to decline. "You haven't been out with us in ages."

"Yes," Breeze, the goaltender, chimes in with his choppy accent. "I owe you drink from last season when we go out. Hell," he goes on, "with all the booze you bought me, I probably owe you twenty drinks."

"One is good," I assure him with a clap on the back. It's not like I've been keeping count, but I do recall buying multiple rounds for everyone after we were knocked out of the playoffs in early May. I guess that's what he's referring to.

"Does that mean you're actually going to hang with us tonight?" Nolan raises a brow.

"Yeah, sure." I shrug. "What can it hurt?"

I regret those words when I walk into the strip club and see how out of control things are. This could end up badly. There are three bachelor parties going on...and now us.

Breeze buys me the drink he owes me. I try to nurse the watered-down vodka and tonic, but various players keep buying rounds for everyone. Before I know it, I'm fucking hammered.

"So much for three months of sobriety," I say to Nolan.

"You're not an alcoholic, Brent," he says. "I don't know why you talk like that." He pauses for a few seconds, then says, "Oh, wait. I actually do know why you say shit like that. It's because of Aubrey and her mouth."

Lifting my fifth vodka and tonic of the night, I murmur, "Yeah, okay, but she has a point. My downward descent always seems to start out this way."

He makes a scoffing noise. "That also sounds like something

Aubrey would say."

Leaning back, I ask him, "Dude, what is your fucking problem with her?"

He blows out a breath. "I like her just fine. It's just that I see the way you look at her. And the way she looks at you."

"So?"

"You've slept with her, haven't you?"

I shrug. "Maybe."

"More than once, I presume?"

I nod, and he says, "Damn it, Brent. What are you two doing? She's an employee of the team, same as you. Nothing good can come of you and her together in any way."

I don't like what he's saying, especially since it's true. So when a skimpily clad cocktail waitress comes along, I order yet another drink.

"Man, you are such a downer," I mutter. "Just because you had a bad experience with love—" I shut the hell up when I realize what I've just blurted out.

Nolan's head jerks up. "What did you just say?"

I wave him off. "Nothing, I was just thinking out loud."

He's not alarmed that I brought up his past. Well, maybe he is, seeing as it's a closely guarded secret that not only was Nolan once madly in love, but he married the girl. Both of them were still teenagers. He was just out of juniors and thought she was the love of his life.

Too bad she loved nothing but dick.

She cheated on him with half the team he was on at the time, as well as many other random men. When he found out about all her flings, he filed for divorce and everything was swept under the rug. No one really remembers since he was a "nobody" at the time. But he sure remembers. He told Benny and me all about it, in confidence, this past summer. He even admitted that he's never been the same since, not when it comes to love. He just doesn't believe in it—at all.

Narrowing his eyes at me, and probably more pissed than I thought that I mentioned his past, he says, "I told you to fuck Aubrey one time and get it out of your system. You weren't supposed to fucking fall in love with the bitch."

"Hey." I shoot him a warning glare. I will throw down, even with a friend, for her. "Aubrey's not a bitch, Nolan."

"Okay, okay." He puts up his hands. "This is me backing the fuck off. But let me put it out there that I think you're both dumb to be playing with fire."

I toss back my drink. "Let me get burned, then. I don't care what the team says or does to me, as long as Aubrey doesn't get hurt."

Nolan rolls his eyes. "Yeah, good luck with that." He only has my best interests at heart, but while drinking at a strip club is not the best time to discuss this in any rational manner.

Just then a bunch of the guys bring over a tall, blonde stripper. She has on nothing but a G-string and an open short robe. When she starts dancing seductively in front of me, I realize they've bought me a lap dance.

This is so not good.

I keep my hands to myself, like a good boy, but there are a lot of cameras flashing. Big fake tits in my face are not going to fly with Aubrey. Nor is the vodka and tonic in my hand destined to bring a smile to her face. Management will be pissed too. I should stop this right now.

But I let it go on.

After the dance, I tip the blonde so she'll take off. I then get all the guys to erase the pics and videos they captured. I hope I didn't miss any, because I know if I did it'll end up on social media. And if that happens, the pic—or worse yet, a video—will show up on a site like Deadspin. I know Aubrey and the team monitor that site and the knock-off ones closely. Everything will be out about this night if something goes viral. And though nothing happened with the dancer, images of her writhing all over my junk wouldn't look good.

Speaking of junk, I'm horny as hell now thanks to the lap dance. "Hey, I'm taking off," I say to Nolan. I'm anxious to get home to Aubrey.

Luckily, he sees how drunk I am and makes arrangements with Breeze to follow us out to my place so he can drive me home in my car, and then have a ride back.

Nolan may be a dick at times, but he always has my back.

I also learn he has a video of me with the stripper. I don't ask him to erase it. He'd never do anything with it.

26

THE REAL WORLD SOMETIMES SUCKS

AUBREY

Brent wakes me from a dead sleep. When I realize he's tugging at my sleep clothes, pulling them off despite my groggy and only half-awake state, I'm surprised, but definitely all in.

But then, when he just about crushes me with his weight, I'm more like, "What the hell, Brent? I can't breathe."

"Sorry." He lifts his body off me enough that I don't suffocate under his very naked self. Not that it'd be a bad way to go. But still, Brent's usually much more smooth and controlled than this.

He nuzzles his nose into my neck and breathes out something that sounds like an apology. And that's when I smell alcohol.

"Are you crazy?" I push him off of me. "You're drunk, aren't you?"

He flops back on the bed. "So what if I am? I haven't had anything remotely resembling alcohol since fucking August. And I'm not an alcoholic, Aubrey. I can go out and throw back a few once in a while."

"Oh, that sounds like Nolan talking."

"Funny. He said the same thing about you."

"So he did say it was okay for you to get drunk?"

"Who cares if he did? It's true."

"Where'd you go?" I carefully inquire.

He looks a little shady when he replies, "There was a bar at the steak place where we ate."

"Hmm..."

I want Brent to feel comfortable kicking back with his teammates—and I really don't think a once-in-a-while night out with the boys will make him spiral—but I do worry if the team finds out they may panic and extend my contract, thinking they still need me. If that happens our relationship will have to continue to remain a secret, a secret that if discovered could sink us both.

I share all this with Brent, and then say, "Do you see now why I'm so upset?"

"Yeah," he says on a sigh. "When you put it like that I do." He pulls me to him and wraps his arms around me. "I wasn't thinking. But I promise you I won't go out drinking again till you're no longer my life coach."

"And even then, Brent, don't let things get out of control. You may not be an alcoholic, but drinking to excess has caused you problems in the past."

"I know, babe." His hand slides down to my bare ass, already distracted. "I won't."

I may complain, but I'm just as bad as him. Dropping the conversation, I get busy Zamboni-ing his ice.

I go on the road with the team the week of Thanksgiving.

Since there's a game the night before the actual holiday, as well as one the following Friday afternoon, I have to inform my family that I won't be able to join them for our big holiday turkey feast this year.

Mom and Dad are disappointed, but understand that my job comes first.

"We'll catch up with you at Christmas," my always supportive dad says after I give him the bad news.

"Yes, definitely," I reply, knowing I'll be out of the contract with the Wolves by then.

I start imagining holidays spent with Brent—putting up a tree, drinking eggnog, and exchanging special gifts, all as an official couple.

I hear my mom sigh and realize Dad has his phone on speaker. "Honey," my mother starts out of the blue.

"Yes, Mom?"

"Please promise me you'll be sure to eat a real dinner on Thanksgiving. I know how caught up in your job you get, but you have to have some turkey. No fast food, okay?"

I assure her, "Mom, I don't really eat fast food, anyway."

"Oh, that's good, honey. But promise me about the turkey."

"Yes, Mom," I dutifully reply. "I will absolutely have some turkey on Thanksgiving."

I talk a bit longer with my parents, and then I call Lainey.

"Sestra!" she sings out when she answers.

I start laughing. "Sounds like someone's been binge watching *Orphan Black* again."

My sister may have a slight obsession with Tatiana Maslany.

"Guilty as charged," she replies. "I just finished with another multi-season viewing. I swear I might die waiting for season five."

"You'll live," I assure her.

"Oh, hold on a minute. I'm getting a text."

I imagine Lainey holding out her phone to read her new message. When she returns to our convo, she huffs.

"What's wrong?" I ask.

"That was from Dad. What's this about you not coming home for Thanksgiving?"

Sighing, I break the bad news to her. "It's true, Lain. That's why I'm calling, to let you know I won't make it home this year. Dad just beat me to it."

"Damn, your job is so freaking all-consuming."

"That's what I've been trying to tell you," I reply, feeling sad.

"I'm seeing it now more than ever, Aubrey. When do you have time to, like, live a life?"

Lainey is right. No wonder I fell for a client. I have no time for anyone other than whoever it is I'm life-coaching. What am I going to do when I'm assigned to someone new? Sure I'll have a little time off, but then another assignment will come along. Do I really want to spend months away from Brent?

"I have a lot to think about," I murmur.

"What's that mean?" Lainey wants to know. "Oh wait. Holy crap! You met someone out there in Las Vegas, didn't you?"

I've been dying to share my new relationship status with my sister, and finally here's a chance. As long as I'm fuzzy on the details she won't guess my new love interest is my client.

"I kind of have," I admit.

Lainey squeals into the phone, "Details, Aubrey, I want details. Tell me everything. Plus, I want to know when I get to meet him. Will you be bringing him home to Pennsylvania for Christmas?"

"Whoa, slow down. We're in the early stages of dating. Although I have known him since August."

Another excited squeal assaults my ear. "What's his name?"

This should be safe. "Brent," I reply.

"How old is he?"

"Twenty-two."

"Ooh, you cougar. A younger man."

"Lainey." I roll my eyes. "I'm only two years older than him."

"Okay, whatever. Tell me more. What does he do? How'd you meet? Is he hot?"

I answer the only question I can, and luckily it's the one I know Lainey wants to hear the most. "He's absolutely gorgeous, Lainey." Now it's my turn to squeal a little. "He's tall, like over six feet, and he has all this nice, thick dark hair. And then there's his face."

"Cute, huh?"

"Gorgeous."

"What about his body?"

"Oh my God, it's to die for. He's built, all masculine and strong."

I sigh, and so does Lainey.

And then she says, "Mmm, he sounds like he's smoking hot."

"He is," I assure her. "He really is."

"So what color are his eyes?" Giggling, she adds, "They're not sunflower brown, are they?"

It's safe to answer truthfully on that one. "Um, no, they're more whiskey colored."

"You were so funny that night, Aubrey," Lainey goes on, referring to the party where I was drooling over Brent, only to find myself waking up in his bed.

If Lainey only knew *that* guy is *my* guy she'd die.

I can't share that with her, but I can say, "You know what's really wild, Lainey?"

"What?"

"The guy I'm dating looks an awful lot like the guy from that night, the one I was drooling over. I swear they could be twins."

"Wow, lucky you," she says. "That dude was sexy as hell."

Smiling at the serendipitous way things sometimes work out, I say, "Yes, he certainly was." *And is.*

Lainey then surprises the hell out of me when she asks, "Are you in love with him?"

"Um…"

"You are, aren't you?"

Yes!

Lainey can't hear my internal thoughts, but she may as well have. "Does he love you back?"

"I think so."

"What? You haven't told each other yet?"

I reply with what I believe is true. "Words aren't everything. I'm sure we'll get around to saying it to each other, but for now I'm good. I *feel* his love for me every day we spend together."

"Ah, that's sweet." She sighs into the phone. "Now we need to find someone for me. Maybe I'll get lucky like you and find *my* Prince Charming. But it'll have to be after I graduate in May."

"Why? Are there no good prospects up there at school?"

"Not really," she says. "I date a lot, but there's no one special emerging from the pack. I can't wait to graduate, Aubs. I'm ready for real men in the real world."

"Ha!" I laugh. "The real world isn't all it's cracked up to be, trust me."

It's true. The real world sucks sometimes, especially when it prevents you from sharing with your sister the complete details of the man you're head-over-heels in love with.

27

WHEN YODA SPEAKS, LISTEN YOU MUST

BRENT

Benny misses one game, and then another. The latter is played the night before Thanksgiving in Toronto, Nolan's hometown.

The crowd is out of control up there. There's blue and white everywhere. Our sad little team colors of black and red are barely represented. But I do spot Aubrey in the players' wives and girlfriends section, wearing my jersey.

She's seated next to Benny, who opted not to watch the game from a luxury box. He said he'd rather hang with Aubrey. Of course that means he'll probably quiz her on every aspect of the game.

Poor girl.

I chuckle, but then I feel bad. I hate that Aubrey has to sit up there under the guise of being my life coach, the same reason she gives to others for why she's wearing my number. I'm still her client, yes, but we're so much more than that. And I want nothing more than to shout to the world that I'm in love with this girl.

That raises the question of why I haven't said it to her yet.

Honestly, I'm afraid if I put it all out there on the line, I'll somehow jinx things. Hey, what can I say? Hockey players are very superstitious, and I'm no exception. Plus, there's the fact that Aubrey and I have been balancing on a damn tightrope lately. This keeping our romantic relationship a secret is really starting to mess me up.

My fucked-up state is evident when I screw up two plays, both resulting in goals for the other team. One fuckup is an errant pass I send directly to an opposing player's stick. He scores and I slam my stick on the ice. The officials overlook my tantrum, but when I hurl the stick across the ice, I'm slapped with a ten-minute misconduct penalty.

While I'm in the box, the Leafs score again.

We lose 2-0.

"We can't generate one fucking goal?" I yell at the guys in the locker room after the game.

I'm mad at myself, but I need to take it out somewhere.

Most of my teammates look away or pretend to be busy with taking off their equipment. Not Nolan, though. He looks directly at me and says, "It's one game, Brent. Calm the fuck down."

"One game," I scoff. "One game, like when we lost in the first round of the playoffs last season? We were up three games to one, as I remember. But that one game was the beginning of the end. They stole the last three out from under our noses, and we fucking let them."

"This isn't the playoffs, dude," Breeze interjects. "No worry so much."

Nolan agrees, "Yeah, you tell him, Breeze."

"You know what?" I snap. "You're both assholes."

Everyone is quiet and on edge because of my behavior. I've been a good leader to the team this season, but not today. I sit down on the bench in front of my locker and place my head in my hands.

Nolan comes over and sits next to me. "What's up, my friend?" he asks. "This isn't like you, not here in the locker room, and not with the way you played tonight."

I raise my head, blow out a breath. "I don't know what's going on with me. But I know I'm feeling messed up in the head again."

"Isn't that what Aubrey's supposed to prevent?" he quietly asks, so no one will hear.

I chuckle. "You'd think so, eh? But it's mostly what's going on *with* her that has me not thinking straight."

"I thought you guys were good? I thought you had this thing under control?"

Nolan may not fully approve of our relationship—and this is probably why—but he's not one to bail when I need him. Nor does he rub shit in your face, even when Yoda has been right all along.

"We're great," I say. "Everything with us is fine. The problem is the fucking secrecy. I've had it with hiding who we are to each other."

I glance around to make sure no one's listening in.

See how fucked up this shit is?

When I'm sure we're good, I add, "I just want to take my girlfriend out in public, you know? Maybe take her to a nice dinner or a goddamn movie. Is that asking for too much?"

"No, no it's not." Nolan is using his soothing sensei voice. I must look like a real wreck. "But how much longer do you have to wait? Only a couple more weeks, eh?"

"Yeah," I grumble. "Though it feels like forever at this point."

He stands and raps me on the back. "Quit thinking about it so much, Oliver. Focus on playing hockey. The time will go fast."

This is one time the great sensei better be fucking right.

SECRETS AND LIES

AUBREY

I sense trouble is in the air. Even from up in the stands, where I'm seated next to an unusually quiet Benny, I can tell Brent's off his game. Passing the puck directly to an opponent is something he just doesn't do.

But that's not the part that worries me. It's his reaction. Slamming his stick on the ice isn't too bad, but sending it sailing across the rink?

That's not Brent at all.

"My man is fucked up," Benny says, sending an accusatory glance my way.

"Why are you looking at me like that?" I question.

He shrugs as he focuses back on the ice, where Brent is skates dejectedly to the penalty box. "You need to life coach the shit out of him if you expect him to make it to December without having a meltdown."

"He's hanging in there," I say, with no conviction whatsoever.

Benny laughs. "Hanging in there, eh? I heard he was out drinking the other night. Word is he got pretty fucked up."

"He did," I admit with a sigh. "But I'm sure that was a one-time thing."

"Sure, Aubrey, whatever you say."

Benny looks guilty as hell, and I sense he knows something and is holding back. I swear these guys gossip worse than little old ladies. If something more happened with Brent, he would know it.

"Am I missing something here, Benny? Did something else happen that night?"

"I wasn't there" is his evasive answer.

I know then that I'll get nothing more from him. Damn bro code. It's a code of silence I have no chance of breaking. I'll have to get to the bottom of this on my own.

The next day, I try.

It's Thanksgiving and the team is holding a big dinner down in the hotel ballroom. Brent stops by my room to pick me up so I can go down with him.

"I hate this fucking shit," he tells me when I come out in the hall and close the door behind me. "I can't even come in your room."

"We could go back in and pretend we're having a meeting," I suggest with a wicked grin.

Brent doesn't take the bait. He's clearly in a mood. Sighing, he says, "No one would buy that."

"Oh, I think they would. After that little tantrum you had on the ice last night, they probably expect me to meet with you."

He pins me with a look of disdain. "Aubrey, don't fucking life coach me right now."

His cranky mood can't bring me down. "Ooh, someone sure is

feeling surly," I tease.

We start toward the elevator, and thankfully no one is around, especially when Brent leans in close and growls, "You bet your ass I'm feeling surly. What I'd like to do is take you back to your room and fuck you so hard you wouldn't be able to walk for days."

"Damn," I mutter, liking surly Brent more and more.

I'm up for heading back to my room, but just as I'm about to say as much damn Nolan comes around the corner.

"Oh, hey," he mutters, looking rather subdued. "Mind if I head down to the meal with you?"

Brent replies, "No, not at all. The more the merrier."

These two seem weird, like they're hiding something.

Frustrated that I'm being kept out of the loop—because that can't be good—I feel compelled to bait Nolan.

"What?" I say. "No smartass commentary today?"

"Nope," he replies.

Brent and Nolan share a look, so I outright ask, "What's going on?"

I receive no answer since the elevator dings at that exact second and the door opens.

Brent, placing his hand on the small of my back, says, "Come on. Let's just get this stupid dinner over with."

In the ballroom, I sit between him and Benny. Nolan and the goaltender, Breeze, are seated across from us. There's a lot of good-natured small talk, but something is off down here too. I sense everyone knows something that I don't. It has to be something related to the night Brent went out drinking.

Where'd they really go?

What'd they really do?

Do I even want to know?

29

MY GENIUS PLAN

BRENT

Two more losses, and then we're back in Vegas. There, the losing streak continues. Management is pissed, and Dolby calls to bitch me out.

Then it's Jock's turn.

"Did you get hit in the head with a puck or something?" he asks.

"No. Why?"

I hear him slamming things around on his desk. "Because your behavior on the ice lately has been unacceptable, Brent. Two brand new endorsement deals I was working on just went south. One bowed out after that stick-throwing incident in Toronto, and the other won't return my calls. Not after that fight last night."

Oh yeah, I got into a fight last game. That wasn't so bad. But punching the linesman—though I swear it was an accident—earned me a two-game suspension.

"I got plenty of other endorsement deals," I counter.

"You're going to lose them too if you don't shape up."

"I promise to behave, Jock."

"You better."

I hang up and go outside for some much-needed air. It's so fucking hot out here in desert-land, even though it's now December.

Damn, I'm looking forward more than ever to spending time out east with Aubrey, where the weather's been cold and snowy.

"One more week," I remind myself. "Then her contract ends."

I can't wait to be with her, all out in the open. We made official plans just the other day to spend the holidays together as a couple. I'm planning to fly with her to her hometown of Butler, PA, so I can spend Christmas with her and her family. I'm thrilled that I'll finally get to meet her parents and her sister. And after our visit with them we plan to head up to Minneapolis so Aubrey can meet my mom and dad.

My parents were going to have a big celebration for the holiday, but they scaled it back. Apparently, my dad hasn't been feeling well.

When I go back into the house, my phone starts beeping. I look down and see it's a text alert from Aubrey.

Hey, I was on my way home, but Mr. Dolby just messaged that he wants to meet with me. Maybe he's ready to sign off on my contract early.

God, I hope so, I text back.

Fingers crossed, she replies.

Mine too, I send back.

I let out a relieved breath, thankful that all the hiding and secrecy may be over sooner than we thought. But when Aubrey returns, looking beyond dejected, I know the news isn't good.

"What's wrong?" I ask. "What happened at the meeting?"

She tosses her purse and laptop case onto the floor by the sofa. And then she flops down on the cushions. "You're never going to believe this," she says.

I sit down next to her and take her hand in mine. "What's going on now?" I warily inquire.

She shakes her head. "Oh, Brent, this is so bad." Tears form in her eyes. "They just extended my contract."

My throat closes. "Shit. For how long?"

She pulls her knees up to her chest and leans her head forward, hiding her face as she says, "Till the playoffs are over."

I let go of her hand and jump to my feet. "What? No way! Aubrey, this is unacceptable. The playoffs start in April. We won't be done till at least May. Maybe not till the month after if we go deep."

Lifting her head, she rests her chin on her raised knees. "Yeah, if you guys go all the way, I'll be with you until mid-June."

I start to pace, muttering, "That's six fucking months away."

"Yeah"—she sighs—"it is."

"Six more months of hiding and sneaking around, all while taking a chance of getting caught."

"Yep."

I stop and turn to look at her. Her expression is so sad that it breaks my fucking heart. "I can't keep up this farce of not loving you for that long," I choke out.

Her eyes widen. "You love me?"

I go to her, take her hands in mine and urge her to stand. "Of course I love you. I have for a while now."

That makes her smile as she rises to meet me. She slides her arms around my neck. "I love you too, Brent."

Leaning down, I press my lips to hers. "This wasn't how I planned to tell you," I murmur against her mouth. "I was waiting for the chance to make a great romantic gesture."

"This is romantic enough," she assures me.

She kisses me, and I kiss her back with everything I've got. I do love her, so very, very much.

We make out for a few minutes, until she has to excuse herself to go to the bathroom. I take the opportunity to take a look at that damn contract. Finding it is easy since it's right where I expect it to be— tucked away in her laptop case.

I read through it quickly. It seems pretty ironclad. Aubrey could quit, but that'd look really bad for her and her firm. Just as it would if they were to discover our relationship had crossed the line.

I search for other reasons why the team might let her go, ones that wouldn't hurt her reputation. It seems the only way they'd terminate her immediately is if something extremely damning came out about me. It'd have to be something awful that happened on her watch, so to speak, something she should've had a handle on. There's no mention of repercussions if that were to happen, but I assume they'd simply let her go so everyone could save face.

That wouldn't be so bad, right?

I think about the night at the strip club, wondering if Nolan still has the video of my lap dance. If that thing goes public, the team would *have* to let Aubrey go. That's definitely something they'd have expected her to contain.

It wouldn't be her fault, though. It's all on me. Aubrey could simply go with the story that I was a terrible client, the kind *nobody* could ever fully straighten out. And yeah, I may lose another endorsement, but that won't affect her.

She'll sure be pissed as hell, though, when she sees what's on that video. I'll have to explain that it looks way worse than it was. I'll also be sure to let all parties concerned know that it also was all on me. I'll say my teammates played no part in the lap dance debacle, even though they did. I'll also stress how Aubrey was doing a phenomenal job, as evidenced by their willingness to re-sign her.

I alone was the one who slipped up.

Convinced that this is the only way for Aubrey to get out of her contract unscathed, and also the only way for us to be together, out in public, before the summer, I pick up my cell and call Nolan.

"You still have that video of me at the strip club?" I ask as soon as he picks up.

"Yeah, I think so. Why?"

"Where are you?"

"Over at my house."

"Great," I say. "Stay put. I'll be over in five minutes. I'll explain everything once I'm there."

"Okay. See you then."

I disconnect, grab my keys and head for the door.

30

WHAT THE EVER-LOVING...?

AUBREY

When I return to the living room, Brent is gone.

"What the hell?"

Did our professions of love scare him off?

I don't really think that's the case, but I have to question why he wandered off so quickly and out of the blue.

Plus, where did he go?

Since I'm still wearing my business clothes, a light blue linen pant suit, and it's kind of warm inside the house, I decide to shower and change. A short while later I bop back down to the living room, dressed in the much cooler outfit of one of Brent's Wolves tees, which is very oversized on me, and short jean shorts. Since Brent's still MIA, I plop down on the sofa and fire up my laptop.

May as well get some work done, right?

One of my jobs is to keep tabs on social media, including all the popular sports blogs and hockey news sites. I don't expect to find anything bad about Brent. Working through a slump and incurring a couple bad penalties, and even a suspension, doesn't make him all that newsworthy. At least not the kind of newsworthy the team frowns on. The Wolves' management worries more about character stuff. That's why Benny was sent to rehab back in August. Couldn't have pics of a raucous drunk representing the team surfacing all the time, now could we?

No.

Benny still whores around, but he's very discreet about it. He sure wouldn't have been if he'd been inebriated out of his mind.

And that's what matters—appearances.

"Everything looks quiet today," I murmur as I scan through the usual sites.

But then, just as I'm about to close the laptop, an alert pops up for a new site that's just like Deadspin.

Crap, this new one always seems to find the most lascivious material. Still, I'm certain this newest story, whatever it is, won't involve Brent.

Geez, I sure hope it's not about someone else on the team. I love the Wolves, and the players have become like an extended family to me.

I click the link to go to the site and discover there's some kind of recently uploaded video. And the buzz is already crazy.

I click and read the headline—*Brent Oliver Gets His Grind On.*

"What the ever-loving…?"

I watch the video.

Good God, it's of Brent, *my* Brent, sloppy and drunk at a strip club.

But the worst and most disgusting part is he's getting a lap dance...and enjoying the hell out of it.

"I am going to kill him!"

I EFFED UP

BRENT

With the deed done, I return to the house.

I need to find Aubrey and engage in some preemptive damage control before she discovers the online video. Hopefully she hasn't seen it yet. Nolan tried to keep me from posting it, but I ignored him. For the record, he thinks I'm a fool for fucking things up on purpose.

I hope he's not right.

I find Aubrey on the sofa, legs curled up under her. She has her head in one hand, her dark hair spilling over it.

Shit, she's seen it.

"Babe…" I stop in my tracks.

She looks up at me. "Brent, what did you do?"

There are tears in her eyes, and her question is murmured in a whisper. I immediately feel like crap. "Aubs, it's not what it looks like."

I go over and sit next to her, but she scoots away. "Just… Give me some space, okay?"

"Yeah, sure." I assume she's angry over the content of the video, so I address that. "Nothing more than what you saw in the video happened, Aubrey. I know it looks bad"—she peers over at me and scoffs—"but I swear that was the extent of it. The guys bought me a lap dance that night, nothing else. It happens sometimes. I know I should've declined, but I was drinking at the time."

"Clearly," she interjects, her voice dripping with sarcasm. And then she asks, "Was that video taken the night you came home drunk? The same night you let me blow you, Brent."

"Yes," I sheepishly admit.

She sighs, and I sense I'm in for it. But I guess we have bigger problems since she says quietly, "Why didn't you tell me what happened? I could've prevented that video from getting out."

I shrug, feeling guiltier than ever.

She shakes her head. "This is so, so bad, Brent. You don't even know."

"Maybe it's not," I counter, running my hand down my face. "We have to look at the bright side here."

"What the hell kind of *bright side* are you seeing in this scenario?" she practically yells at me. "'Cause, really, Brent, if there is one, I'd like for you to share it with me."

I move closer to her, and this time she lets me close the gap. I think she's just too upset to stop me.

With my hand on her leg, I say, "Of course there's a bright side. The Wolves will let you out of your contract now. We won't have to wait until the summer to tell the world we're in love."

She stares at me like I'm speaking another language. "Are you smoking crack?" she asks.

I mutter a confused, "Um, no."

Slipping out from under my hand, she stands abruptly. "Do you not realize how bad it is for me to be terminated for something like this?"

Wait a minute. She just used the present tense.

"Are you saying the team already contacted you?" I ask.

To say I'm surprised things are moving so quickly is an understatement. Maybe I *have* fucked things up.

"Yes," she replies, "they have."

I run my hand through my hair. "Jesus, talk about not wasting any time."

"I told you this is bad, Brent."

She hands me her phone, where a text is pulled up. I start scrolling the long and full-of-legalize message.

The gist is summed up in the final paragraph: *Your contract is hereby rendered null and void, as per our agreement. Your employment with the Las Vegas Wolves is terminated, effective immediately. As agreed upon in the new addendum, dated December 4, you are to have no ongoing relationships with any parties associated with the Wolves, or any of their affiliates. A formal letter outlining these details will be forthcoming via certified mail.*

"No ongoing relationships? What's this shit?" I spit out, angry at myself for my impulsive act. "You never told me there was a clause like this in the contract."

"There wasn't," she says flatly. "At least, not in the original one I signed."

Aubrey looks completely defeated, especially when I stupidly ask, "What exactly does this mean?"

I read the text, sure, but a part of me is hoping I missed something, some sort of out.

Aubrey crushes all hope, though, when she confirms, "It means we can't be together, Brent. And now it's not simply a 'wait until the summer' condition. It's a wait till freaking *forever!*"

"That can't be," I murmur, still resistant to accepting the truth. "I paged through the new paperwork you signed, and I didn't see anything like that—"

"Wait. What?"

She's staring at me, confused, her brow furrowed.

Feeling like the world's biggest ass, I struggle to explain. "I, um… I may have taken a peek at what we were up against."

"You read through my new contract?" Her tone is pure shock. "You went into my laptop case and took it out?"

"Yes," I admit, guilt consuming me. I can't meet her gaze. And that's how she knows I did more than read the contract.

"Oh my God, Brent. Please tell me what I'm suspecting right now isn't true."

I say nothing, and she crumples to the floor right in front of me. I hate myself for causing her this much pain.

With her back against the coffee table, she brings her knees up to her chest and wraps her arms around them. "*You* released that video, didn't you?"

"Yes," I admit.

Choking back a sob, she asks, "Why would you do something like that? Why?"

"I did it for us, babe."

"Jesus, don't you realize you've just made it so there is no more 'us'? Everything is ruined now. You may have read the contract, but you missed the extra page in the back. Like the text laid out, the extension I signed contained an addendum, stating that if I'm terminated early I'm to have no contact with anyone associated with the team in any way, shape, or form. That includes *you*, Brent."

I slide down to the floor next to her, broken and shamed. "Aubrey, babe." I take her in my arms. "They can't hold us to something as ridiculous as that. It's far too extreme."

"It is extreme," she cries. "But the fact remains that I signed it and fully agreed to it."

She loses it then, sobbing and shaking. All the composure she's maintained over the past four months of dealing with me crumbles right before my eyes. Aubrey's petite frame is racked with big choking sobs, and my heart shatters to a thousand *I-fucked-up* pieces.

I try to comfort her, but I know then that I've already lost her.

32

LEAVING MY HEART BEHIND

AUBREY

My boss calls an hour after the video is released and orders me to return to Chicago immediately.

Surprisingly, he's not angry. He's just resigned.

"We'll find you another assignment," he says, in a meant-to-be consoling tone. "The management team out there is completely unreasonable. As far as we're concerned, Aubrey, you did a phenomenal job. I think the best thing going forward is for us to get you on another contract with a new client as soon as possible."

I pretend to agree, but truthfully I feel like I need some time off.

I feel the same way a day later when I'm packing, which I find is far from easy. I've been here so long that I've had to have most of my things boxed up and designated to be shipped to my townhouse in Chicago.

But I still have a few final things in Brent's bedroom. I'm waiting for a time when he's at practice. We've avoided each other really well the past twenty-four hours, ever since our little "talk" in the living room.

Damn it, I'm so angry at him. If he'd just spoken with me first, I could've told him that releasing that video would be the worst move ever.

I love Brent, but we need time apart. That's why I plan to be gone by the time he comes home. Not only do I have no reason to be here anymore, but having a relationship with him, even if we pretend it just now started, is no longer a possibility. I can't throw away my career for him. And that's what I'd be doing. My firm would terminate me for violating the contract I signed, and my reputation would be for shit.

If Brent had just waited till summer, when the contract ended by reaching its full term, then that new addendum would've meant nothing. It's because I was terminated that it went into effect.

The team now expects me to stay away from everyone.

With my carry-on strap swung over my shoulder, the same piece of luggage Brent made me carry way back on that fateful day in the arena parking lot, I step into the room he and I have shared for over a month.

It's so overwhelming to me that I'll never again be in here that I have to stop for a minute and catch my breath.

"I can't believe it's really over," I choke out.

I also can't believe I'm a bad cliché—a woman caught between love and her career. Love might have won out, if I weren't so mad at Brent. But the more I think about it, the more I question if this relationship is really all that healthy. He kept the strip club incident from me. And that's like lying by omission, right?

He also went behind my back and released that video. Not only was the content humiliating for me to watch, but Brent made that decision all on his own. I can't be with someone who doesn't even think to consult me before making such a sweeping decision.

It seems that, for as much as Brent Oliver has changed, he's still pretty much the same self-centered prick I woke up to that morning in his bed. And that's why I can't sacrifice myself to be with him. It was bad judgment to get involved with him in the first place.

But you fell in love. You're just trying to talk yourself out of it now.

"Shut up," I hiss. "I have to convince myself of something or I won't be able to leave."

Then stay.

"I can't."

I angrily start stuffing clothes in my bag, starting with things in the closet. When I reach the nightstand by his bed I come across my red panties.

"I knew he kept these!" I exclaim.

Instead of tossing the lacy undergarment into my bag, I leave them where they are. He may as well keep his pervy reminder of the morning we first met.

A short while later, I place my key to his house on a table by the door.

And then I leave.

I don't write a note or a letter.

I don't need to, as I've already left my heart behind.

I'M NUMB, BUT NOT COMFORTABLY SO

BRENT

When I return from practice, Aubrey is gone.

There's no note, but I view that as a good sign. Maybe I'm delusional, but I don't think we're done.

Still, I'm numb as I walk around in the house. My home has never felt so fucking empty. Aubrey gave this place life, with her laughter and her love.

"God, I miss her already."

As the days pass, I miss her more and more. And I never stop loving her. I want to pick up the phone and call, but I don't want to cause her any more grief. If she feels anything like me, though, she probably has a big hole in her heart too. Mine is tearing me to pieces.

I finally decide to fill that hole with the only good things I have left—drive and determination. Maybe if I show Aubrey how she really changed me for the better, she'll say "fuck the contract" and come back.

With newfound hope in my heart I start playing better hockey than ever before. We win game after game and easily move back into first place in our division.

"I hope Aubrey's watching all these games," I confide to Benny one night after a particularly satisfying victory. "If she is, I bet I end up hearing from her soon."

We're in the locker room, and Benny just stares over at me. "Dude…" He sighs and shakes his head.

"What?"

He gives me this most sorrowful look, like I'm a lost cause. Maybe that's not it, though. I know he's still pissed at me for fucking things up. Aubrey was not only the best hockey student he ever had, but she was also his bud. Believe it or not, I think Nolan misses her too. More likely, he misses their verbal sparring. But I know he feels some kind of loss, seeing as at the end of a long plane trip out to a game in New York City, he starts in on me about how traveling is so fucking boring now that he has no one to ride me about.

"We need to find you someone new," he says, teasing. "Maybe the team can hire another life coach."

Joking aside, I take that shit seriously.

"I'm not interested in any other women," I snap, making all the players seated around us turn and look.

Once they resume what they're doing, and their eyes are off me, I hiss, "For the record, I sure as fuck don't ever need another goddamn life coach."

He pauses for a beat, and then says, "Eh, maybe not. But what you *do* need is to get out more. Come with us tonight. Breeze has a friend who just opened a new club in the city."

Breeze is from Russia originally, but he has a lot of friends out on the East Coast, especially in New York City.

I think about joining them, but in the end, once we're checked in our hotel, I decline.

"I think I'm going to stay in my room and watch highlights from the last game we played against the Rangers," I tell Nolan when he calls my room. "There are a few plays I'd like to dissect, maybe figure out how we can do better."

"Isn't that Coach's job?" Nolan replies dryly.

"It's my job too," I counter. "I'm captain of this team, remember?"

I'm deflecting, and he knows it. "Whatever, Oliver," he retorts.

He disconnects, and that's the end of that.

So here I sit, dissecting footage of plays, and still miserable as hell. I'm still doing all this for Aubrey, still hoping that if I show her all the time she spent with me wasn't a waste she'll see that falling in love with me wasn't a mistake.

She's bound to recognize that eventually, right?

Of course she is. She just needs time to sort things out. I suspect I'll hear from her once she sees the light.

Though, I sure hope she comes around before the holidays, which are quickly approaching. If she does maybe we can still spend Christmas together like we originally planned.

That's what I tell myself day after day.

And that's what keeps me going—my house of cards, built on a shaky foundation.

But as Christmas nears, and I've still not heard a word from her, I finally begin to lose hope.

34

MOVING ON SUCKS

AUBREY

Life without Brent is hard.

The first thing I do when I'm back at my townhouse is go up to my bedroom and pick up the pillow he slept on after our day of nonstop sex.

Inhaling deeply, I murmur, "Thank God it still smells like him."

I've never been happier that this place has been closed up, preserving all the scents and memories from our visit in October. Even Al is still on the floor, crumpled to where we tossed him in the heat of passion.

I pick him up and laugh. "I can't believe Brent was jealous of you." The bright green alligator stares back at me, and I smile sadly. "How ridiculous that he thought you were a real guy, and that Lainey and I shared you."

I start laughing at the silliness of it, but soon my laughter turns to sobbing.

Curling up on my bed with the stuffed toy held close to my heart, I cry out, "I miss him so much, Al. What am I going to do?"

Depressed, I hole up in my place and do nothing but watch hockey. I immerse myself in the NHL channel, watching every game and all the coverage. What I live for, though, are the Wolves games.

I also monitor every move Brent makes off the ice. It's as if I'm still his life coach. To my relief, there are no reports of crazy shenanigans, and he plays phenomenal hockey. A few paparazzi shots turn up one night. They're pics of Nolan, Benny, and Breeze hitting the town in New York City, going into some new club. Nothing looks out of the ordinary; they're just guys out for a night. Even the club they're going to looks rather tame.

Everyone is clearly behaving. And it shows in their play. The team holds on strongly to first place in the standings.

The week before Christmas—a holiday I'm not celebrating now on account of my broken heart *and* the fact that I was supposed to spend the day with Brent—my boss calls.

"It looks like we found you a new client," he says. "I'd like you to fly out to Los Angeles the first week in January to meet him."

I'm torn by this news, caught between wanting to move on with life and wanting to stay in this state of inertia where I have all the time in the world to focus on Brent.

"Aubrey, are you there?" my boss asks.

"Yes, yes." I draw in a breath, then release it slowly. Guess it's time to move on, whether I want to or not. "LA, huh?" I say with no enthusiasm whatsoever. "Is the new client an actor, then?"

"You know we like to keep those details confidential till you're actually on the job."

"Because that worked out so well last time," I can't resist retorting.

My boss huffs. "Ms. Shelburne, that was inappropriate."

If only he knew how inappropriate I really was in Vegas—falling for Brent, fucking Brent. I almost tell him everything, since it's messing me up, this keeping it in. But in the end I do no such thing. I simply say, "Sorry."

He forgives my indiscretion, and we wrap up the conversation shortly thereafter. With that out of the way, I turn on the TV and search for tonight's Wolves game.

Settling in on the sofa, I watch the man I love play amazing hockey. He scores a goal and racks up four assists, and that's just after two periods of play.

He's fine without me. So I should be fine without him, right?

Lots of people go on with their lives with broken hearts.

Brent sure seems to be doing that.

Why can't I?

By the third period, it's clear the team will win this game. It takes all I've got, but I make myself turn off the TV. It's the first time I've done such a thing since I've been back in Chicago.

"It'll be a new year soon," I remind myself. "And that means it's time to move on."

But God, I don't want to.

Every fiber of my being fights it, but I force myself to do what I must in order to move forward with my life—I let go of Brent Oliver for good.

35

MOTHER KNOWS BEST

BRENT

We win the last game before the holidays, and then we go on what amounts to a mini-break. There's not another game till two days after Christmas.

It doesn't always work out this way, but I'm glad it has this year. I was supposed to spend this time with Aubrey, but since I haven't heard from her I can only assume she doesn't want me in her life anymore. She was serious about us being over.

With no hockey to immerse myself in to distract me, I feel like crap. I decide to go home to Minneapolis to spend the holiday with my parents. My dad still isn't feeling well, so maybe a visit from me will be good for him. That stubborn bastard refuses to see a doctor, according to my mom. I'm hoping maybe *I* can talk some sense into him if I'm up there.

Unfortunately, I never get the chance.

When the plane lands in Minneapolis, I discover I have twenty-eight messages waiting for me—an assortment of texts and voice mails—all from my mom.

I check the texts first, and they're enough to start my heart racing.

Call home immediately, Brent.

It's an emergency.

Son, please, get back to me as soon as you can.

And then I reach the one that throat punches me: *This is regarding Dad. Something terrible has happened.*

I grab a cab, and on the way to my parents' house, which isn't far from my lake house, I call my mom.

"Oh, Brent," she cries into the phone. "Thank God you're finally getting back to me."

"Mom, Mom." I'm frantic. "I was on a plane and had no idea you were messaging me. But I'm here in Minneapolis now, heading to the house. What's going on with Dad?"

I hear her sniffle and then, "He had chest pain early this morning, but he blew it off as heartburn. We started putting up the Christmas tree, at his insistence, and he suddenly keeled over. Oh, Brent..." My mom chokes out a sob, and I suck in a stunned breath.

"Mom, where's Dad now?"

I'm scared to hear her answer. What if he's gone? God, I'd never forgive myself for not being there.

Thankfully, though still disturbing, my mom says, "He's at the hospital, Brent. Your father had a heart attack."

"Jesus, Mom."

"I know, honey, I know. But the good news is he's stabilized. I'm with him right now."

"Where are you? Lakeside General?"

It's the closest hospital to my parents' house, so that would make sense.

"Yes," she confirms.

I lean forward and redirect the cabbie to that location instead of their house.

"I'll be there soon, okay?" I say.

"Hurry, Brent. He's been asking for you."

I promise the cabbie an extra twenty if he gets me there fast.

Eight minutes later I'm at the hospital. My dad looks terrible. He's only in his fifties, but today he looks seventy. I can't believe how gaunt and pale he is. Where's the strong man I remember from my youth? Even a few months ago he didn't look like this.

"What's wrong with him?" I ask the cardiac surgeon when he comes by to check in on my father.

He hustles me outside the room, and Mom follows. Leading us to a private lounge where we can talk, he tells us some decisions have to be made.

Fuck. This can't be good.

The surgeon takes a seat across the table from me and my mom. Clearing his throat, he says, "As you know, Mr. Oliver suffered a very serious heart attack today."

Mom, though this is not news, gasps. I grab her hand, and she smiles over at me.

"Mr. Oliver is stabilized now," the doctor is quick to add. "But imaging shows us he has multiple blockages."

Now it's my turn to suck in some air. Mom squeezes my hand.

"Those blockages are what's causing the chest pain and contributing to his general feeling of malaise," the surgeon goes on. "That's why Mr.

Oliver hasn't been feeling well for a while now. But we can remedy that. He needs to have this condition treated, and soon. Unfortunately, I'm ruling out angioplasty—"

"What's that?" my mom interjects.

"It's a less-invasive procedure that essentially involves threading a balloon up to the blocked artery and inflating it to allow for more normal blood flow."

"And that not an option, why?" I ask.

"There are too many blockages, and some are quite severe."

"What can be done, then?" my mom inquires, her tone shaky.

The surgeon smiles empathetically. "Your husband needs coronary artery bypass surgery. What that means is we'll create a new pathway away from the blocked artery to improve blood flow to his heart."

"That sounds very serious," my poor mom whispers. Looking down, her dark hair falls in such a way to frame her face.

"It is very serious," the doctor confirms. "But the long-term outcomes are very positive. If all goes well, your husband can still expect to live a long and happy life."

"When can my father have this surgery?" I ask.

"Day after tomorrow," the surgeon replies.

"That's Christmas Eve."

"Yes, it is. We'll schedule Mr. Oliver for the first surgery that morning."

Mom sighs, relieved I'm sure that help is on the way. I, however, remain unsettled.

When Mom returns to Dad's room, I wait out in the hall. I don't want my father seeing me messed up like I am right now.

"Fuck," I hiss under my breath.

I feel so damn alone. I need someone to talk to. If I could just share all the fear I'm feeling I might be okay. But I can't put this on my mother; she has enough to bear. If Aubrey were still my girlfriend I'd lean on her.

Shit, I wish she were here. I could use her style of comforting. She'd tell me everything is going to be okay, and she'd make it feel like it really would be. That's how she made me believe in myself. Well that and the occasional kick in the ass.

Mom comes back out of Dad's room and informs me he's sleeping and that she's going to grab a coffee since it promises to be a long night.

Eyeing me intently, her eyes the same color as mine, she says softly, "Can I talk to you about something, Brent?"

I nod. "Of course, Mom."

She gestures to a row of vending machines down the hall, beckoning for me to follow. "Come. Walk with me."

As we walk, she asks me about Aubrey. "Why isn't she here with you, honey?"

I never told my parents that we're finished. The plan was that after we spent Christmas with the Shelburnes, we were to come up here to Minnesota. I only told my mom that plans had changed. I never specified why.

I have no choice now but to fess up now. "Mom, Aubrey and I are done."

My wise mother retorts, "From that tone, it doesn't sound like you're done."

We stop, and she levels me with a single look—you know *that* look, the one only moms can give to make you feel about two inches tall.

"Mom," I begin, sighing. "Aubrey doesn't want me, okay? But it's all my fault. I screwed up big time."

"So fix it," she says. "Relationships are messy things, Brent. It's not all good times and happy days. Look at what's happening with your father right now."

"That's totally different," I counter. "Dad's sick. Aubrey left me. Though, like I said, she had a good reason."

"Brent, whatever happened between you two, it's just a different kind of adversity. How we handle the bad things in life is what defines us." She pauses, then asks, "Can I ask you something?"

"Sure."

"Do you love Aubrey?"

"Yes. I do."

"Then go get her, son. Tell her what's happening. Let her know that you need her. If she loves you, she'll forgive whatever happened enough to come back to Minnesota with you. She should be here with you for your father's surgery. You can figure out everything else later."

"It's more complicated than that," I murmur, thinking of the addendum in that fucking contract.

"It's as complicated as you make it," Mom says. "Go get your girl, Brent."

She's right.

To hell with the contract. To hell with the team and their ridiculous demands. My dad is sick, and I need Aubrey. Damn it, I *love* Aubrey. And I don't want to spend another day without her.

It's time to do what Mom just suggested. It's something I should have done from the start.

It's time to go get my girl.

36

A SURPRISE ARRIVAL

AUBREY

My damn stubborn sister won't leave me alone for the holiday. At my parents' insistence, Lainey arrives at my townhouse two days before Christmas.

"No more pouting," she declares not five minutes after walking through the door. "Look at this place." She gestures around wildly. "You don't even have a tree. Mr. Whiskey Eyes may be gone from your life, but that doesn't mean life is over."

That's debatable.

"I should never have told you we broke up," I complain as she drags me up to the shower.

She turns on the water, and I sit down on the closed toilet seat.

"Look, Aubrey." She points to the pulsating flow coming from the shower head. It does look inviting. "This is water. It'll make you clean.

All you need to do is stand under that little nozzle thing. Maybe even add a little soap, and watch the magic happen."

"Ha-ha. Smartass," I retort, though I do grudgingly give her a smile.

I haven't showered in days, but Lainey has me considering it.

When she heads for the door to leave me alone, it's not without a warning. "I'm checking back in here in five minutes. You better be in that shower, Aubrey, or I swear I will drag your ass in there."

We're about the same height and weight, so she may be able to take me. Worried that my little sis might actually beat my ass, I put up my hands and say, "Okay, okay."

I stand and tug my Wolves sweatshirt over my head, leaving me in an old ratty bra and sweatpants, my uniform of late. I toss the shirt at my sister and, catching it, she says, "I didn't know you were a hockey fan. Oh, wait." She turns it over. "This is for that team out in Las Vegas."

I quickly look away.

When I venture a glance over at her, her eyes are wide and her mouth is agape.

"Don't say a word," I warn.

Of course, that doesn't stop Lainey.

"Holy crap, Aubrey, Whiskey Eyes is a hockey player, isn't he? He must've been your client. What'd you say your guy's name was? Brent, right? What's his last name? I'm so Googling him once you're in that shower."

"No, don't," I plead.

And that confirms it for my sister. "Oh my God, you fell for your client. I knew it was bound to happen. I'm right, aren't I?"

I sigh because, really, wait till she hears the rest. Like the part where she and I were at Brent's party the day before I met him.

For now, though, I stick with, "That's the short version, but yes, you're right. I fell for a damn freaking client."

The room's filling with steam, so she points to the shower and says, "Get in there. I'll put some clean clothes on the counter. But after you're dressed you are so telling me every detail."

I shouldn't divulge anything, but I don't care anymore. "Okay," I agree. "We'll talk when I'm done."

When I emerge from the shower, there's a pair of skinny jeans, a black tank with spaghetti straps, and a plaid button-down shirt waiting for me on the counter. The clothes are neatly stacked, and they're in Al's fuzzy green lap. Lainey has one of his long green arms positioned high in the air, like he's waving at me.

It's a silly but sweet gesture that brings a much-needed smile to my lips.

I blow-dry my hair and dress in the clothes Lainey set out. I even put in my contacts. Though they're extended-wear, I haven't worn them in days. I've been living in my glasses.

Finally feeling much better, and certainly much cleaner, I head down to the living room.

My sister, bless her heart, has cracked open a bottle of wine. I'm going to need some in order to tell her the whole Brent story.

"Here," she says, holding out a full wineglass to me by the stem. "I poured one for you, already."

"Thanks," I reply.

I take the glass and sit down next to Lainey on the sofa. Her legs are curled up under her, so I follow suit. This is how we've hunkered down a million times, ready to dish. Only this time Lainey is one step ahead of me. She has her laptop open, and when I lean in to take a peek I see there's a team pic of Brent filling the screen.

She taps the screen. "So it seems you've been holding out on me big-time, haven't you? Brent Oliver is gorgeous, yes. And he was your client, yes. But there's more. You never told me Whiskey Eyes is freaking Sunflower Eyes!"

"Um…" I take a small sip of wine. "I couldn't say anything, remember?"

Lainey shakes her head. "Wow, still…the same guy from the party ends up being your client. That's crazy. What are the odds of that happening?"

"Extremely low, I'm sure."

"You must've died when you first saw him."

"You don't even know the half of it, Lainey."

"Good thing he didn't recognize you. You were *so* drunk that night."

"Uh, who said he didn't recognize me?" I mumble.

"What? How could that be? You never talked to him, at least not when I was there. Did you meet him before your Uber got there that night?"

Taking another tiny sip of wine, I smile to myself.

"Aubrey," Lainey begins in her best warning tone. "What are you not telling me?"

I cock my head and roll my eyes up to the ceiling. Tapping my chin, I say all evasive-like, "Oh, I don't know. I may have neglected to mention that I never left that night. And I may have kind of ended up in Brent's bed."

"Holy shit!" Her eyes, same turquoise color as mine, widen. "You slept with Sunflower Eyes that night?"

"No," I clarify. "I passed out drunk in his bed and just happened to wake up next to him."

"That must've been a sight," Lainey says, chuckling. "Did you fall in love right then and there?"

"Hardly," I scoff, recalling the encounter. "We kind of hated each other at first." I can't help but smile when I add, "I thought he had stolen my panties and called him out for being a sick pervert and a pig. He didn't appreciate that very much."

"How romantic," my sister says dryly. "I can see how that all led to love."

I throw a pillow at her. "You're such a bitch."

"And you're such a slut."

I laugh. "With him, you bet I am. Or…was."

Her expression turns serious. "Seriously, Aubrey, what happened between you two? Why'd you break it off with him?"

"I'll tell you everything, but first—" I pick up the bottle and swish around the pinot noir. "—I think we need more wine."

By the time the pinot noir is empty, Lainey knows everything.

"There has to be a way for you to be together," she says wistfully.

My sister, the romantic.

"I wish." I sigh. "But the new contract with that addendum is pretty much airtight."

"Yes, but…"

"What?"

Lainey taps her finger to her chin. I've seen that look before; she's trying to find a way around this for me. "You mentioned that you only had to sign the addendum that day, right? The rest of the contract was just a copy of the original, not technically 'new.'"

"Right."

"Well, I happened to take a class in contract law this past semester. I took it as a business elective, thinking it'd be a breeze, but it was actually kind of tough. Anyway, the professor was super thorough."

Lainey falls silent, and I have to prompt, "Okay? So how does your difficult class help with my situation?"

"Well, one of the things we studied was exactly what you said you signed. An addendum, right?"

"Uh-huh."

"Did their representative sign it, as well?" Lainey asks, wheels clearly turning.

I try to recall. "Hmm, come to think of it, I don't remember seeing Mr. Dolby sign anything that day."

"You should take a look at the paperwork, Aubrey. Our professor was clear that if an addendum isn't signed by *both* parties it's not enforceable. Everything reverts back to just the original contract."

I jump up from the sofa. "Shit, Lainey. We have to find that addendum, like, right now. And not the digital one they e-mailed me. That's just a copy from before we signed. I need to find the original from that day."

"I'll help you look for it," she says, standing. "Just point me in the right direction."

I stand up, bite my lip and glance around the room. "Where *did* I last see the damn thing? I think I saw it lying somewhere just the other day. I've been so damn disorganized lately. But the good news is I'm sure it's somewhere in this place."

I'm all set to begin the search, and so is Lainey, but just then the doorbell rings.

"Expecting someone?" she says.

I shake my head. "No."

Since I'm just standing there like a goober, my thoughts on the contract and where it might be, my sister says, "Don't worry, I'll get it."

When she opens the door, I can only see her. Part of a wall blocks the rest of my view, including who's at the door.

"Who is it?" I yell when she continues to murmur with whoever is on the other side. If it's a cute door-to-door sales guy who has pulled her attention away from our task, she's never going to hear the end of it.

I start over to her. "Come on, Lainey. You can flirt with men at your own damn pl—"

I'm silenced when the guy she's talking to walks in. "Hey, Aubrey."

"Brent?" He's as hot as ever, but his expression is oh-so-broken. "What's wrong?" I ask, suddenly scared for him.

With a raw pleading in his voice, the likes of which I've never heard, he rasps, "I know I shouldn't be here, and I know I have no right to ask anything of you. But damn it, I need you, babe."

37

F*CK THE STUPID CONTRACT

BRENT

I need her, and I'm not afraid to admit it. My dad's life is on the line. Fuck the stupid contract.

Maybe Aubrey feels the same way, seeing as her sister seems to know who I am when she opens the door. On a side note, damn, she looks so much like Aubrey.

It's a little odd, though, when she calls me "Sunflower Eyes" and not Brent.

Where the fuck did that come from?

She holds my gaze, staring deeply into my eyes, and then says, "Hmm, Aubrey is right. They are more of a whiskey shade."

Alrighty then. Aubrey's sister is obviously as quirky as Aubrey described her. She would be a great match for Benny. Or maybe she'd actually be a better fit with Nolan. God knows he needs someone to lighten his ass up. Plus, they have the sex toy connection, as in they both love them.

Oh well, too bad I'm not here for something as simple and lighthearted as matchmaking.

I step inside just as I see Aubrey coming to the door. My whole world stops. "Hey, Aubrey," I so eloquently say.

"Brent?" she replies. "What's wrong?"

"I know I shouldn't be here, and I know I have no right to ask anything of you. But damn it, I need you, babe."

I take a tentative step toward the woman I love and have missed like nobody's business. "Did you hear what I just said?"

She looks at me, tears forming in her eyes, as she replies, "Yes. I heard you."

"It's my dad," I go on, choking up. "He had a heart attack, Aubrey."

"Oh my God, Brent—"

"He's in a hospital right now, up in Minneapolis. He needs surgery, Aubs. They scheduled him in for the morning after tomorrow." She closes her eyes, and I continue. "I'm not afraid to admit that I'm scared as hell. Please, babe, please come back with me to Minnesota."

Opening her eyes and holding my gaze, she says, "Of course I'll go back with you."

"Thank you," I murmur.

We take each other in for this one long moment, and then we fall into each other's arms.

"Brent, I want to be there for you." She buries her nose in my neck and inhales me. "I've hated every day I've been away from you. I never knew I could miss someone this much."

"I've missed you too, babe." I hold onto her tightly, like if I don't she may get away again. "God, it's been hell."

Nothing has ever felt as right as this does. We have to be destined to work this thing out, right? I tell myself we are and I already feel renewed, like I can now be strong for my dad.

Lainey helps Aubrey pack a few things, and then we're off.

When we arrive in Minneapolis, it's the middle of the night. The SUV I keep at the lake house is parked at the regional airport where I chartered the private jet that flew me to, and now us back from, Chicago.

As Aubrey and I walk across the tarmac, I ask her, "Are you okay with staying at my house out by the lake tonight?"

She takes me hand. "I'm more than okay with that."

I stop and turn her to face me. I don't want to make assumptions, not on this. "Aubrey, I know we still have a lot to talk about—"

She shushes me. "Brent, we'll get to all that later. Let's just focus on your dad's surgery for now."

I love her so much. "You're right," I say, nodding.

Back at my place, the mood shifts. As I carry in Aubrey's bags, I sense mounting tension. I sure don't want to push her into something she's not ready for, especially when we've not yet talked about where we stand.

At the base of the stairs, I set her bags on the floor.

Turning to her, I ask, "Um, do you want your own room?"

She shrugs. "I don't know. What do you want?"

"I want what's most comfortable for you."

"Brent"—she rolls her eyes—"that's not an answer."

"Neither was yours."

She chuckles. "Yeah, I guess you got me there."

"Seems neither of us knows what we want," I say with a smile.

But she doesn't agree. "No, Brent. I know what I want." She blows out a breath. "It just feels weird, is all."

"What?" I motion between our bodies. "Do you mean this unresolved stuff between us?"

"Well, there's that, for sure. But there's more to it." She glances around. "Being back in this house, where it all began. It's just a little overwhelming."

I know exactly what she means. "Yeah, it feels like we're back at the beginning, eh?"

She smiles and touches my arm. Shaking her head, she says, "I thought you were so hot when I first saw you at that party."

I take a step toward her and tentatively place my hand on her hip. "I wanted you like crazy that morning in my bed."

"More like you wanted to kill me," Aubrey corrects, laughing.

"Not before I fucked the crap out of you."

My eyes burn into hers, and she murmurs, "Brent..."

I pull her to me and whisper in her ear, "I still want you like crazy. Let me fuck you now... in this house... in the bed where it all began."

I feel her melting, giving in. Yet still resisting. "A lot has happened since then, Brent."

"Yeah, I know." With my hands wrapped in her hair, I nudge her head back so I can kiss softly along her neck. "A lot," I murmur against her soft skin. "Like me falling in love with you."

And that's when I feel her surrender.

Up in my bed, the same bed we woke up in four months ago, I lay her back gently.

And then I undress her.

When my own clothes are discarded, I lie down next to her.

There are kisses and there is laughter. There's even a little awkwardness when I roll on top of her and slide an arm under her and her hair gets stuck.

"Ow, ow. Brent, hold up."

"Oh shit, sorry."

It's back to smooth after that, especially when I slide into her. "God, fuck."

She gasps.

And I thrust.

Again, again, one more time.

And then there's more.

Shit, was it ever as good as it is right now?

"No, no, this is the best," Aubrey pants.

Guess I asked that question out loud. But it's true—this is incredible. I can't get deeply enough inside her. And I can't taste her enough times. I want to consume this woman I love. I literally *need* her to be a part of me. Because what if this is it? What if this is all a one-time shot?

We've discussed nothing. She's here for me now because of my father. And sure, we've admitted we've missed each other, and there are still strong feelings between us, but once my dad's better—and he *must* get better—this could all disappear.

And where would that leave me?

38

WOO ME, BRENT. WOO ME

AUBREY

Despite everything going on in his life, Brent seems determined to woo me.

He cooks me breakfast the next morning and serves it to me up in bed.

"Sorry, babe," he says as he places the tray of food on my lap. "All I had in the fridge that was even remotely breakfast-y were liquid egg whites, some assorted cheeses, and a couple of sweet peppers."

It's cute that he's apologizing for making me a cheese and sweet pepper egg-white omelet. He needn't be, as this is what he eats back in Vegas. And I like this kind of healthy food too. It's delicious.

"S'okay," I murmur around a delectable bite. "This is awesome. Everything tastes really fresh."

"You have my mom to thank for that," he says, chuckling. "She somehow found time to sneak into my house and stock the fridge."

"She sounds like a sweet mom," I say softly.

"She's amazing," Brent agrees.

As I devour breakfast, I take note that Brent is already showered and ready to go. He looks great in his distressed jeans and a long-sleeved gray tee. It's clear, and understandably so, that he wants to head over to the hospital as soon as possible.

I eat faster so we can hit the road.

A few minutes later, as I'm finishing with breakfast, I say, "Let me jump in the shower real fast. I can be ready to go in less than half an hour. Is that okay?"

"Perfect," he replies.

We have so much to talk about, especially after last night, but the drive to the hospital doesn't seem the place.

Outside his dad's room, I meet his mom. She's a beautiful lady—petite with whiskey-colored eyes—just like Brent—and long chestnut-brown hair.

"Mom, this is Aubrey," Brent says with a big, beaming smile.

Placing her hand on my arm, she smiles warmly. "Ah, Aubrey… Brent's told us so much about you. It's good to finally meet you." She sighs. "Though I wish it were under different circumstances."

"Me too," I reply. "But it's still wonderful to meet you, as well."

"Come, now." She locks her arm with mine, and I like her already. She seems an easy person to be around. "You must meet Brent's father."

In his hospital room, I meet the famous Billy Oliver. He's like an older version of Brent in many ways. They share the same strong facial features, though Mr. Oliver's hair is much lighter, and he has a fair amount of gray at his temples. All in all, though, Brent is a perfect blend of his mother's coloring and his dad's face and build.

After formal introductions are made, Brent's dad says, "I can't believe I'm finally meeting the famous life coach."

"Probably more like infamous," I murmur.

If his dad knows anything about my termination, or that video leaked by Brent, he probably questions my abilities.

But instead of nodding in agreement at my own slight against myself, he smiles up at me, kindness in his eyes. "Infamous, my ass," he scoffs. "I've only heard great things about you, young lady."

"Thank you," I reply, blushing.

Mr. Oliver goes on, "In fact, too bad my son didn't have you come up here sooner. You probably could've straightened out this old-coot-with-a-bad-ticker's way of thinking. Up until this wake-up call, I thought I was invincible."

"Too stubborn for his own good," Mrs. Oliver chimes in.

I nudge Brent. "Sounds like someone else I know."

Mr. Oliver lets out a chuckle. "Ah, your woman knows you well, son."

Turning about six shades of red, Brent murmurs, "Dad, please." And then, leaning down to me, he whispers in my ear, "Sorry about that."

His parents don't know we've not yet talked things out, but they are clearly Team Braubrey.

Mr. Oliver, pushing around the pillows behind him and getting more comfortable in his hospital bed, asks Brent to fill him in on all the latest hockey games and scores, which Brent does. Since I've been diligently following league action I'm able to throw in a few updates of my own.

"This one's a keeper, for sure," he says to Brent after I give him a pretty thorough recap of a Minnesota Wild game from the other night.

"Billy," Mrs. Oliver chastises.

I suppose she's beginning to sense her son's—and my own—uneasiness at all these relationship references.

Clearing her throat, she brings up what everyone seems to resort to when at a loss for words—the weather.

"Has anyone noticed lately how unseasonably warm it's been up here? I sure hope it cools down soon. I was hoping for a white Christmas, but I don't think it's in the cards for us this year. Maybe we'll have some snow by New Year's."

"Mom loves snow," Brent then informs me.

Mr. Oliver interjects. "That's only 'cause she doesn't have to shovel it."

Brent's mom reaches over and caresses her husband's face lovingly. "There'll be no shoveling for you, mister, for a good, long time."

"Guess that means we'll have to think of *other* things to occupy our time when we're all snowed in," Mr. Oliver says to his wife with a suggestive wink.

"Annnnd that's our cue to go," Brent says.

"Oh, stay, honey," his mother replies. "Your father's just being silly. Must be all the drugs they have him on."

Mr. Oliver harrumphs, and Mrs. Oliver shushes him.

Brent, chuckling at his parents' cute banter, and clearly loving that they care so much about each other, says, "I'm kind of hungry, anyway, Mom. Aubrey and I can come back up after we grab a quick bite down in the cafeteria."

"Don't be too long," she says.

"We won't," he assures her as we head for the door.

Down in the cafeteria, as we move through the line, picking out sandwiches and a side of carrot sticks with dipping sauce I insist on having, I finally share with Brent what Lainey told me about how contract addendums have to be signed by both parties to be enforceable.

As I finish with my explanation, I add, "And I don't think Mr. Dolby ever signed the addendum that day we met."

"Whoa, what?" Brent stops in his tracks, but I can't go on since we're at the register. He pays for our food quickly, and then says, "Let's talk about it once we sit."

"That works for me."

We choose a table far away from everyone, and once we're seated, he clears his throat and asks, "So what is it exactly that you're saying about the updated contract?"

I take a bite out of a carrot stick. "It may not be valid."

"Have you checked to see if Dolby signed it?"

I shake my head. "Not yet. I was about to search for the paperwork when you arrived at the townhouse last night. But I'm almost certain he never signed anything."

Brent leans back in his chair, his sandwich untouched. "Shit, if that's the case then we could've been together all this time."

I nod as I dip another carrot in a cup of yogurt sauce. "Hmm, maybe."

He must sense my reticence, as he's quick to add, "Aubrey, I know I have a lot to apologize for. And I've had weeks to go over everything that happened. I think it comes down to three things." He pauses, then releases a breath, like he's gearing up. "One, I never should've gone through your laptop bag. Two, I shouldn't have released that video without talking to you first. And three, I definitely should've told you about the strip club *and* the video right from the start." Sighing, he adds, "I'm sorry I fucked up so epically, babe."

I know Brent's sorry, and frankly I can't hold something against him that I'm not even mad about anymore. Plus, his dad is sick, and I'd be a real bitch to drag this thing out, especially when I want to be with him.

"You're forgiven, Brent," I say. "And actually you have been for a while. It's all water under the bridge."

"That may be true," he says. "But I think if we're getting back together I still need to own up to what I did."

I like his accountability—it's a good change for him—but right now I'm more focused on the first part of what he said. "Are we getting back together, then?" I ask.

"I want to. As long as you do too, Aubrey."

Why fight what my heart is telling me to do. "I want to be back with you, Brent. I want us to be a couple again."

Reaching across the table to place his hand over mine, he says, "I guess it doesn't much matter what we want. We still have to wait till you find the new contract, the one with the addendum, to see if we're free to pursue this relationship."

"No." I shake my head. "I don't care if the addendum is signed or not. I want to be with you no matter what."

He raises a brow, making him look more adorable than ever. "Are you saying fuck the consequences, Aubrey?

Rising from my seat and leaning my whole body across the table, I press my lips to his. "Absolutely," I murmur.

AL IS FOREVER MY BITCH

BRENT

My dad's surgery goes extremely well. He comes through the operation with flying colors.

With my father out of the woods, on Christmas Day I fly back to Chicago with Aubrey to search her apartment for the contract. Her sister is gone, having flown back to Pennsylvania to spend time with her folks.

Good ole Al is still with us, though.

When we take a break from searching, we order ham dinners from a little café around the corner that's open for the holiday. We eat with the green alligator at the table with us.

Afterward, when Aubrey's busy clearing our plates, I make her stop so I can bend her over the table.

"What are you doing?" she asks, laughing.

"Having dessert," I inform her.

I make sure Al has a good view when I lift up her pretty velvet skirt and pull her panties down her legs.

When I start pounding into Aubrey, she finally notices Al. "We should turn him away," she breathes out roughly, breathless from our activity.

"No," I counter. "I like that he's watching. He's forever my bitch now."

She stills and looks back at me over her shoulder. I stop moving, but remain inside of her. "What?" I ask.

"I can't believe you are seriously this jealous of a stuffed alligator."

I shrug. "Maybe I am, but just a little. What can I say? I hold grudges. And that little stuffed bastard deserves it. He had me so worked up that day back in October."

"You're silly, Brent."

"I'll show you silly, woman," I warn. And with my eyes on my new bitch, Al, I add, "I'm gonna show him how it's done." I pull all the way out, and then slam back into Aubrey at a new angle, one that has her grabbing the sides of the table and screaming out my name.

I smirk at Al. He wishes he could be me.

After the exhibitionist sexing, the table is cleared—with a time-out for showering—and then Aubrey and I resume searching for the addendum.

"I found it!" Aubrey calls out from the kitchen an hour into the hunt.

I'm in the adjoined dining room so I rush in to where she's standing, contract in hand.

"Did Dolby sign it?" I ask, knowing this is still important, even though Aubrey claims she wants us to be together regardless of what we find.

She hands the document to me. "I'm afraid to look. You check."

I peer down at the paper, an innocuous document that still ultimately holds our fate.

It only takes a few seconds for me to find the line I'm searching for.

"Babe…" I look up from the papers, smiling. "He never signed shit. The line for his signature is completely blank."

Her eyes widen. "Holy crap, no way! Do you know what this means, Brent?"

I grab her up in my arms. "It means we can be together, Aubrey. We can tell the world how much we love each other. And there's not a damn thing anyone can ever do about it."

40

LAINEY LIKES THE WRONG DAMN HOCKEY PLAYER

AUBREY

"Too bad I have that stupid work assignment coming up," I say to Brent.

I don't want to rain on our parade of happiness, but the truth remains that I have a job commitment—the upcoming client in LA—that promises to separate us.

"Shit." He rubs his hand down his chiseled face. "I was hoping things could go back to the way they were. You know, you coming to the games to watch me play, traveling with the team, that sort of thing."

He doesn't add that he simply likes me being there for him. And I *want* to be there for him. Hell, I want to be Brent's, well, everything.

Blowing out a frustrated breath, I say, "There's another issue we have to address."

"What's that?"

"I have to call my boss. He needs to know about our relationship, and it's better he hears about it from me, as opposed to through the media."

"True," Brent agrees.

I contact Mr. Delahunty the very next day and inform him of the change in my relationship status. I'm careful to let on like our romantic relationship started *after* the contract was terminated, a minor detail to protect us all.

Mr. Delahunty seems to suspect otherwise—he's no dummy—but he leaves it be. He then tells me the celebrity in LA I'm supposed to take on as a new client in early January has been admitted to the hospital for "exhaustion," a common code word for rehab.

This dude is sure to be a pain in the ass, I can tell already. But then again, aren't they all?

Mr. Delahunty finishes the call by saying, "We don't need you to fly out to LA until February."

I'm thrilled, and when I disconnect I relay the good news to Brent.

"This is awesome, Aubs. That gives us the whole month of January before you have to leave."

I'm excited to have plenty of time ahead to spend with Brent, but there's another concern we've neglected to address. "How should we announce to the world—to the hockey world, at least—that we're together?"

"Maybe we should release a sex tape?" he suggests with a waggle of his brows.

"You're twisted," I retort.

But then he leans back against the counter in my kitchen, and for this one crazy minute I don't want him to be kidding. In his faded jeans and white button-down shirt Brent looks sexy as hell, so much so that

I actually find myself considering the sex tape idea.

Taking a step toward him, I suggestively throw out, "Whether we make a tape or not, we should rehearse first."

"Definitely," he wholeheartedly agrees.

There's never going to be a sex tape release, but that afternoon we rehearse as if there is.

Later that night we return to Las Vegas for Brent's game, which is the next day. It's not until seven in the evening, though, so when he arrives home after an early morning practice, we end up hanging out and talking in his living room.

Talking of course leads to making out. And then things, as they always do, get heated pretty quickly.

When half my clothes are scattered across the living room floor, I remember to remind Brent to close the blinds.

"Eh, no one can see us in here," he says. "And even if they could, who cares? I say we leave the blinds as they are."

He's hovering over me, and I smack one of his rock-solid biceps. "Ow." I shake out my hand. "Your damn muscles are getting harder all the time. I swear they're like freaking steel."

Brent chuckles smugly. He loves when I stroke his ego like that. But it's true, so once I've determined nothing is broken, I go on, "For the record, the answer to your big idea of leaving the blinds open is a big fat *no*. Get up and close the freaking things, Brent."

"Okay, okay." He stands and heads over to the windows. "It was just a random thought."

I flip over onto my stomach and stare at him, shaking my head. "What is it with you and exhibitionism?"

He cocks a brow as he looks over at me. "What do you mean?"

"Well, yesterday there was the sex tape idea."

"That was a joke, Aubrey."

"Still, you were *really* into having sex in front of Al back in Chicago."

Brent levels me with an *oh-please* look. "He's a stuffed animal, babe."

"A stuffed animal you're clearly jealous of. Like, insanely so."

"So what if I am?" When I start laughing, he warns, "You're going to pay for giggling at me like that."

With the blinds all closed, he stalks toward me.

I scoot back.

When he continues his pursuit, I stand and try to take off. But Brent's way too fast. He catches me in a heartbeat and scoops me up in his arms. Amid my half-hearted protests, he tosses me onto the sofa. He joins me and the rest of our clothes are discarded.

Safe to say there's no more talk of Al.

Afterward, the issue we never resolved comes up—how should we let everyone know we're officially dating.

I suddenly have an idea. "Hey, New Year's Eve is coming up. Didn't you mention something about Nolan throwing a party?"

"He is having one," Brent confirms. "But I have to warn you now it'll be a huge drink-fest."

"*We* don't have to get drunk." I turn in Brent's arms to face him. "I mean, I'm sure we'll have a glass of champagne to ring in the New Year. But we can pass on the hard stuff. Besides, Benny will be there, right?"

"He's supposed to go."

"Well, he won't be drinking at all. We can hang with him."

Brent nods. "Okay, sure, that'll work." Suddenly, after a moment of contemplation, he throws out, "Do you think we should invite Lainey to the party? She's on Christmas break, and we could finally introduce her to Benny."

Though we've always believed those two would be a cute couple, I have my reservations.

"Uh, I don't know," I hedge. "Benny may be clean and sober these days, but he still has a raging puck bunny problem."

Brent can't argue with me on that one. But he does bring up a good point when he remarks, "It's not like anyone is suggesting marriage here. We don't even know if they'll like each other."

"True." After a long pause, I carefully inquire, "Benny doesn't have any diseases, does he?"

"God, Aubrey."

"What? I need to know for Lainey's sake. He's a super slut, so it's not an outrageous thing to ask."

Brent sighs, and then he assures me, "He's clean, Aubrey. Not only does he use protection, like, all the time, but we get tested for shit like that every couple months. You know that. That's why you agreed to go on the pill. You told me you wanted to ditch the condoms as much as I do, remember?"

He's right. We're tired of the hassle. Plus, since we want each other pretty much *all* the time, it'd be nice to be more spontaneous.

With my worries about Benny lifted, I invite Lainey out to Las Vegas for Nolan's little gathering. She accepts, and I fly her out the next day.

New Year's Eve rolls around, and as planned we all convene at the party at Nolan's palatial home down the street. Brent and I don't make a formal announcement that we're together, but it's pretty clear to everyone when we walk in the door arm-in-arm that we're official.

Funny, no one seems surprised. A lot of the guys knew all along, but like Benny and Nolan, they were trying to be cool about it to keep our secret under wraps.

The one person our relationship is news to is Brent's agent, Jock. He's at the party too, so we spring it on him at his favorite spot to hang—the bar.

Surprising to both Brent and me, Jock loves that we're together.

"This is going to do a lot to rehabilitate your image after that lap dance video," he tells Brent before downing what's left of his whiskey on the rocks.

Sad to report that, yes, Brent lost two endorsement deals because of that stupid video. Consequently, Jock is not about to let an opportunity to remake Brent's image as a committed relationship guy flitter away.

As the next hour goes by, Jock remains by our sides. He makes certain we're in lots of selfies, mostly with other players and their significant others, ensuring we'll be plastered all over social media by tomorrow.

Lainey hangs with us as we make the rounds with Jock, but she's sure to bow out of the photos, lest she be pegged as Brent's girlfriend, seeing as we look so similar.

Another scandal is all we need.

"So, Aubrey," Lainey begins as she pulls me away from Brent and Jock so we can talk.

I almost topple over in the five-inch heels I'm wearing, leaving me to mumble, "I swear I'll never get used to high heels." Lainey crosses her arms, looking impatient, and I ask, "What?"

"Where's Thor?"

She remembered Benny from the party way back in August, but as Thor. When I told her Thor and Benny were one and the same, she was all about meeting him tonight.

"His name is Benjamin, not Thor," I remind her as I smooth my flowy red sequin halter down over the low rise of my skinny jeans.

"Yes, yes, I know." She glances around the packed living room. "So where is he?"

Brent comes over to where we're talking, having lost Jock in the crowd. I can't take my eyes off him. You'd think we'd been apart for days, as opposed to five minutes. Oh hell, what can I say? Brent is stunningly handsome in the sleek black suit he chose to wear tonight, leaving me simultaneously in awe of and in lust with him.

But my libido is put on hold when I see he's frowning. "Uh-oh, what's wrong now?"

He sighs as he throws an apologetic glance at Lainey. "I have some bad news. Benny just sent a text. He's decided to stay home tonight."

Lainey is clearly disappointed, but takes it well. "Maybe we can meet another time," she says.

"Yeah, maybe." I sigh.

Brent opens his mouth to no doubt chime in with something reassuring, but just then Nolan, clad in a dark suit of his own, one that makes him look like a spy or a secret agent, comes over and puts his slimy arms around me and Brent.

He's a little drunk and his words are slightly slurred, especially when he says, "Which one of you lovebirds is going to introduce me to this gorgeous creature hanging out with you tonight?"

He then nods to my sister.

Yes, my sister, who instead of being offended like she damn well should be, starts lapping up Nolan's pervy attention like a thirsty bitch in heat. The two of them can't hide their lust when they start undressing each other with their eyes.

Ugh.

"Not me," I announce as I hip-check Nolan away from me and into Brent.

He laughs. "Damn, Oliver, maybe we should get Aubrey on the roster."

Brent laughs right along with his friend. "I told you, Solvenson, don't mess with my girl. She's back, and she's feistier than ever. She'll lay you out in a minute."

"Clearly," Nolan mutters.

Brent then does the honor and introduces Lainey to Nolan.

Lainey, eyes dreamily focused on Nolan, says to him in her most sultry tone, "For the record, Nolan, you can mess with *me* anytime you want. And you might like the way *I* lay you out."

What the ever-loving...?

Brent and I gape at each other, and then at my deranged sister. Nolan, loving it, slips away from us and goes to stand next to her, where they engage in flirty conversation.

"How much champagne did she have?" Brent murmurs to me.

"I don't know, but apparently enough that she's totally channeling her inner puck bunny."

"Who knew she had one?" he remarks.

"Not me. She usually hates sports."

"Like someone else I know."

"What? I love sports."

He gives me a look, and I quickly amend, "Well, I love hockey."

"You didn't at first."

"Yeah, and that's a tragedy. I didn't know what I was missing."

Draping his arm around me, he says softly, "I'd like to think I've been a part of the reason for your change of heart."

"Part of the reason?" I peer up at him, hoping he sees the love in my eyes. "More like pretty much the whole reason. You're a good hockey ambassador, Brent Oliver."

We share a quick peck, but then I notice Nolan is successfully charming Lainey.

When he makes her laugh, I elbow Brent and say, "Seriously, we need to stop this from happening."

I do *not* want Nolan and my sister hooking up. I hate him, and I love her. This has the makings of an epic disaster.

But before Brent and I can intercede, Nolan and Lainey stroll away from us. I overhear him asking if she'd like a refill on her champagne. *Damn charmer.* I also don't miss the way his hand is resting low on the small of her back, which is totally exposed in the short, shimmery gold lamé dress she has on.

"He better not sleep with her," I warn Brent.

"Why are you griping to me?" he retorts. "They're two consenting adults."

"I guess you're right," I grudgingly concede.

Brent then has the balls to say to me, "Word is Nolan has a way with the ladies. If they do hook up tonight Lainey might end up having the time of her—"

I smack his arm. "What the hell, Brent? Whose side are you on, anyway?"

Leaning down to kiss me, and thus placate me, he says, "Yours, babe. I will always be on your side."

I make out with him for a few minutes because, well, he's freaking Brent Oliver. And we're in love. But then I come to my senses and pull back. "Brent, seriously, can you try and save my sister from your hockey-whore friend?"

Sighing, he steps back and says, "Let me see if I can get him alone for a minute and talk to him."

"Be sure to warn him that I'll castrate him if he hurts Lainey."

Brent mutters, "Damn, Aubrey, that's a little harsh. Remind me never to piss you off."

"Aw..." I go to him and slide my arms up around his neck. And then I whisper, "Don't worry. I'd never, ever, ever harm *that* part of you."

Grinding *that* part of him against me, he murmurs, "No, I have a feeling you wouldn't. You like what I do to you with it way too much."

I grind right the hell back, and he gets hard instantly. "Yes, sir," I breathe out. "I sure do."

Brent glances around. "We should get out of here."

"What about Lainey? What about talking with Nolan?"

"They'll be fine. Nolan is probably about to pass out anyway."

I'm not so sure about that—Nolan's not known for passing out when he drinks—but I know in my heart that my sister can take care of herself.

Sliding my hands down to Brent's firm ass, I say, "Okay. Let's go home."

We take off to ring in the New Year the best way I can think of— with Brent Oliver buried deep inside me.

A WALK OF SHAME. BUT NOT MINE THIS TIME

BRENT

The next morning I get up extra early. Aubrey is still sleeping, satisfied and exhausted. Brent 51 and DPMB are lying on the floor. Yeah, I made sure she celebrated the New Year with multiple orgasms. The toys filled in—quite literally—when I had to wait to get hard for the next round.

As I make my way downstairs, I catch sight of Lainey slipping in through the front door. It's a walk of shame if ever I've seen one. And I've seen a lot. Hell, I've had many of my own, from before I met Aubrey.

"Oh, hey, Brent," she says shyly when she sees me.

"Have fun last night?" I ask, cocking a brow as I take in her disheveled appearance—rumpled dress and heels in hand.

Yawning, she says, "Yeah, I had far too much fun. I think I'm going to crash till my flight leaves later."

As she heads to the bedroom we gave her on the first floor, I can't resist asking, "Nolan treat you okay?"

She stops, turns around. A blush creeps up her neck as she demurely replies, "Yeah. He's an, uh, interesting guy."

"That he is."

I'm dying to know if he nailed her, and I kind of think he did, but I'm not about to ask directly. I may not even find out from Nolan. He usually keeps that shit quiet, especially if he really likes the girl he's hooked up with.

Before Lainey continues on her way, she hesitates. "Is Nolan, like, seeing anyone?"

I shake my head. "No."

She smiles. "Okay, thanks. I better go get some sleep."

I should warn her not to get her hopes up—Nolan isn't a relationship kind of guy—but she's gone before I have the chance. Maybe it won't matter anyway since she has to go back to Minnesota. Her final semester starts in a couple of days, and I'm sure she'll forget all about Nolan Solvenson soon enough.

With the contract worries out of the way, and no hard feelings between Aubrey and team management—it was their mistake, after all—she and I have a blast. She comes to every home game, and I pay for her to travel with the team when we're on the road. No one has a problem with her presence. In fact, all the guys love her, even more so than before since she's officially with me. I think they realize what a positive influence she's been, and continues to be, in my life.

There's no question about that, seeing as I'm leading the league in scoring and the team remains securely in first place.

Benny is still her bestie on the team. Breeze likes her a lot too. She and Nolan verbally spar all the time, like always, but I've come to accept that it's just their way. It makes me glad that anything going on between him and Lainey fizzled out. That is, if there ever was something there to begin with.

Nolan hasn't owned up to sleeping with her on New Year's Eve, and Lainey's not mentioned a word to Aubrey.

If she had, I'd surely hear about it.

Aubrey still has no idea Lainey stayed over Nolan's house the night of the party. I thought about saying something, but, really, it's Lainey's tale to tell. Not to mention, I've learned enough to know to stay out of their sisterly crap.

I do get a little suspicious from time to time that something *is* going on with Lainey and Nolan, especially when we have a road game against the Minnesota Wild and Nolan goes MIA, save for practice, which is not like him at all. When I ask Benny if he knows where Nolan's been wandering off to, he tells me he has no clue and I believe him.

The real kicker, though, is when Aubrey can't convince her sister to meet her for lunch on game day.

"Lainey's acting really sketchy," Aubrey complains to me when she puts down her phone. "She claims she has exams to study for and can't get away to go to lunch. Something feels off, Brent."

"What do you mean?" I carefully inquire.

She shrugs. "I don't know, but I bet it has to do with a guy. Maybe Lainey has a secret boyfriend or something."

Oh, fuck.

Sighing, she adds, "I guess she and I will have to hang another time."

"Guess so, babe."

I'm trying to maintain a nonchalant tone, and I guess it works since the subject is dropped.

Shit. I don't have the heart to tell Aubrey that Lainey may be holed up with Nolan, banging the day away till game time. I don't know if it's true, so I keep my mouth shut. No need to get shit stirred up.

Further bolstering my suspicions, however, Nolan arrives at the arena shortly before game time looking rather satiated. He plays really well, scoring late in the third period on a drop pass from me. That breaks the tied score and we end up winning.

We actually do a lot of winning throughout all of January, and into February. Things are great with my family, as well. Dad continues to improve, and my mom is back to her usual happy self. Also, for me, life remains incredible with Aubrey in it. The only thing threatening to fuck things up is that damn upcoming LA assignment.

Fuck that celebrity dude. I don't want her to leave me.

Two days before she's set to fly out of Vegas and onto LA, I am miserable. Still, I keep my promise to be supportive, even offering to help her pack.

Up in our bedroom, grasping at straws, I sit down on the bed and say, "Do you really have to go, babe? Playoffs are only a little over two months away. I need you here with me now more than ever."

She sighs. "Brent, what can I do? This is my job we're talking about."

She's been pretending to be committed to this new assignment, but I can tell she wants to stay with me as much as I want her to. I haven't told her yet, lest I get her hopes up for nothing, but I talked with Dolby the other day. I asked him if there's any way the team can hire Aubrey on in a permanent position.

Before you laugh and think I'm just a fool in love, it's not that far-fetched of an idea. The team's ownership likes her being around all of us. And why wouldn't they? We're winning like crazy, in part because Aubrey keeps us all grounded.

Just the other day, Benny was jonesing for a drink. "One won't kill me," he said on the flight home from an away game.

"Dude, don't do it," I warned.

"You're an ass if you ruin your sobriety now," Nolan threw in, shaking his head.

It was Aubrey, though, who got Benny over the hump.

She moved next to his seat. And though she knows enough about hockey these days that she could probably teach a class of her own, she started asking Benny about game strategy and plays.

Of course, he was into that. So much so that the old dry-erase board was dusted off and brought out. Unfortunately, its emergence came just as Coach Townsend was heading up to the lavatory in the front of the plane.

"Hey," Coach T said, stopping in the aisle. "Is that one of mine?"

"Uh…" Benny turned beet red. "Yeah, uh, I may have borrowed it a while back." Sheepishly, he added, "You have a bunch, so I didn't think you'd miss just one."

"Maybe not, but even so…" Coach sighed. "I've been looking for that particular board since October. See that heart drawn on the back?"

Benny flipped over the board, and we all leaned in to have a peek. And wouldn't you know it, there was a little heart drawn on the back.

"That particular dry-erase board," the coach went on, "was a gift from my wife."

Benny's eyes widened. "Wow, I never noticed that heart there before. I'm really sorry, Coach."

He started to hand the board back, but Aubrey put out her arm. "Can you hold up a minute, Coach T? This is actually all my fault. I asked Benny way back in the fall if he could teach me the game. He borrowed the board so he could diagram a bunch of plays for me."

Coach smiled. He clearly liked what the board had been used for and immediately softened, which you don't see much of with him.

Easing the dry-erase board back to Benny, he said, "Ah, hell. My wife gives me one of those things at the start of every season. That's why I have so damn many. Just go ahead and keep that one, Perry."

Even Coach T is positively affected by Aubrey, lending further credence to my assertion that hiring her makes total sense. She hasn't worked for the team since the contract termination in December, but business is business. If they believe she's worth the investment they'll hire her in a minute.

Only problem is the minutes are ticking away. The day Aubrey has to fly to LA is almost here.

And I've still not heard a thing from Dolby.

GOOD-BYES SUCK

AUBREY

The day I leave for LA arrives.

This is it, another sad good-bye. Only this one is harder than any before because I've fallen more in love with Brent.

There are tears, lots of tears, and promises to Facetime every single day. It won't be the same, though.

Damn it all to hell! I want to stay here with Brent. I don't want to go live near—or God forbid, with—some problem actor in LA. But I need my job. I refuse to become one of those player girlfriends or wives who do nothing but gossip, shop, and stir up drama.

Yeah, I've watched *WAGS*.

And hell no, that's so not me.

On the way to the airport, I notice Brent is exceptionally quiet. So, clearing my throat, I try to draw him into a conversation.

"Maybe I won't have to stay all that long in California."

I'm throwing something out, however lame, to maybe make this easier for both of us.

But Brent's not buying it. "You stayed with me, under contract, for four months," he replies. "And it would've been longer had I not fucked up."

I place a hand on his hard thigh, and he hits the gas. He's frustrated, wound up.

"Brent, please." I blow out a breath. "Don't kill us on the way there, okay?"

"Sorry, babe." He slows down.

Still, even going the speed limit we reach the exit ramp leading to the airport way too soon. "I'm going to park and come in with you," Brent suddenly declares.

We discussed it before we left and agreed that dropping me off at the curb would make this easier. But, really, nothing is going to do that.

Squeezing his thigh, I tell him, "Good. I want you with me till the last possible second."

Inside the terminal, Brent uses his charm and convinces the ticketing agent to give him a pass to allow him to go to the gate with me. On the way there he seems distracted again, like something is weighing on his mind. I'd chalk it up to him being upset about me leaving, but it seems the phone in his hand is what's occupying him. He keeps checking it every couple of minutes.

I look over at him as we walk and raise a questioning brow. "Are you waiting for an important call or something?"

He looks guilty, even as he insists, "Um, no."

I stop and make him look at me. "Hey, you don't have some former puck bunny lined up to meet you after I'm gone, do you?"

I'm kidding—sort of—but Brent doesn't find it funny. "That's not even remotely amusing, Aubrey," he tells me.

Trying not to be overly emotional, I admit, "I'm making stupid jokes 'cause I don't want to leave you." I lean my forehead against his chest. "Maybe I should just quit."

Wrapping his arms around me, he says, "But you love your job."

Stepping back, I stare up at him like he's nuts. "I do not love my job. I like working, yes, but I haven't loved *this* job for a long time now. The only fun times I've had in the past year were the days I spent with you."

"Aw, babe, that's sweet of you to say."

He tries to pull me in for another hug, but I place a hand on his chest. "No, wait. You know what?" I let go of Brent and start rummaging through my carry-on bag, searching for my phone. "I'm calling Mr. Delahunty right now. I'm handing in my resignation. I haven't been happy working this position in ages. I even remember bitching about it to Lainey, before my work assignment with you even started. I'm done, Brent. I'll worry about finding something else later, but I'm making sure, first, that it's something that'll make me happy, something that'll make us *both* happy."

He starts to reply, but his own cell goes off, blaring out the lyrics to KC and the Sunshine Band's song "Don't Go."

"Oh my God, I love that song," I say as I nod along to the beat. "It's such a classic."

"It is," he agrees. "And I remembered you saying once that you loved it. Anyway"—he blows out a breath—"it seemed particularly fitting for today. I downloaded the ringtone last night."

"Aww, Brent," I murmur.

I'd love to listen to the song all day, but Brent silences KC and the boys when he answers the call.

When he steps away so I can't hear, I can't help but wonder, *Why the secrecy?*

After another few minutes pass, I'm all like, *Crap, I hope he doesn't really have a puck bunny lined up.*

I know I'm being silly, so I squash that thought. Still, it's a little worrisome when Brent moves farther away *and* becomes more deeply engrossed with whomever he's talking to.

When he ends the call, he slides the phone back into his jean's pocket and walks back over to me, beaming. "What's that smile for?" I ask, wary.

He grabs me up in his strong, capable arms and says, "Make that call to your boss, babe. You already have another job lined up."

"Huh?"

I peer up at him. He's never looked as happy, or as handsome, as he does right now.

God, how did I get so lucky?

I quickly get back to the point. "What do you mean I have another job lined up?"

"Well," he begins, "I spoke with Dolby a few days ago. I asked him about giving you a permanent job with the team, some kind of consulting position, but more office-based than the one you had with me. The guys love you, Aubrey, you know that. And Dolby knows it too. You'd be a good fit with the organization."

"What are you getting at, Brent?"

"Well, that was Dolby on the phone just now. He met with ownership earlier today and there's an offer on the table for you. If you want it, that is."

"What do you mean 'if I want it'? You bet your hot ass I do."

I snuggle in closer, and he murmurs in my hair, "Hot ass, eh?"

Leaning back, I pretend to push him away. "Stop. You know how I feel about you."

"I do, Aubrey. I do."

He looks content, but then, as he's peering down at me, his brow suddenly creases with worry.

"Hey, you're not mad I worked on this without talking to you first, are you? I just didn't want to get your hopes up unnecessarily. But I probably should've cleared it with you first."

Is he crazy? "Are you crazy?" I say. "I completely understand the need for secrecy on this one. But the bottom line is I'm glad you did whatever you did to get this thing rolling. And for the record, I'm the exact opposite of mad. I'm grateful and happy."

And with that, I make the call to my boss. Since there's no point in flying to LA for two weeks, my resignation is accepted as effective immediately.

I can't wait to start my new job…with my new guy…and my new life.

THE LUCKIEST GUY IN THE WORLD

BRENT

L ife with Aubrey is better than ever when her leaving is no longer a concern. And as far as hockey is concerned, the team is on fire.

WOLVES LEAD THE LEAGUE

WHO CAN BEAT THIS TEAM?

Apparently, not many teams can. We roll into April, stacking up victory after victory.

And then it's time for the playoffs!

"No fucking things up this time," I say to the team before Game One of the first round. We're in our home locker room, ready to hit the ice against the Arizona Coyotes. "We've been here before, boys, and this is where we always forget who we are. That can't happen, not tonight.

And not the next game, either. Let's go for four in a row and close this thing out fast. Let's make it to the second round of the playoffs for the first time in Wolves history. Can we do that, eh?"

"You bet your ass we can!" Benny yells out.

"Fuck, yeah," Nolan chimes in.

There's a flurry of other assents and agreements, and then the guys start tapping their sticks on the ground, a show of solidarity. I know then that this year is going to be different.

Turns out, I'm right—we win the first round of the playoffs in what I asked for, four in a row.

Round two is a little tougher. We're matched up against the Sharks, and they're no slouches.

I prepare for the series, which includes wanting everyone who's important to me in attendance. My father is feeling fantastic, so he and Mom come into town. I'm more motivated than ever, knowing I came so close to losing my dad. I think about how you can't put things off in life. If my dream really is for my dad to watch me hoist the Stanley Cup up over my head I better keep my ass focused.

That's where Aubrey really helps. She keeps me on task, like always. She also sits with my parents during the games, cheering me and the team on. The love I feel every time I look up in the seats and catch sight of the three most important people in my life is overwhelming. I know what really matters in life now, and no matter what happens in this series I'm still the luckiest guy in the world.

But, apparently, our team is pretty damn lucky too. We keep on winning. Though maybe it's not luck, after all. Maybe we're just a damn good hockey club.

We win against San Jose in six games and move on to the conference final against the Dallas Stars.

We take the Stars in seven, and holy shit!

"We're going to the Stanley Cup Finals, babe," I say to Aubrey as I pick her up and spin her around.

We're in the team locker room, albeit alone. All the interviews have concluded, so the other players have left.

When I put her down, I take a seat on the bench and start unlacing my skates. "Let me shower and we can finally get out of here."

"Wait." She wedges her cute little self between my legs and smiles down at me.

"Oh hell, I know that look," I say.

My upper body is already bare and Aubrey traces a finger down my chest, lingering down around my abdomen. "Everyone is gone, right?" she murmurs.

"Yeah, yeah, they're gone." I glance around the empty space. "It's just you and me."

"Hmm, then I have an idea."

I suck in a breath when she starts toying with the tie on my hockey pants. "Babe, I'm really sweaty," I warn her. "I should take a shower first if we're going to—"

She silences me with a finger to my lips. "I want you all dirty and sweaty, Captain. I'm not going to Zamboni you, but I want you on top of me, doing what you do best."

"Shit."

I have Aubrey naked in no time. And then I dirty her up like she wants, on the bench, on the floor, up against the wall…

A day after we clinch the conference title, the series out in the east ends.

"Looks like we'll be playing the Red Wings," I say to Aubrey, who's been watching the game while sitting next to me on the sofa.

"Too bad it isn't the Blackhawks," she says. "We could've stayed at my place for the games in Chicago."

"Hey, speaking of which…" We've not yet discussed what to do with Aubrey's townhouse since she's no longer living there. "Are you planning on putting your place on the market any time soon?"

Chewing at her lip, she contemplates my question. "I don't know, Brent. Should we keep it for when we're in Chicago? Or, I could maybe rent it out."

"It's up to you, babe."

We table that discussion for later, and instead work out the logistics for the upcoming games.

"I'm glad you have home ice advantage for this series," Aubrey says. "Playing the first two games here in Vegas will be huge."

We've built a rather good fan base, so I agree. I then inform Aubrey, "Hey, do you remember that limo driver from the day you first arrived?"

She rolls her eyes at me. "How could I ever forget anything about that day, Brent? As I recall, you schmoozed the guy into leaving so you could drive me to your house and torture me along the way."

I laugh since she's so right.

Scooting over to her, I murmur in her ear, "Hey, it all worked out okay."

Leaning her head on my shoulder, she agrees, "It definitely did."

After a beat, she pulls back and asks, "Oh, so what were you about to tell me about the driver?"

"Just that I got him and his kid tickets for the first game."

Aubrey sits up straight. "Wow, that was really sweet of you. I remember the driver talking about how he couldn't afford to take his kid to even a regular season game."

"Yeah, he told me the same thing."

She places her hand on my cheek, rubbing at the playoff beard I've been growing. "You're a good man, Brent Oliver," she tells me.

And, for once, I feel like I am.

Epilogue

THE BEST HAT TRICK EVER

BRENT

We take the Red Wings in seven.

It's a grueling, grinding, hard-fought series, but that just makes our victory that much sweeter.

There is nothing I can compare to the moment I lift the Cup above my head. I look for my dad up in the stands, and when I find him I see he's crying tears of joy. Mom and Aubrey are there too, hugging and jumping up and down.

I kiss the Cup…and savor the moment.

After the initial hubbub wraps up, my family and my girl join me on the ice. We take a bunch of pics with the Stanley Cup. Aubrey even kisses it, just like I did when I held it above my head.

There's a parade down the Strip in Las Vegas a few days later. It's hot as hell, but no one cares.

We won the motherfucking Stanley Cup!

Aubrey and I decide to spend the summer in Minneapolis, at my lake house. We'll come back to Las Vegas in August, before training camp starts. Benny is heading back to his hometown of Surrey, BC for the off-season, and Nolan is spending the summer in Toronto.

Nolan seems pretty intent on making time to come up to the lake house to visit with us, which is interesting when we find out, after visiting Aubrey's parents in Pennsylvania, that Lainey plans to stay in Minnesota for a while.

"Did she get a job there?" I ask Aubrey.

"Not that I know of," she tells me.

"Hmm…"

Guess I'll find out this summer if she and Nolan have been dating on the sly. It'll be hard to keep that shit hidden when he stays with Aubs and me.

Before we leave Vegas, there's one thing I want to do—propose to Aubrey. Like I said before, you can't put things off. I love her, and I want to spend the rest of my life with her.

I choose an evening when the sunset is stunning for us to drive out to the desert. I take Aubrey to the same spot where we viewed the stars way back in the fall. Only now, instead of a black velvet night sky above our heads, one dotted with a zillion stars, the horizon is streaked in shades of crimson, orange, and purple.

"God, it's so pretty out here at this time of the day too," Aubrey says when we step from the car.

"It is," I agree.

Cocking her head and looking over at me, she asks, "Do you still come out here to think, Brent?"

"Nah, not as much. But it's still a special place to me."

"It's becoming special to me too," she says.

I know then I've chosen the perfect place to ask her to become my wife.

While she's smoothing down her short cream-colored dress, I walk out into the desert, where I stealthily remove from a light blue Tiffany's box a multi-carat diamond set in platinum.

I bought the ring just the other day, and I sure hope she loves it.

I set the ring gently on top of a smooth boulder, and then call out, "Hey, Aubs, come check out this neat rock I found over here. It's crazy-sparkly and really cool. I don't think I've ever seen anything like this out in the desert."

"Okay, hold on."

She makes her way over to me slowly, since she has on sandals with heels. When she reaches me, she says, "I didn't know we were going hiking, Brent. I would've worn something different."

"No hiking," I assure her. "I just want you to see this shiny little stone."

She looks down at the boulder just as the setting sun hits the ring. The resulting sparkle is dazzling.

Looking up at me, she whispers, "Oh my God, Brent. Does this mean what I think it means?"

I drop to my knees. To hell with sand and pebbles and even the little lizard that just ran by. I'm doing this right.

Taking her hand, I say, "Aubrey Shelburne, you're not just the love of my life, you're my everything. Will you do me the honor of becoming my wife?"

With tears in her eyes, she replies with an enthusiastic, "Yes!"

I stand and pretend I didn't hear her. Cupping my ear, I lean in close and say, "Wait, what was that?"

Her arms fly around me. "Yes, yes, yes. I will absolutely marry you, Brent Oliver."

As we seal the deal with a kiss, I know for certain that this moment outweighs even winning the Cup. Because *now* I've truly won it all—I'm a Stanley Cup champion, Aubrey said "yes," and I'm finally the man I was destined to be.

This is, by far, the best hat trick ever!

If you enjoyed Destiny on Ice, *be on the lookout this spring for the second novel in the Boys of Winter series,* Resistance on Ice, *which is Nolan's story.*

ABOUT THE AUTHOR

S.R. Grey is an Amazon Top 100 and a #1 Barnes & Noble Bestselling author. She is the author of the brand new Boys of Winter hockey romance series, the popular Judge Me Not books, the Promises series, the Inevitability duology, A Harbour Falls Mystery trilogy, and the Laid Bare series of novellas. Ms. Grey's works have appeared on multiple Amazon Bestseller lists, including Top 100 several times. She's also a #1 Bestselling Author on Barnes & Noble and a Top 100 Bestselling Author on iTunes.

S.R. Grey Facebook:
http://www.facebook.com/SRGrey

Author Website:
http://srgrey.com/

Sign up for S.R. Grey's exclusive-content newsletter and never miss an update, cover reveal, or release:
http://mad.ly/signups/106801/join

S.R. Grey on Twitter:
https://twitter.com/AuthorSRGrey

S.R. Grey Goodreads Author page:
http://www.goodreads.com/author/show/6433082.S_R_Grey

S.R. Grey on Instagram:

http://instagram.com/authorsrgrey#

S.R. Facebook Reading Group (join now for giveaways galore!):

https://www.facebook.com/groups/SRGreyHardAbsandHotBooks/

ACKNOWLEDGEMENTS

Maybe the hardest thing to write, next to those blasted blurbs, is this section. I don't want to miss anyone, and I always fear I might.

So, here goes everything and nothing....

Thank you first and foremost to the readers. Without you, I'd have no voice, no stories to share, and, God forbid, there'd probably be no Brent Oliver! *GASP!* I know, right? See how important you are?

Next, thanks to all the bloggers and loyal readers of my work. I love you all!!

Thank you also to Christopher John, who is not only a great photographer, but a friend, as well. Your fabulous photo of Assad Shalhoub, the one that now adorns this cover, captured Brent Oliver so perfectly. Speaking of the cover, big thanks go out to Najla Qamber for designing a book jacket that completely captures the feel of the novel.

Thank you, Franci N., for taking the first look and giving me early feedback on Brent, Aubrey and the gang. That includes Brent 51 and Al. *insert alligator emoji here*

Thank you to Kristin S. and the amazing editing team over at Hot Tree Editing. And thanks to Emily and her team at E.M. Tippetts for formatting services that go above and beyond. I always seem to end up in some kind of last-minute panic, and they always calm me down.

Last, but not least, thank you to my hockey "consultants." You guys rock!

If you enjoyed *Destiny on Ice*, check out S.R. Grey's standalone New Adult Romance novel, *The After of Us*.

When Will Gartner finds out he has a five-year-old precocious little daughter named Lily, his world is turned upside-down.

Read the first chapter now....

ONE

Will

"College graduate, that's me."

It's so hard to believe that I have to utter those words again, out loud, one more time. And then I need more, just to make it really real.

Leaning my head back to stare up at an azure-blue sky, I rise up in the seat of the nice, new BMW convertible I'm driving and scream as loudly as I can, "I'm a goddamn college graduate, motherfuckers."

Take that, all you pricks who didn't believe in me.

I jerk the wheel back just in time to keep from veering off the road, and thus into vast desert nothingness. But yeah, once I'm back on track I think about how no one thought I'd succeed. Not my ex-girlfriend, Cassie, not my mom, and certainly not my stepdad, Greg. I should mention that Greg's not technically my stepdad. Dude never bothered to "officially" adopt me. Not that it matters, not anymore. I'm about to turn twenty-two.

I'm all grown up…and a fucking college grad, as established.

As I hit the gas, the Mojave Desert becomes a hazy blur, my great trek to Las Vegas almost near its end. Yeah, good ole Sin City is where I'm headed. So many Californians take this trip for pleasure. But me, I'm going home.

I estimate I should hit the state line in about another hour—maybe less, at the rate I'm flying—then I'll be back in my home state of Nevada. Of course, I won't be there for long. I'm all set to fly to New York City at the end of the week.

Shit, I have to laugh. I'm a goddamn coming-home success story, if ever there was one. That's right—I, Will Gartner, former fuck-up extraordinaire, have not only graduated from a prestigious college—with honors, no less—but I've also lined up a sweet-ass job in the largest city in the country.

As of next Monday, a week from today, I'll be putting my fancy new graphic design skills—some taught to me at college and others I just have an innate talent for—to work.

And for fat stacks, no less.

When I arrive in New York I'll have a couple of days ahead of me in which to settle in, which is good. Gotta get myself set up in the cool apartment I *think* I want. If I back out, though, it doesn't matter. Mom and Greg have me booked in some fancy Manhattan hotel for however long I need.

Still, what I really want is to do this shit on my own from day one. It's time to cut the ties to my past and quit relying on other people to do shit for me, especially when I can manage things for myself. This is the new me, you see: A Will Gartner who is finally free.

Funny how I don't feel so very free.

I guess I've always seen myself as more of a freelance kind of artist. My dream was once to publish a comic book line, one I created a long time ago. I used to hope maybe I could turn my early work into a graphic novel, and possibly create a whole series from there. I dreamed of bringing to life in vivid color the characters on my sketch pad, praying one day they'd be seen by others, even if it only ever turned out to be a few.

Oh, well. Guess I'll learn to adjust and be content with the knowledge that my ad work will be viewed by thousands—probably tens of thousands.

Should make me feel good, right?

Yeah, it should. So why is it I feel like nothing but a sellout to corporate greed?

"Quit thinking that stupid idealistic shit," I chastise myself. "Get real."

Refocusing on my itinerary for when I arrive in Vegas, I ponder the one last blowout I plan to have at my parents' house. Not that I've done much planning on it, but the groundwork is set. Mom and Greg are gone, so they aren't a factor. My folks took off for an extended three-month vacation, following my graduation ceremony. That means they won't be back for several weeks. Those two are always traveling, jetting from one place to the next. They were so anxious for this trip to begin that they flew out of LA on Saturday, the day of my graduation. In fact, they even had me drive them to the airport that very night.

I blow out a breath, recalling our final moments at the curb of the passenger drop-off area.

As I helped Mom unload her baggage from the trunk of the graduation present she'd given me—the ice-blue convertible Bimmer I'm driving this very moment—she gave me free rein over her not-so-humble Vegas abode. She has no problem with me staying at her and Greg's oversized McMansion, seeing as I'm about to become what she always dreamed I'd be—a clean-cut business professional.

Nonetheless, my mom, knowing my background and no doubt recalling my reckless younger days, was sure to add, "Have fun, but don't trash the place, Will."

I feigned indignation, placing my hand over my heart and acting hurt. "Would I do such a thing, Mother Dear?"

She gave me a withering look, and Greg chimed in with, "Seriously, Will. No parties."

He returned to his task of loading their bags onto a cart and didn't see me roll my eyes at him. I swear that man will forever view me as fifteen.

Mom, always quick to defend me, dressed Greg down immediately. "Oh, Greg," she said, "a tiny party is fine. My son"—she reached up and ruffled my hair—"can have a few friends over if he likes. I'm sure they'll all behave like perfect ladies and gentlemen."

Ha!

Another eye roll was in order, but I played along, knowing it was to my advantage.

Don't think I can't recognize how fucked up our family dynamic is, with Greg trying to set boundaries and Mom continually shutting him down. That's just her, though. My mom, Abby Gartner Vintner, simply sucks at discipline. I guess that's part of the reason why my brother, Chase, and I had so many problems growing up. Losing our real father and living on the streets for a while didn't help matters, nor did Abby's onetime-pervasive gambling problem, but her overall permissiveness led me and my brother to make a slew of bad choices.

That's all in the past now. Chase is a success story these days.

The one-time felon, who spent four years in prison, runs a thriving business and has a great family. He and his wife, Kay, plus their young children, Jack and Sarah, all came to my graduation this past weekend.

They had to fly back directly afterward, however. Chase told me he had work to do on Sunday, something about checking in on a job site that's running behind schedule. He builds homes—like our father once did—in Ohio.

And then there's me. "College graduate," I murmur, savoring the sound of those words one more time.

Still, though. Despite how many times that phrase passes my lips, it just doesn't feel real. But it *is* real. I did it. I survived the fancy school in Malibu that Mom and Greg paid far too much for. And now it's on to the big city to live out my dream.

Or live out someone's dream, a little voice whispers.

"Think about the party," I mutter in response.

Yeah, the party…

I'm thinking one low-key bash at the house won't hurt anyone. No one will probably show up anyway, seeing as I've lost touch with most of my old friends. Probably a good thing, considering how my early high school years were filled with drugs and partying with those exact same people.

Oh, and with my one-time girlfriend, Cassie Sutter.

That chick and I were bad news once we got together. Shit, we were high more often than not. She was my enabler, and I was hers. She also holds claim to the title of "my first love." Walking away from her was one of the hardest things I ever had to do. But if ever there was a toxic love, it was ours.

Think I'm over-exaggerating? I'm not. Hell, I almost killed a man in cold blood for Cassie, if not for Chase intervening.

Chase. Reaching up from the steering wheel, I run my hand through my hair. It's the same light brown color as his. My hair used to be lighter, much lighter. I was once a towheaded blond, back when I was a little kid. My hair also used to be wilder. Not all that long ago, either. Sadly, I had to get a haircut last week, to appear more "professional" for my new job.

What is it that people say? Need to look the part to play the part, right?

Chuckling, I rake my fingers through my hair once more. Thankfully, there's still enough there to grab and pull. Chase does the same thing, all the time. Family trait, I suppose. Wonder if our dad had the same hair-raking quirk?

I can't ask him, seeing as he's dead and gone. Suicide, back when I was eight. My dad drove off a cliff, located in the same exact mountain pass I'll be driving through in roughly thirty minutes.

How fucked up is that? *Thanks, Dad.*

My father, Jack Gartner, is part of the reason why Cassie and I fell in together. She lost her dad when she was young, just like me. And let me tell you, that shared sympathy bonded us hard and tight.

But our woven-together grief, sadly, led to disaster.

On those days when finding solace in each other's arms just wasn't enough, we searched for outside sources to ease the pain. And, oh, did we find shit to do—weed, Oxy, X, cocaine, and other drugs Chase would kill me for if he ever knew I even tried them.

Bad enough he knows what he knows. But there is more, so much more.

Chase also thinks Cass and I never spoke to one another after I broke up with her, back when I was fifteen. For a while, it was true, we didn't talk. I was clean, and Cassie…well, she wasn't. She had done a stint in rehab back when we were in high school, but it didn't stick. Her mom ended up transferring her to a private school on the outskirts of Las Vegas. I guess she was hoping the move would get Cassie in with a different crowd, a straight-laced crew of kids.

It didn't work. Cass was still using, only with a whole new set of people, kids that were far from straight-laced. She still texted me too, all the time, even when I told her I didn't want to see her anymore.

I knew it was time to move on. Like, for real.

But, I had just turned sixteen and was horny as hell. So when Cass started asking me to meet her just to hook up, I'd go.

Every … single … time.

As a result, we ended up having sex all over town—in the backseat of the car my mom had given me for my sixteenth birthday, in alleys where we once scored drugs, and in cheap motels, located in the parts of Vegas tourists never see.

I wasn't doing any drugs that summer. Except for one—Cassie.

I'd given up all the bad things, but I couldn't quite give up on her. Not until her mom found out we were seeing one another did it end. Mrs. Sutter made sure it was over for us when she moved away. Taking Cassie with her, of course.

Off to a different state, they flew. At least I think they settled in a different state. I don't really know for sure. All I *do* know is I haven't seen Cassie since the last day we were together, almost six years ago.

That doesn't mean I still don't think about her from time to time. Not a lot, granted, but sometimes, like now.

I wonder if she ever got her life together, the girl I once loved. I wonder if she got clean. Did she go to college? Maybe she got married? Hell, she could even have a kid by now, for all I know.

But mostly, beyond all those things, I hope my first love found the inner peace she so desperately sought.

Read the rest of the standalone novel *The After of Us* now….

Amazon (US): http://amzn.to/1qefx0V

B&N: http://bit.ly/23aR0I4